LOVE AND REVENGE

A LEGACY OF WAR

PHIL SILLS

PANDA PUBLISHING, INC.

PANDA PUBLISHING, INC.

4255 US HWY 1 South, STE 18-125

Saint Augustine, Florida 32086

United States of America

Library of Congress Control Number: 2020912792

Paperback Edition ISBN Number: 9781733544368

Kindle Edition ISBN Number: 9781733544375

*To my wife and life partner Jackie and my sons,
Mike and Chris and their spouses Jenna and Josh.*

And the new addition to our family, Aubrey Sills.

ACKNOWLEDGMENTS

The author wishes to acknowledge the very talented editor Jessica Hatch of Hatch Editorial Services, LLC (jessica@hatch-books.com). This is the second book Jessica has worked on with me, and with her guidance and support, my previous book, *The Hunt For Madoff's Treasure*, was a semifinalist in the prestigious Royal Palm Literary Award Competition. Smart, perceptive, intelligent, she's one of the best in the business.

The author also wishes to acknowledge the multitalented Robin Phillips of Author Help (robin@authorhelp.uk) Staffordshire, England. Over the years, Robin has been my go-to person on a host of publishing and website endeavors. Once my manuscript is edited by Jessica, I send it along to Robin who takes it from there. Robin does everything—formats print and Kindle editions, secures ISBNs, creates artwork and cover design, and uploads the finished product onto Amazon, who then handles print production and advertising. Soup to nuts, Author Help provides a complete publishing package.

The author also wishes to identify the painting on the front cover as the work of Pablo Picasso entitled "Massacre in Korea," depicting the barbarism of the Korean War, which indescribably killed millions of Korean men, women, and children.

CAST IN ORDER OF APPEARANCE

Si Woo - *Assassin*
Amon-ra - *Si Woo's wife*
Neeku - *Si's three-year-old daughter*
Leia - *Si's five-year-old daughter*
Kim Jong-un - *North Korean Supreme Leader*
Dr. Hyeon - *Neeku's doctor*
Ri Sol-ju - *Kim's wife*
Captain Judy Sluzac - *Drone and F-15 fighter pilot*
Joey Sluzac - *Judy's brother*
Rose Conway - *Judy's amigo at the air base*
Kylo-ren - *Director of the National Police*
Sejong - *Kim Jong-un's brother*
Elizabeth Kleinshure - *Led covert CIA operation to kill Kim*
Amor-ra - *Sejong's partner*
Thi-sen - *Amor's father and drug kingpin*
Officer Brenda Carson - *Judy's amigo*
General Zoko - *Leader of conspiracy*
Colonel Prescott - *Judy's commanding officer*
Pamela - *Derek's daughter and Joey's friend*
Derek Navarro - *Pam's father and Judy's love interest*
Admiral Shumi-un - *Organizes Victory ship*
Allison Brant - *Elizabeth's first alias*
Sara Murphy - *Elizabeth's second alias*
Grace Hayworth - *Elizabeth's third alias*
Moe Shorthair - *Prescott's drinking buddy*
Betty Ann Monroe - *Woman molested by Colonel Prescott*

Juan Carlos - *Elizabeth's lover*
Brad - *Derek's brother*
Mrs. Romano - *Juan's client in Milan*
Kitty - *Victim of Senator Levitt*
Senator Rollins Levitt - *Rapist*
Doris Kearns Goodman - *President of the United States*
Commander Paul Steele - *F-22 Raptor pilot*
Gayle Santos - *Juan's client in London*
Marco - *Gayle Santos's boy toy*
Attorney Josh Davis - *Brad's attorney*
Maria - *Juan's daughter*

PROLOGUE

Peoples Housing Unit T-5486
29 Clelu Boulevard
Pyongyang, North Korea

After a quick shower, Si Woo made his bed and laid out his green army uniform. As he stood there looking down at his uniform, a chill came over him with the realization that today would be the last time he would wear the uniform of the Supreme Guard. Si took a deep breath and walked around his small, four-room apartment, trying to catch his breath and collect his thoughts. After the death of his wife, Amon-Ra, five years ago in a bicycle accident, he was eligible to move into a new People's Housing complex with his mother-in-law, Eeth-so, and his two daughters, Neeku, age three, and Leia, age five. *Life's been good here*, he thought, scanning the simple artifacts he treasured—a family photograph by Lake Gungi, a photo of him and Amon-Ra at a popular restaurant, and a photo of him in his green-and-white dress uniform. In the space of a mere five years, Si had risen in the ranks of the Supreme Guard to now become one of the personal guards protecting the presidential palace, which housed the Supreme Leader Kim Jong-u, his family, and high-ranking government officials. The palace and its sub-buildings were located on a 247-acre site surrounded by a fifteen-foot stone wall in Pyongyang, the capital of North Korea. A complement of three hundred guards rotated twenty-four hours a day both inside and outside the palace grounds. The defense of the site was accomplished using what was considered a multilayered military concept: the guards that carried high-powered weapons, submachine guns, and assault rifles were stationed farthest from the palace; the guards stationed on the first two floors wore sidearms; and the guards on the third and fourth floors were unarmed. This was based on an age-old Korean theory that the greatest danger was from without, not within. In close proximity to the palace was a military compound housing an anti-aircraft battery of surface-to-air missiles, two helicopter gunships, and several armored personnel carriers of various sizes. In fact, most international defense experts considered the presidential palace in Pyongyang better defended than the White House in the United States.

. . .

Si quickly dressed and went into his daughters' bedroom, which the girls had shared with their grandmother. Everything looked the same as it had four days ago, when the girls were spirited out of Pyongyang on their way to South Korea and freedom. What precipitated this sudden move was Si learning that his three-year old daughter, Neeku, was suffering from juvenile leukemia and that there was nothing they could do for it in North Korea.

"You mean there are no drugs or treatment for my baby?" Si asked Dr. Hyeon, the pediatrician at his local clinic.

"In the west, yes, but not here," Dr. Hyeon said.

"What about in Beijing?" Si asked.

"Yes, Beijing, but that's impossible. China's health care system services over a billion people; she'd never qualify for treatment," Dr. Hyeon said.

"Why do other counties have a cure for this... this disease and we don't?" Si implored him.

"Here in North Korea we have a national health plan for all the people, and it's free. If you're a citizen, it's free. But that comes with some tradeoffs. We're a small country, and in order to provide free health care, there are many procedures that are not covered. For instance, bone marrow transplants are too expensive," Dr. Hyeon said.

"You're telling me there is nothing I can do to save my baby?" Si said, shaking his head in despair. Dr. Hyeon didn't immediately reply but rather went over to his computer and scanned it, looking for something in Si Woo's file. He then rose and told Si that he had to make a phone call and that he'd be back in a few moments. Confused, Si picked up his daughter and pressed her softly to his chest and walked around the examination room whispering in her ear that Daddy loved her and would find a way to save his little bundle of joy.

After what seemed like an eternity, Dr. Hyeon returned and, taking Si by the hand, asked, "Would you give your life for your daughter?"

Si didn't hesitate. "Yes, yes… anything… yes."

Dr. Hyeon squeezed Si's hand. "I thought you would. Say nothing to anyone… anyone. I can call you at home?" he asked.

"Yes," Si replied, shaking the doctor's hand.

"Good. I will call you with a time and place for you to meet a man named Sam; he will tell what you must do. Again, tell no one," the doctor said as he left the room.

Si, overcome with grief, sat on the edge of his daughters' bed and took one of their pillows, pressing it to his face. He could still smell their sweet aroma, and as he closed his eyes, he could see their happy faces as he kissed them on their rosy cheeks.

Glancing at his daughters' Minnie Mouse alarm clock, Si quickly gathered what he'd need to accomplish his mission, locked his door, and proceeded to the bus stop to be on time at his guard post in the palace to accomplish his mission. Today was the day he would assassinate the Supreme Leader, Kim Jong-un.

1

North Bus 3
To the Presidential Palace

Si let the women enter the bus before him, then made his way to the center. As he did so, the passengers gracefully bowed their heads in recognition of his army uniform. In the capital city of Pyongyang, most of the residents held positions within the government, and it was common for military personnel to use public transportation. Pressing his right hand against his side, Si felt the bayonet hidden in his pocket. He was given the bayonet when he met with his contact at the park several days ago. Sitting on a park bench his contact reviewed his assignment. He was told to place the bayonet through a hole in his pants pocket and that when it came time to attack the Supreme Leader, he should grab him around the neck and plunge the bayonet below his rib cage on the left side of his torso. He was told to plunge the blade as many times as he could before swallowing the poison pill taped to the inside of his wrist.

When he examined the weapon for the first time, he saw that it was actually a twelve-inch plastic ruler fashioned into a bayonet; it was designed to pass undetected through metal detectors. With so many people entering and exiting the palace, in many respects, the security checkpoints were a mere formality, as people were usually in a hurry to get to their assigned duties. Yet as Si got in line, he began to perspire and hoped that his nerves would not betray the fear that he had brewing inside him. When it was his turn to pass through the metal detector, the guard merely smiled at him and waved him through.

Since he was twenty minutes early, he decided to stop at the commissary and get a cup of tea. Fearful of taking a seat with a twelve-inch bayonet in his pocket, he leaned against the wall and watched the men and women who worked at the palace dunk their donuts in their hot cups of tea. For one brief moment, he felt that his assignment was madness and that killing the Supreme Leader made no sense. For it wasn't Kim's fault that his daughter had juvenile leukemia; it wasn't Kim's fault that his daughter couldn't get a bone marrow transplant. But his family, his mother-in-law and precious daughters, were now safely out of North Korea.

"What's done is done," he said to himself. He must

rid himself of these thoughts and carry out his mission. However, just before returning his cup to the kitchen, he noticed a young couple standing in the doorway, just a few feet from him, holding hands and looking lovingly into each other's eyes, just like he and his late wife, Amon-Ra, would do when he went off to officer training school. She meant so much to him; she was his whole world, and his sudden, inexplicable loss was more than he could handle. A stupid bicycle accident, the truck driver hadn't seen her; he was momentarily blinded by the sun, and like that... Si's world was gone... gone forever.

Si took a tree-lined path to the palace. The path took him around a retaining pond with a jet sending water twenty feet into the sky. During his walk his thoughts went to the meeting he had had with the man who had given him his assignment. He was young, tall, and spoke with an unfamiliar accent. Si guessed that the man came from one of the northern provinces. He said if Si was successful, the United States would not attack North Korea. He said that plans were underway in the United States to conduct a preemptive strike against North Korea's atomic weapons program. He said that the Supreme Leader would not listen to reason and that millions would die; that Si was really a patriot by killing Kim; and that his daughter would receive the treatment she needed and his family would enjoy a better life in America.

Si was now approaching the second checkpoint leading to the palace. He hoped that it would be as smooth as it had been coming through the main gate entering the grounds... and it was. The plastic bayonet didn't set off any alarms, and Si was free to enter the palace to start his shift. Taking the freight elevator to the fourth floor, Si relieved the sentry by the passenger elevator. Across the way, another new sentry took his post adjacent to the door to the Supreme Leader's quarters. Now was the hardest part of Si's assignment: waiting for the Supreme Leader to come close enough to him that he could stab him to death.

For the next several hours, the comings and goings of people to the Supreme Leader's quarters were normal. Most were support personnel: maids, tutors for the children, kitchen staff, messengers, office staff with papers for Kim to sign, and guests invited to meet with Kim and his wife, Ri Sol-ju. Deliveries to the Supreme Leader's quarters were brought through a separate rear freight elevator, which was guarded by five military officers who inspected everything.

Then, just as Si feared that Kim had different plans for the day, the door to Kim's residence opened, and out strolled Kim, dressed in a white, terrycloth bathrobe, and beside him, holding his hand, was his three-year-old son, Ling-tu, wearing an identical, white bathrobe. Instinctively the guard across from Kim pressed a wireless switch on his belt, alerting the elevator operator to come to the fourth floor. Happy and smiling, Kim and his son proudly marched hand in hand to the elevator. Si, realizing that this was his opportunity to attack, placed his hand in his pocket and gripped the bayonet. Just then, Kim's son broke free from his father's grasp and raced to greet the friendly man in the elevator. The elevator operator greeted the boy by lifting him into the air and turned, effectively blocking Si's path to stab Kim, then gently deposited the child into his father's outstretched arms. With the opportunity to stab Kim dashed by the impromptu movement of the elevator operator, Si took his position alongside the elevator and waited for his next opportunity.

However, the wait was not long in coming. After only forty-five minutes the elevator door opened, and out stepped Kim, this time without his son. Seizing his opportunity, Si quickly withdrew the bayonet, grabbed Kim from behind by the throat, and pulled him toward himself, stabbing Kim exactly where he was instructed: into the left side of Kim's body bellow the rib cage.

Shocked by the attack, the elevator operator lunged at Si, throwing him to the floor just as Si was preparing to withdraw the bayonet and stab Kim again. Si could feel the blade snap in his hand and feverishly attempted to bite the poison capsule taped to his wrist. The next thing Si felt was the guard from across the hall kicking him in the head and stepping on his hand. While the guard restrained Si, the elevator operator sounded the alarm and tried to comfort Kim, who was lying on his back in great pain. Almost instantly guards rushed to the fourth floor to help apprehend the attacker and to call the medical staff on the first floor of the palace. While the guards restrained Si, a medical doctor arrived carrying a first aid kit. Opening Kim's bathrobe, he inspected the wound and what appeared to be an object in his abdomen. Opening his kit, the doctor withdrew an auto-injectable device and said to Kim, "This will relieve your pain." He then plunged the morphine into Kim's hip. A few moments later, two ambulance technicians came running from the freight elevator pushing a gurney. Lowering the gurney to the ground, they quickly and painlessly lifted Kim and placed him on it. After strapping Kim to the gurney, they adjusted the height and raced back to the freight elevator and down to a waiting ambulance.

2

Creech Air Force Base

I t was show-and-tell day at Creech Air Force Base, located on the outskirts of Indian Springs, Nevada. The base had billed it as a once-in-a-lifetime opportunity to see America's newest, biggest, bad-assed weapons system, up close and personal. The MQ-9 Reaper, a hunter-killer drone also known as "the Grim Reaper," was a seventeen-million-dollar sci-fi monster, twenty-seven feet long with a wingspan of sixty-six feet. It was an unmanned aerial vehicle that the military expected to one day replace today's fighter pilots. The base was spit-polished and ready for the arrival of most of the 1,991 residents of Indian Springs, Nevada. The festivities were set begin at 1200 hours with a rendition of the US Airforce song, sung by a chorus of Indian Springs High School students.

"Off we go into the wild blue yonder, climbing high into the sun," played over a loudspeaker.

The information officer then told the crowd to watch for a small, birdlike object approaching the base from the north as it made its turn to land on the runway adjacent to where they were standing. The crowd got a good look at this amazing bird as it slowly approached the runway, lowered its landing gear, and gently raised its nose, rotated its flaps, and touched down like a feather to the cheers of the crowd.

"The Reaper hunter-killer has landed," the officer shouted as the drone came to a stop in front of the crowd. In attendance on this hot, sunny day were Captain Judy Sluzac and Joey, her twenty-two-year-old brother. Judy was one of the twelve UAV pilots stationed at the air force base, and she thought it would be nice for her brother to see what she actually did for a living.

"How'd you like that?" Judy asked Joey.

"Awesome," exclaimed Joey.

"You see those rockets under the wings?" Judy said, pointing to two red-and-white, cigar-shaped missiles.

"Are those real?" Joey asked.

"Real and super deadly. Each one can knock out a tank," Judy said.

"Did you ever fire one of those?" Joey asked.

"Not one of those, but yeah, I've fired missiles in Afghanistan like those," Judy said softly.

"Did you kill anyone?" Joey asked.

"Let's talk about it at home," Judy said as she saw her friend Rose approaching.

The women embraced as Judy said to Rose, "You know my brother, Joey?"

"Yes, and boy has he grown," Rose said to the shy young man. She switched tacks, her voice turning low and husky. "Is he here?"

"I haven't seen him. So far, so good," Judy said, looking around.

"I've got to get back. Call me," Rose said, squeezing Judy's arm.

"Right, we'll talk." Judy nodded as Rose cut through the crowd heading for the parking lot.

"Who isn't here?" Joey asked.

"Oh, this is the part of the show I wanted you to see," Judy said, changing the subject as the information officer requested the crowd to direct their attention to a sleek fighter plane taxiing out of a hangar on the other side of the field.

"That's my F-15 fighter jet," Judy said proudly.

"You fly that jet?" Joey asked.

"We practice. The other UAV pilots and I take turns flying it," Judy said softly as not to call attention to herself.

"Now, like the drone, the F-15 is under the control of a pilot in one of those trailers over there," the information officer said, pointing to a row of forty-foot, tan trailers parked adjacent to a hangar to his right.

"Inside those trailers are command and control facilities to send our drones into reconnaissance, surveillance, or to carry out attacks on people or other targets deemed a threat to the US," the information officer boasted to the crowd.

The F-15 turned onto the runway and came to a stop, awaiting its command to begin its demonstration flight. And what a flight it would be; a flight no one in the crowd would ever forget.

Teasing the crowd, the information officer recited the F-15's specifications. With a length of forty-nine feet and a wingspan of thirty-two feet, the F-15 was the perfect fighter plane to be modified into a UAV. It already had advanced, aerodynamic avionics, a fly-by-wire flight control system, and it was highly maneuverable. "And get this," the officer said, "its top speed is fifteen hundred miles per hour... twice the speed of sound." It was the perfect answer to an enemy drone or cruise missile strike because of its speed and maneuverability, he said to the oohs and aahs from the crowd.

"Now just before I give the OK to begin the show, I do want to advise you if there are any people who are faint of heart, you might want to call it a day and watch the show in the safety of your car or off the base. That's OK, don't be shy," he said as some took him up on his offer.

"OK, I'm going to advise the pilot to begin the demonstration of the newest member of the UAV. Ladies and gentlemen, the F-15." That being said, the information officer took out his walkie-talkie and told the pilot to begin the show.

At first, the plane's movement was slow as it moved

down the runway; then, with a jolt, the plane perked up and began racing down the runway faster and faster until it reached takeoff speed; as flames tore out of its exhaust system, it rocketed off the runway in an incredibly vertical manner, straight into the cloudless sky. Leveling off, the F-15 banked to the right and performed several upside-down loop-the-loops and figure eights, to the delight of the crowd. This went on for several minutes as the F-15 showed how effortlessly it maneuvered at high speeds.

At that time, the information officer interjected that if a real pilot were in the cockpit, they would probably be unconscious due the g-forces on their bodies.

"As I mentioned, the F-15 will now approach the field at an elevation of five thousand feet above ground and will be moving at seven hundred miles per hour, breaking the sound barrier. HOLD ON... HERE SHE COMES." With that brief warning, the F-15 engaged its afterburners, and as the engines screamed overhead, a bone-jarring explosion rocked the field. Some people were frozen in place, and others fell to their knees in utter shock.

"Are you OK?" Judy asked Joey, who stood there motionless.

"Joey," Judy said, shaking Joey by the shoulder.

"Holy shit, I couldn't breathe. Is my nose bleeding?" Joey asked.

"No, are you having difficulty breathing?" Judy asked, concerned.

"It's like someone hit me in the head with a shovel," Joey said; he seemed shaken.

"Can you walk?" Judy asked, holding Joey's hand.

"Yep, but look at all the people on the ground," Joey remarked.

"That didn't go well," Judy said. "Look, come with me to the car. You'll wait there for me while I help out here."

"No. No, I'm OK now. I want to help," Joey insisted.

Judy could only look on in awe as her little brother got on his knees to help an elderly man trying to get to his feet. Joey, God bless him, had been beset with health problems his entire life. Spinal curvature as a child left him with back and leg deformities. Only after years of surgery and physical therapy was Joey able to walk with a cane, and here he was on all fours, comforting those in shock. Seeing the kindness Joey had for strangers in need, Judy got down on her knees and embraced her baby brother and cried.

3

People's Hospital of Pyongyang

Soon after the ambulance left carrying Kim to the hospital, several black, unmarked police cars arrived at the presidential palace. Their first order of business was to lock down the building until the staff were interviewed. In charge of the investigation was Kylo-ren, the director of the National Police. However, before leaving his office to investigate the crime scene, he had personally assigned over one hundred of his top detectives to drop whatever they were doing and find those responsible for this heinous act. He also received permission from Pak Thae-bok, the chairman of the Supreme People's Assembly, to be in direct control of the investigation, superseding the military police, since it was their breakdown in security and the attacker was ostensibly a member of the MP. Kylo-Ren also put in call to Kim Jong-un's brother, Sejong, and gave him a brief rundown of what he knew at that point in time and agreed to meet him at the hospital within the hour.

Sejong and Kylo met in a conference room in the surgical ward just steps away from where Kim was undergoing surgery. The doctors had decided that Kim's spleen had to be removed since there was no way to stop his internal bleeding. Kylo described in vivid detail what the elevator operator and the guard on the fourth floor saw and did during the attack on the Supreme Leader. Kylo had them reenact, in slow motion, what each person did. Kylo said that by their quick and selfless actions, they had saved Kim's life.

"And where is the assassin? You said his name was Si Woo?" asked Sejong.

"He's at the National Police Headquarters under constant surveillance," Kylo said.

"Has he been interrogated?" asked Sejong.

"Not yet, but as soon as I leave the hospital, I will join my detectives in conducting his interrogation. I want to be there when they interrogate him... and at this point in time, we need more information," Kylo said.

Sejong kept his thoughts to himself until more was known about the attacker Si Woo, but his gut feeling was that the CIA was behind it. They probably sold the idea to a renegade group of disgruntled military men as a 'regime change' and an opportunity for the military to take over the government.

Impatient to get back to headquarters to begin the interrogation, Kylo went over to the nurses' station and requested an update on Kim's status. Recognizing that Kylo was not one to be ignored, the nurse donned a sterile gown and went into the operating room. She returned a few moments later with news that the Supreme Leader's vital signs were improving and that they would know more in a few hours. What she did not tell Kylo was that Kim had a low-grade fever and that they were running an IV with a broad-spectrum antibiotic in hopes of staving off a postop infection.

Just as Kylo and Sejong were making their goodbyes, in marched a contingent of police surrounding a frantic Ri Sol-ju, Kim's wife. Seeing Sejong, she ran over to him and asked, with tears in her eyes, "Where is Jong?" Sejong took Ri Sol-Ju's hand and softly reassured her that Kim was doing fine.

"The nurse just spoke with the surgeon and reported back to us that Kim's vital signs were good," said Kylo.

"Ri Sol-Ju, this is Kylo-Ren, the director of The National Police," Sejong said by way of introduction.

"I was told you have the man that attempted to kill our Supreme Leader. Why? Why did he do it?" Ri Sol-Ju asked.

"I will have more information after he's interrogated at headquarters, and I will advise you at that time," Kylo said with a slight bow.

"I want to see my husband. I want to see Jong... I want to see him now. Can you arrange that?" Ri Sol-Ju asked Kylo.

"Let me speak with the nurse. I'll be right back," Kylo said softly and went to find the nurse.

"Ri Sol-ju, can I get you something to drink?" Sejong asked, seeing how distraught his sister-in-law was, but she didn't reply. Kylo returned to tell her that Kim was being brought to the intensive care unit and that a room was being organized for her to wait in until she could see him.

Approaching Ri Sol-Ju, Kylo said softly, "My lady, I will do everything in my power to see that the people who are responsible for this crime against our Supreme Leader and our wonderful nation are brought to justice," Kylo said with a slow and meaningful bow. He then instructed his policemen to protect her with their lives. The nurse approached and informed them that a suite had been prepared for the Supreme Leader's wife, but before Ri left with her escort, she approached Sejong and thanked him for always being there for his brother.

Sejong replied, "I am your servant and will always be here for you and our Leader."

Kylo, seeing an opportunity to make a graceful exit and return to police headquarters, turned, extending his hand to Sejong. "I must get back to begin the interrogation."

Taking Kylo's hand and holding it firmly, Sejong came eye to eye with the director. "I don't care what you have to do to find out who was responsible for this attack on my brother," he said, "just do it." With that, Sejong released Kylo's hand. Stunned by Sejong's un-orthodox invasion of his personal space, Kylo bowed to acknowledge his instructions. Instead of making an issue of it, he put Sejong's strange behavior down as brotherly love.

4

National Police Headquarters

Racing back to police headquarters, Kylo found dozens of people milling around the building as cadets tried to keep them behind hastily erected barriers. Getting out of his car, he found that these people were shouting questions as to the Supreme Leader's condition.

Before entering the building, he turned to the crowd to say, "Our Supreme Leader is strong and mighty and is attending to the business of the state. I will keep you informed as we proceed with our investigation. For now, I implore you to return home as updates will be posted on your televisions. We thank you for your support."

With that Kylo quickly entered the building to take

charge of the investigation. His first order to his staff was that no one was to discuss the case with anyone not directly involved with the investigation. He then directed his lead detectives to begin the suspect's interrogation. Dressed in a green jumpsuit, Si Woo was brought in handcuffs and leg shackles to Interrogation Room B1 in the basement. The room had a metal table, which was bolted to the floor and had a steel hoop on top to attach the suspect's handcuffs. There were two steel chairs for the investigators and one steel chair directly across from them in which the suspect sat, but in this case the suspect's chair was bolted to the floor. Si Woo sat erect, staring at a four-by-six-foot black sheet of plate glass mounted to the wall, behind which police detectives were observing his every remark. Si's face showed signs that he had recently been in a fight, with welts around his eyes, bruises on his neck, and a cut on his lower lip. Glancing around, Si noticed several small video cameras mounted to the ceiling and walls. He had no doubt that everything he said would be recorded and analyzed by teams of investigators.

The detectives began by establishing for the record the people in the room. The detectives gave their names, rank, and the day, date, and time of the interview. After reviewing some notes, they asked Si to state his name, military rank, and address for the record. To this, Si sat back in his chair, glared at the detectives, and said nothing. Seeing no response from the suspect, one of the detectives, reading from the binder, stated the suspect's name, military rank, and address. The detectives then tried a number of simple, mundane questions to merely break the ice; again, Si was nonresponsive. In the observation room, Kylo made notes on a yellow legal pad and, turning to a police psychiatrist called in to give his opinion of the suspect, said, "This is getting us nowhere; let's go on to plan B." Kylo told his team to cancel the interrogation and meet him in his private conference room in an hour with everything they'd collected so far. When Kylo entered his conference room he was surprised to see crowded around the table seven of his detectives and piles of papers, photographs, and video-recorded testimony from dozens of character witnesses.

"Well, let us start with the suspect's family. Who covered that aspect of the case?" Kylo asked.

A bright-eyed, young-looking detective raised his hand and said, "I did, sir."

"OK, who are you and what have you found?" Kylo asked.

"I am Plo Kon, sir. The suspect, Si Woo, a widower, lived at the People's Housing Unit T-5486, 29 Clelu Boulevard, with his mother-in-law, Eeth-so, and his two daughters, Neeku, age three, and Leia, age five. Neither his mother-in-law nor his daughters have been seen in four days. The examination of their apartment indicates that they packed up and left. Security cameras at Moria, a local department store, show the suspect purchasing two large, khaki duffel bags three days before they disappeared."

"Excellent," Kylo said to his young detective. "Who checked his mobile phone records?"

Up shot the hand of a plainclothes detective.

"Sir, the suspect made twenty-six outgoing calls and received fifteen over the past thirty days. I've made copies of the calls," he said as he passed sheets of paper to the group. The majority of outgoing calls were made to his five-year-old daughter's grade school, his local medical clinic, the presidential palace switchboard, and to his mother-in-law. "Now, his incoming calls are suspicious in that, of the fifteen calls, twelve were from untraceable, disposable mobile devices unavailable in our country. The other calls were from his medical clinic," said the plainclothes detective.

"Did you follow up on any of the outgoing calls?" Kylo asked.

"Yes, sir. According to their records, most, if not all, pertained to a serious, life-threatening condition his three-year old, Neeku, had: juvenile leukemia."

"At that time was she undergoing treatment?" Kylo asked.

"No, sir. The clinic said it's not part of the patient's coverage."

"What does that mean in laymen's terms? Are they treating her? Yes or no?" Kylo asked, getting irritated by the medical doublespeak.

"No, sir, it's not offered under Si Woo's medical coverage," the detective responded.

"And it's fatal?" Kylo said.

"Yes, it's fatal," the detective said hesitantly.

With that, the room went silent as each officer pondered whether this was the straw that broke the camel's back.

5

Central Intelligence Agency
Langley, Virginia
Annex Room M-3668

Elizabeth Kleinshure was a low-level CIA paper pusher assigned to liaise with field agents requiring travel arrangements. She loved the word, liaise; it sounded very important and Elizabeth always wanted to be important. When asked what she did at the CIA by family and the few friends she had, Elizabeth would look from side to side, then whisper, "I'd tell you, but then I'd have to kill you," holding her finger to her lips and blowing the gun smoke from her imaginary 007 Beretta semiautomatic. Sadly, Elizabeth was nothing more than a travel agent making $29.23 per hour, but she acted like she ran covert operations from her office. As part of the charade, everything in her office was under lock and key, as if field agents' lives depended on her ability to keep a secret. In addition, being a spinster didn't look good in the button-down world of the CIA, so Miss Kleinshure filled her office with pictures of her nieces and nephews and friends and acquaintances. In some cases, they were merely the photos that came with the frames, but unbeknownst to everyone except a few trusted subordinates, Elizabeth was conducting a covert operation of her own, an operation that was guaranteed to catapult her within the ranks of the CIA.

Confidential Phone Call 4:05 p.m.
From: Elizabeth Kleinshure
To: Muriel Cook, secretary
Start Recording:
Kleinshure:
"There's a fly in my office and he's driving me crazy.
Hello, hello, is there anyone there?"
Cook:
"Yes, I'm sorry, but... did you say a guy is driving you crazy?"
Kleinshure:
"Yes, yes, are you deaf?
"I'm in my office, Annex Room M-3668, and I'm being harassed by a large, black, ugly fly."
Cook:

"Did you say that you were being harassed by a large, ugly Black guy?"
Kleinshure:
"No, no, listen to me. It is a fly... you know, it has wings and flies. Send someone to kill him."
Cook:
"Have you tried to kill this Black guy?"
Kleinshure:
"Are you stupid or deaf?"
Cook:
"Neither and I'm going to report this conversation to HR to follow up on your threat to kill an ugly Black guy."
Kleinshure:
"Go to hell."
Stop Recording 4:07 p.m.

"Marylou, come in here and bring a newspaper," said Kleinshure into the intercom.

"Ms. Kleinshure, the *Washington Post* has not come yet. Is yesterday's paper OK?" replied Marylou.

"I don't give a shit if it's last years. Any paper will do; I gotta kill this fly," Kleinshure said, looking at the ceiling and muttering to herself, "Why me, God? Why me?"

As things happen for some unforeseen reason, when Marylou came in with the previous day's *Post*, the ugly, black fly had disappeared. Obviously, he had been tipped off.

"Marylou, as you're here, tell the team we're having a meeting at

0900 hours in my office and tell Jerry I want the room swept for bugs." As Marylou left Kleinshure's office, she thought of the déjà vu moment that had just passed.

After everyone refilled their coffee cups, four members of her team, who were stateside—Jerry, Sal, Larry, and Bill—settled into chairs around a circular conference table.

"The room's clean?" Kleinshure asked Jerry.

"As my baby's ass," Jerry responded.

"Fine. What's the word from NK?" Kleinshure asked.

"You know Si Woo failed in his attempt to kill Kim Jong-un," Sal said.

"Yes, yes, that's old news, but how did he survive the polonium?" Kleinshure asked.

"Beats me," Sal replied with a shrug.

"They'll probably be rounding up the general and his people," Bill added. "Yeah, but it was a good operation. No one ever got that close before," Jerry said.

"And they got the money to the general before the shit hit the fan, right?"

Kleinshure asked. "Well then, we're covered. Get the boys out of harm's way before the South Koreans find out this was an off-the-books CIA operation."

"Oh, one last thing, boss: What about Si Woo's kids?" Larry asked.

"How much did we give that guy in SK?" Kleinshure asked.

"One fifty big ones," Jerry said.

"In that case, he'll deal with them," Kleinshure said.

"Any other new business?" she asked. "None? OK, this meeting is over." She rose from her chair as a large, black fly buzzed near her ear.

6

"Is everyone here?" asked Director Kylo. "Alright, let us start with Si Woo's missing family. Anything new?"

"There's some chatter amongst police in the south that there's a security detail assigned to a young, female patient in a hospital. That in itself is highly suspicious," a detective said.

"Unless she's a movie star," another detective quipped to some muffled laughter.

"That's enough of that. Do you know the hospital?" Kylo asked.

"No, but we know the police district has four hospitals in it, and our people in the south can check them out," the detective said.

"Good. Have them find her and get us a copy of her chart," Kylo said. "Well? Any word on how they got to the south?"

"An old woman and two young kids? No, this was carried out by professionals. The car that collected them was black and looked military, an eyewitness said. Most likely it rendezvoused with a fishing trawler that took them south and passed them off to the police," a seasoned detective mused.

"What about this pediatrician's cell phone calls?" Kylo asked.

"He's under twenty-four-hour surveillance. It seems Si Woo and the doctor shared common incoming calls from an untraceable phone," said a detective.

"Anything else?" Kylo asked, looking around. "OK, then it's time to get theatrical. This is what I want: some props. We'll pretend that the trawler never got to the south. That it capsized and all on board were killed. That the only body to wash ashore was Si Woo's three-year-old daughter, the little girl with juvenile leukemia. Now we know that Si Woo purchased two duffel bags at a department store—get me an exact copy of one of them. Then go to his apartment and get a bag filled with the children's clothes and shoes. Don't take clothes that are laying about; get clothes he may not have noticed after they had gone—you know, in the bottom of their drawers. Look for some memorabilia, too, also hidden and out of sight. Then go to the morgue and get me some black-and-white photos of children who died in the flood six years ago. We need individual photos of little girls whose bodies were face down in the mud. Now this is important; throw everything in a large bucket of muddy water and leave it out to dry in the sun. When it's dry and covered with caked-on mud, place some items in evidence bags; then take one of the three-year-old's shoes and have our photo lab insert the shoe into one of the children's facedown pictures. When the props are ready, call me and I'll show you how to set the stage."

A few days later, after what many detectives in the investigation referred to as "Kylo's Scavenger Hunt," the duffel bag, the children's clothing, shoes, and mementos all looked like they had come out of the sea and ended up drying on the shore. The most time-consuming and depressing part was sifting through the hundreds of photos of children who had died in the flood six years ago. Confident that all was ready, they brought the props to the interrogation room and called Kylo to set the stage. Eager to see the fruits of their labor, Kylo wasted no time in getting to the interrogation room and was amazed, simply amazed, at how thoroughly his men had carried out his instructions. He asked that a table be brought into the room to display the props. He then selected two evidence bags and, after wrinkling them up, put the mud caked clothing in them. He let some of the items overflow as he positioned them on the prop table. The duffel bag was also left open and additional clothes and items were seemingly, carelessly placed in it. This, too, was placed on the prop table. Then Kylo examined the doctored photographs and placed them between the detectives, in sight but out of reach of the handcuffed prisoner. For the coup de grace, a single little shoe was placed on the table between Si Woo and the interrogation team. Finished, Kylo announced with a broad smile that it was, "Show time. Bring in the prisoner."

Si Woo entered, looking tired. It seemed the guards had removed everything in his cell and forgotten to shut off the lights. He slept on a cold concrete floor next to a hole where the toilet once sat. Once his handcuffs were attached to the table, Si Woo sat back and took in the items all around him—the evidence bags, duffel bag, photographs—and fixed his eyes on his baby's shoe sitting in front of him. The detectives could see a visible tremor as Si Woo took in his children's belongings.

The detectives followed protocol, reciting their names, ranks, the date and time. They requested the same information from Si Woo. Still looking at his daughter's shoe, he remained silent. One of the detectives, reading off a card, recited the information for him. The detectives then gave Si Woo the bad news in a somewhat roundabout way.

"In this world there're some people you can trust and some you can't.

Unfortunately, you picked the wrong ones. The enemies of our great nation fed you lies and misinformation, and you blindly accepted them. You were given the most important responsibility, the protection of our Sovereign Leader, our Supreme Leader, Kim Jong-un, all of which you cast aside, and in doing so you lost everything. Si Woo, I must advise you that the ones you trusted, the ones you put your faith in, killed your mother-in-law and your dear little ones, Neeku and Leia."

Hearing this Si Woo lost control of himself and tore at his handcuffs. "What have I done? What have I done?" he screamed. "All I wanted was for my baby to be saved; it was my life for our Leader. Kill me; just kill me," he said over and over again as he cried. Sensing that they had broken through his wall of silence, the interrogators carefully and gently began extracting the information they needed to pursue the ones who put him up to it.

"And the doctor, Dr. Hyeon at the clinic, proposed a life-for-a-life scenario. If you killed our Leader, they, whoever they are, would smuggle your family out of the country for medical treatment to cure your daughter and ultimately resettle them in the United States. Is that correct?"

Nodding, Si Woo was asked to answer in the affirmative for the record.

"Now you said that you met a man named Sam in the park to receive instructions and the weapon to use in the attack on our Supreme Leader. Is that correct?"

Si Woo answered yes.

"You will also cooperate with our artist to help us in creating a likeness of this person?"

Si Woo answered yes, shaking his head.

"You will also bear witness at the trial of Dr. Hyeon and a person you know as Sam."

"Yes," replied Si Woo. "And my family... my babies?"

One of the detectives placed his hand over Si Woo's. "They have been cremated and their ashes dispersed at sea as is the custom." After the prisoner was led away to his cell, Kylo entered the interrogation room and shook hands with his detectives, saying that he pitied Si Woo and wanted the ruse they used to coax the truth out of the man kept a secret.

"Now, take him to our artist and have him come up with a likeness of this conspirator named Sam. And arrest Dr. Hyeon for the attempted murder of our great Leader," Kylo ordered.

7

Sejong's Estate
Thirty Miles from Pyongyang

On his way back from the hospital, Sejong called his partner, Amor, and asked her to invite her father, Thi-sen, to their home for dinner. When Amor asked Sejong about Kim's condition, Sejong parried her request, saying, "My love,

I will share what I know when I get home," meaning that he would rather tell her in person than on a mobile device.

When Sejong arrived home some fifteen minutes later, an orange sun was setting in the west over the estate's majestic facade. It was the first home that Sejong had had the privilege to build, based on his memories of the architecture in Switzerland and France, where he and his brother were students. He remembered vividly the quaint, narrow streets and outdoor cafes, the smells of fresh bread and garlic, and the rich, full-bodied carafes of local wines. But most of all, he remembered the close bond that Jong-un and he had developed during those magical years together.

Greeting Amor with a hug he asked her if she had been able to contact her father and was told that he was on his way. Sejong was anxious to ask Thi-sen if he could lend a hand in the investigation. Thi-sen was the only official in North Korea secretly allowed to import narcotics into the country for sale and distribution to the country's elite—senior military officers, medical practitioners, industrialists, members of the ruling class, and manufacturing magnates. The two main classes of drugs were cannabis and cocaine. He was also privy to the diplomatic agents who frequented Hong Kong and Singapore where he did his drug business. In this area of the world, the back channels were sometimes the only way to gain useful and sensitive information, and being a drug dealer, this was a natural asset.

Thi-sen arrived soon after. Having kissed his daughter on both cheeks, he embraced the man he called his 'favorite son.'

"Tell me, how is Kim?" he asked Sejong, stepping back and sipping his drink.

"The surgeons removed his spleen. That's all they're willing to say," Sejong said.

"Have you seen him?" Amor asked.

"No, he's in intensive care. However, I did see Ri Sol-ju at the hospital. They've made a suite available for her," Sejong said.

"And the perpetrator?" Thi-sen asked.

"He was one of Kim's palace guards."

"Tell me how I can help you," Thi-sen said, taking a long swig of his drink.

"Information, basically… who was behind the attack for starts," Sejong said.

"Who's heading up the investigation?" Thi-sen asked.

"Kylo-Ren."

To this, Thi-sen merely nodded.

"He's OK?" Sejong asked.

"Oh yes, he was trained by the best—Scotland Yard and the French Sûreté," Thi-sen replied, shaking his head to emphasize his point.

"Excellent. Please let me know only me what you learn. We cannot trust anyone at this stage of the investigation," said Sejong.

"I will contact my trusted sources tonight and let you know what I learn," Thi-sen said with a reassuring smile.

"Now, shall we eat?" Amor said, signaling her cook to serve dinner.

After a slow-paced, enjoyable dinner Sejong and Amor walked Thi-sen to his sleek Mercedes-Benz, and as his driver opened the door for him, he turned and gracefully bowed to his two children and was off in a flash to his next appointment.

After lighting up a joint, Sejong and Amor relaxed on their sofa, sipping a French wine while passing the joint between them.

"I thought it went well," said Amor, taking a drag.

"Your father continually amazes me... the charm that pours from him, the theatrics, the instincts, knowing just what to say and do without a script... I learn something every time we speak," Sejong said, taking a hit on their communal joint. Changing the subject, he reiterated a theme that his partner and love had heard many times before...his hatred of the western colonial powers and their part in the genocide of the Korean people during the Korean War.

"I know in my heart and soul that the United States was instrumental in the plot to kill Kim" Sejong began, though he was interrupted by Amor requesting the joint.

"They thrive on war. Whereas other nations seek peaceful resolution of their differences, the United States looks for excuses to attack—usually smaller, poorer, less industrialized countries that have natural resources, tin, copper, aluminum, and such, that they want for their war machines.

"You know when I was adopted by Kim's father, Kim Jong-il, there were few orphans like me compared to the thousands of orphans after the bombing campaign during the war. That killed more than five million men, women, and children—in only three years! They destroyed every city, town, village by carpet-bombing, and if you survived? Well, you were incinerated with gelatin gas bombs that the bastards then used in Vietnam," Sejong said, running his fingers through Amor's hair.

"You were one of the lucky ones," Amor said, kissing his hand.

The two retired to their bedroom for a well-deserved sleep, yet all was not well at the hospital. Only an hour later they received a call from Director Kylo that Kim had been placed in a medically induced coma.

"But we were told that his condition was stabilized," Sejong said. He had been in a stoned state of torpor, but the call had flung him out of bed, and he stumbled through the process of getting dressed.

"I wasn't given any word that he required this type of aggressive treatment at this time. I'm leaving for the hospital and will call you—" Kylo began to say when Sejong said, "I'm on my way. I'll meet you there," and hung up.

"What's wrong?" Amor asked, looking for the light switch.

"Kim's in a coma, a medically induced coma," Sejong said, looking for his pants.

"What does that mean?" Amor asked, going into her closet for something to wear.

"I don't know, but you don't have to go. I'll call from the hospital when—"

But she was already out of the closet, dressed and ready to go, saying, "I should be there for Ri Sol. Besides, we're not in any condition to drive after partying. Call Tasu to drive."

"You're right," he said, picking up the intercom and telling Tasu, one of their bodyguards, to bring their car around. Tasu had been one of their many bodyguards for many years and was a jack-of-all-trades, an excellent marksman, an IT graduate in computer technology, an ex-commando, and knew his way around the kitchen... and makes excellent omelets.

8

Indian Springs, Nevada
High School Baseball Field

"You coming or do you need a ride?" Rose asked Judy.

"I'm coming, I'm coming. What time is it?" Judy responded.

"It's time for a cold one. I have a six-pack on ice and a bag of salty chips."

"I'll meet you there in fifteen," Judy said.

"Roger dodger, 10-4," Rose said, cutting the connection.

The 'there' was the back of the Indian Springs High School baseball field, their chosen meeting spot to discuss the events of the world as they unfolded in the soap opera that was known as the Creech Air Force Base of Indian Springs, Nevada. While Judy flew unmanned F-15 fighter jets, Rose had administrative duties at the air base.

"Well, did you pull an all-nighter?" Rose inquired as Judy pulled up next to her.

"How can you tell?" Judy responded, getting out of her car and into Rose's Caddy convertible.

"'Cause you look like shit, that's why," Rose exclaimed, handing Judy a Bud Light.

"Well, how about you?" Judy asked, opening the Bud and sucking up the foam.

"Could be better," Rose said with a smirk.

"What's it now with Tony?"

Tony was Rose's ex and the thorn in her side.

"The SOB is hustling on the side," Rose said.

"What's wrong? He's a businessman," Judy said with a smile.

"Businessman my ass. He's a bartender at an Italian restaurant on the Vegas strip," Rose barked.

"What's it this time?" Judy asked, opening a bag of potato chips.

"He's moved a couple of young hookers into his bungalow and is pimping their asses at his restaurant, that's what." In her agitation, Rose spilled some Bud on her white T-shirt, which had stenciled in black the words 'Mean Bitch.'

"You mean when a john enters the restaurant and swaggers up to the bar and asks for a scotch, Tony asks if he wants a J&B or a BJ?" Judy laughed, realizing how funny her remark was.

"Not funny. My kids are down the street at Caesars

Palace dealing blackjack," Rose sadly remarked.

"You miss 'em?" Judy asked.

"Don't ask 'cause I'll start balling," Rose said, looking away and drying her nose on her sleeve.

"Did I tell you about my tours in Afghanistan?" Judy said, trying to change the subject.

"Only a thousand times," Rose replied.

"Good. So, I had recently lost my copilot, so to speak, in my trailer. The guy transferred stateside, and they sent me his replacement. So, when I heard a knock on the door of my trailer, I got up to let him in, and there, standing in the doorway, was the most beautiful man I'd ever seen. I didn't know if I should shake his hand or drop my drawers, so I stood there staring at him. I didn't know what to say; words didn't come out of my mouth like, you know, how humans speak. I must have looked like a complete idiot. I think I said, 'Well, well, come in, big guy,' like Mae West in a John Wayne western. Then I said, 'Why don't you shit over there?' He was gracious and, oh did he know what to do. He fucked me this way and that for the next eight months... constantly, continuously, passionately," Judy said until Rose was able to stop her before she wet her pants in her car.

"Wait, wait, you've got to see this," Judy said as she took out her iPhone to show her pictures of her lover boy dancing.

. . .

"Jesus he's pretty. Believe me, I got the drift," Rose said with a faraway gaze and sniffle.

"Here's another episode from my years in Afghanistan," Judy began to say.

"Do I have to listen to more 'humping my way around Kandahar'?" Rose asked with a smile.

"Just sit there and be quiet. This is important," Judy said.

"Oh, am I goin' to get a test? I'll take notes," Rose said.

"Don't worry, it's multiple choice and I'll grade you on a curve, OK?" Judy began.

"OK. I got this drone out fifteen, twenty clicks from Kandahar just looking for the Taliban when my communications officer tells me to turn a one-eighty. A convoy of marines is pinned down, taking fire from a building full of Taliban. I spun around and let it all hang out and lickety-split I'm there, but what building was he talking about? He, whoever he was, couldn't paint the building for my laser-guided rocket. Give me a fuckin' landmark and I'll fire, I told him.

"Negative, we're pinned down and taking fire from the building, he said. Are there Taliban on the roof of the building? I asked.

"How the fuck do I know? I can't see what's on the roof, he said sounding desperate. Let me take a pass and see what's up, I told him. Then, out of the blue, he asked me, 'What's your name and what do you drink?'

"I told him Judy and I drink Bud Lite. So, I went sideways and skirted a couple of buildings until I leveled off and spotted a group of Taliban on a roof with a rocket-propelled launcher. I radioed the marine that I spotted the Taliban, and the next thing he had to do was take cover. So, I went out a couple of clicks from the target, leveled off, and sent a Predator rocket at the center of the fuckin' building, then turned and high-tailed my ass out of range. The Predator blew the shit out of the building, and kaboom, everything in the vicinity... Then guess what? The marine came back with, 'Bull's-eye, baby... I owe you big time.'

"Well, a few days later I'm in the mess and I notice this guy. He was tall, wearing his battle gear and flak jacket, asking around for someone, and one of the other soldiers turned and pointed at me. So, this guy marches toward me and standing at attention asks if I'm Judy, a drone pilot. I mumbled yes, and he said, 'Stand up, soldier,' which I did, whereupon he grabbed me by the shoulders and lifted me off the ground, gave me a hug, and whispered, 'You saved me and my men's life. I owe you big time, soldier.' He then gracefully placed me back on the ground. Reaching into his jacket he took out a can of Budweiser. We then came to attention and saluted each other. I remember vividly his smile as he turned and marched away. I never saw or heard from him again. I pray that he survived his tour of duty in Afghanistan."

"Wait, what happened to lover boy... what was his name?" Rose asked.

"His name was Billy, and I was crazy about him, but

he was married with young'uns in Georgia. After he left me, I was at my wits' end until I hooked up with Sergeant Flower, one of the camp shrinks. When I first met her, I couldn't get over her appearance to jive with the thought she was a psychiatrist. She didn't look like a psychiatrist; she was a large, Black woman of maybe fifty with a matron's hairdo and large, white teeth. Don't get me wrong—it wasn't her; it was me and my twisted upbringing. I mean, shrinks are supposed to look like Sigmund Freud, not Oprah Winfrey. Anyway, she showed me how destructive my relationship with Billy was and that everything I did was perfectly normal given where I was at that point in time and what I was doing. Look, I woke up every day hoping to save the men and women I worked with and kill all the Taliban I rightfully could. It was war, kill or be killed. It wasn't one of my childhood video games. I remember what she said to me after our last session. She said, 'Judy, someday you're going to save the world,' and gave me a hug. She was one smart lady, and it didn't cost me dime."

"Oh stop, you're goin' to make me cry," said Rose as she got a small yellow, tube from her glove box and handed it to Judy.

"What's this? It's too small to be a dildo," Judy said, inspecting the device.

"It's mace. I told you I'd get you some," Rose replied.

"But it's so small," Judy said, reading the instructions on the tube.

"Look that shit will stop the SOB in his tracks," Rose said, raising her Bud.

With that the ladies clicked their cans together as a toast to better times as a police car arrived with its lights flashing.

The officer rolled down her window and indicated that Rose should do the same. "Ladies, are you consuming alcoholic beverages within five hundred feet of a public school?" the police officer asked.

"No, Officer Brenda! This is an herbal tea," Rose exclaimed, showing her the can.

"Well, from where I'm standing, it sure looks like a Bud Light," Officer Brenda fired back.

"Negative. Looks can be deceiving, Officer Brenda," Judy responded.

"So they can, so they can," Officer Brenda said. She grinned at the two women, who just happened to be her best friends in Indian Springs and tilted her head to enjoy the sun.

"Fine day, isn't it? What brings you to our neck of the woods?" Rose asked the officer.

"Quite a show you put on at the base the other day. I think a few of our fine residents are still in the hospital with STDs," Officer Brenda remarked.

"You know our work at the base is secret and dangerous and beyond your paygrade, Officer Brenda," Judy snapped.

"Heavens to Murgatroyd! Did I inadvertently overstep the bounds as a duly authorized servant of the people of Indian Springs?" Brenda said.

"Yes, and you are on notice that this conversation is at an end. I am a captain in the United States Army and demand that you cease your questioning forthwith," Judy said, getting out of the car. Officer Brenda exited her car and approached Judy. The girls then laughed and embraced each other.

"So, why are you out here this morning?" Rose asked Brenda.

"We got a call that someone was in the woods flashing the kids," Brenda said.

"Did they say it was two ladies running around in their bloomers?" Judy asked.

"No, I knew instantly it couldn't be you; everyone knows you don't wear underwear," Officer Brenda said getting back in her patrol car.

9

People's Hospital of Pyongyang

When Sejong and Amor arrived at the hospital, Kylo and several of his men were in a lounge adjacent to the intensive care unit speaking to Kim's wife Ri Sol. When Ri Sol saw Sejong and Amor, she ran over to Amor, and the women embraced and began crying. Kylo, not knowing what to do or say, nodded to Sejong to help so that they could talk. Sejong gracefully suggested that the ladies retire to Ri Sol's suite to talk while Sejong and Kylo gathered information so that they could brief the women later. This seemed to assuage Ri Sol, and the women, hand in hand, retreated to her suite just down the hall for a cup of tea.

"Have you spoken to Kim's doctor?" Sejong asked Kylo.

"No, I've just arrived like you, and Ri Sol was here," Kylo said.

"Did someone tell her that Kim's in a coma?"

"She said she asked a nurse as to his status and the rest is history," Kylo said, shaking his head at the incompetence shown by the nurse.

"What's done is done. Let's get a doctor to explain what's going on," Sejong said.

"I've sent two men to find—" Kylo began when he saw one of his detectives approaching, accompanied by a man in a long, white lab coat. "This must be one of the doctors," he said.

"And you are?" Kylo asked, extending his hand in greeting.

"I'm Dr. Numsi, one of the Supreme Leader's doctors. Forgive me if I haven't had the pleasure of meeting you," he said, shaking Kylo's hand.

"Well, I'd be suspicious if you had, doctor, since I am Kylo-ren, director of the National Police," he said with a smile.

"And I am Sejong, Kim's brother," Sejong said. Dr. Numsi bowed and invited the men to follow him to his office.

"I've heard that one of our staff inadvertently told our Supreme Leader's wife that he was in a medically induced coma. That is true," he said, reviewing Kim's chart on his monitor.

"Why intentionally place Kim in a coma?" Sejong asked.

"Yes, a good question but first let me review with

you the underlying facts that brought us to this somewhat drastic move on our part. If I may, I'll use the
word 'patient' in lieu of our Leader's name. Therefore,
to continue, the patient presented with an object in the
shape of a blade embedded in the left torso, below the
rib cage some four inches below the skin line. We assume the handle of the weapon broke off during the attack. Our surgeons determined that since the spleen
was punctured through and through, a splenectomy, removing the spleen, was necessary to stop the bleeding.
The wound was irrigated; vessels were cauterized, su-
tured; a drain inserted and the wound closed. Medica-
tion for pain and antibiotics were administered by IV,
and the patient was transferred to the ICU. Now, here's
where it gets problematic. The weapon was sent to
pathology for testing, and a white residue was found in
a groove in the blade. If our suspicions were accurate
the weapon was designed to be a bayonet. That being
said, one of the features of a bayonet is a long channel
on the blade that, when plunged into the victim, allows
blood to flow out of the wound thereby causing the
victim to bleed out, to bleed to death. However, after
testing the residue, we were unable to determine what
it was beyond the fact that it was a mineral in the form
of a powder, like a talc."

"Is it a poison?" asked Kylo.

"Not a poison we could identify with what we had
available," Dr. Numsi said.

"What do you mean, 'we had available'?" Sejong
asked.

"The spectral analysis consumed most if not all of our sample," Dr. Numsi replied. "However, the next part of my presentation is more immediate and touches on the need for the medically induced coma. We saw in examining the patient's blood under the microscope, at various intervals, changes in the shape and volume of his red blood cells. They began to shrink, become distorted, like a raisin, then would shred apart. To supplement the red blood cells being destroyed, we administered a continuous transfusion of whole blood until we could get a handle on the condition's causes."

"Have you determined its cause?" Sejong asked.

"No, but I have reached out to Tasu So Lu at Beijing Royal Hospital and sent her by email our test reports and microscopic images of the patient's blood," Dr. Numsi boasted.

"Who is this doctor and why go so far for an answer?" Kylo asked.

"She is one of China's eminent hematologists, and if anyone can solve our problem, she can," Dr. Numsi emphasized, staring back at Kylo.

"When will you hear back from this eminent doctor?" Sejong asked.

"Well, that's the good news; she recognized the cells and asked us to check the patient's lymph nodes and blood for radioactivity," Dr. Numsi replied.

"And is he radioactive?" Sejong asked, sitting on the edge of his chair.

"Yes. We've tested the patient's blood samples in

the laboratory, and they've tested positive for Polonium-210, a deadly poison."

"Is there a cure?" Sejong asked, holding his breath.

"Yes. Meso-Dimercaptosuccinic acid," Numsi replied with a wide smile on his face. "We've dispatched our helicopter to the Yongbyon nuclear facility and it's on the way back to the hospital. It should be here in twenty minutes."

Sejong and Kylo looked at each other and smiled.

With the good news, Kylo took his leave to return to police headquarters, and Sejong asked Dr. Numsi if he could spend a few moments with his brother.

"You know he's still in a coma?" Dr. Numsi replied.

"Yes, I won't be long," Sejong said quietly.

"Of course. Let me have a nurse dress you for the ICU," Dr. Numsi said.

In the ICU, Sejong pulled a chair over to Kim's bed and was shocked to see that his brother's lips were a crusty shade of blue. With his hand resting on his brother's arm, Sejong whispered his often mentally rehearsed recitation of his plan to seek revenge on the CIA for their attack on his brother and the US for the massacre of his people during the Korean War. Finally, with tears streaming down his face, Sejong lifted his mask and gently kissed his brother's arm and told him he loved him.

Once out of the ICU, Sejong told Ri Sol-ju and

Amor of the good news and called for their car to be brought around. Amor asked if Sejong wanted to celebrate the good news, but his mind was far off, planning his next move in his quest to destroy the enemies of his beloved nation.

10

Police Headquarters
Interrogation Room B1

"Dr. Hyeon, I see from your record that you have
been a pediatrician for seven and a half years
at the People's Clinic, and during that time, Si
Woo's three-year-old daughter, Neeku, was your patient," the detective stated. Dr. Hyeon, sitting across
from the detective, merely nodded in agreement. "And
you diagnosed Neeku with juvenile leukemia. Is that
correct?" asked the detective. Dr. Hyeon didn't answer.
"I have for the record a copy of your notes regarding
this child's medical diagnosis, and they clearly state
that Neeku has juvenile leukemia," the detective reiterated. "Is the record correct? Does she or doesn't she
have juvenile leukemia?"

Once again Dr. Hyeon refused to answer.

"Isn't it true that you used Si Woo's daughter's fatal disease to convince him to kill our Supreme Leader?" the detective asked, letting the gravity of his accusation sear into the doctor's mind.

"We claim in our indictment that you found a desperate father who would do anything to save his child and convinced him to kill our Supreme Leader. What do you say to these charges?" the detective asked. When Dr. Hyeon refused to answer, the detective reminded him that under the law a person who refused to answer a direct question was interpreted as assenting to the validity of the question. After a brief break, Police Director Kylo entered the room and began interrogating the doctor.

"Dr. Hyeon, we have a sworn statement from Si Woo that you told him to meet with a man named Sam who would furnish him with a weapon and instructions on killing our Supreme Leader. Isn't that true?" asked Kylo impatiently. When Dr. Hyeon refused to answer, Kylo quickly stood and, leaning on the table, looked directly into his eyes. "I'm through with your games." Rising upright, Kylo tapped one of the detectives on the shoulder. "Take him back to his cell and hang him by his neck until he's dead. Record his death as a suicide and erase the interview tapes of this traitor." With that, Kylo picked up his notes and left the room. The detectives briefly looked at each other and were slowly reaching across the table to unlock Dr. Hyeon's handcuffs when the doctor completely lost it.

He crumbled onto the table, flailing like a wild animal, screaming, "No, I'm not a traitor, I'm not a traitor! I did it to save our nation from nuclear annihilation. The Americans are planning a preemptive strike!"

"It's too late now; you should have cooperated when the director asked you to," the detective said, removing the doctor's handcuffs from the table.

"No, please," the doctor begged as they dragged him by the shoulders out of the room. "I'll tell you everything I know. Please, I don't want to die." He cried as he sank to the ground in heap.

The detectives looked at each other; then one of them said, "I'll speak to the chief. Just let him lie there on the ground while I get further instructions."

He stepped over the crumpled body of the doctor. The detective entered an anteroom adjacent to the interrogation room, where people could watch the proceedings, and was met by Director Kylo.

"It worked. He'll be more cooperative now," said the detective.

"Good. Bring him back into the room. I'll be there in a minute. Let him stew for a while with the thought that next time he'll twist from the ceiling of his cell from a bedsheet," the director said.

After a twenty-minute break, Director Kylo and his two detectives resumed their interrogation of Dr. Hyeon.

"For the record, you instructed Si Woo to a meet with a man named Sam. Is that correct?" one of the detectives asked.

"Yes," answered Dr. Hyeon without hesitation.

"And this person Sam gave Si Woo a plastic ruler fashioned into a bayonet and instructions on how to use it to kill our Supreme Leader. Is that correct?"

"Yes," the doctor said, nodding.

"Do you know the identity of this person, this Sam?" the detective asked.

"No," the doctor replied.

"Then where did you get his name?" Kylo asked.

"I was instructed that a person named Sam would contact Si Woo and arrange a meeting where Si Woo would receive a weapon and instructions. That's all I know."

"I want to show you this artist's rendition of Sam. Do you know this man?" Kylo asked, showing Dr. Hyeon the drawing.

The doctor looked at the drawing and instantly recognized the person. "Yes, I've seen this man before but never knew his name."

"Where did you see him?" Kylo asked.

"He was at a meeting I went to a few weeks ago," the doctor replied.

"Where was this meeting held?" Kylo asked.

"At a country estate thirty miles southeast of Pyongyang."

"And who owned the estate?" Kylo asked, sitting on the edge of his chair.

"The estate is owned by General Zoko," the doctor replied to the astonishment of the detectives and especially to the director of police, who knew General Zoko personally. Shocked by this revelation, Kylo announced that they were taking a break to discuss this matter. He and his team retreated to a conference room to discuss how to handle this very sensitive matter.

"First of all, remove all of the audio and video recordings of Dr. Hyeon and bring them to me. Next, we have to get the doctor out of police headquarters and keep him in a safe house. We'll continue our interrogation after we are sure that he's secure. At this point in time, no one must know about General Zoko's involvement in the plot to kill the Supreme Leader. Do you understand me?" Kylo said to his men.

Each man nodded in agreement.

"Now get me his street clothes and bring him to my office."

In the interim, Kylo called Sejong to enlist his support in securing a safe house to keep the doctor in while they got to the bottom of this ever-expanding conspiracy. At first Sejong was full of questions, which Kylo deflected by saying he'd explain matters later. Sejong then called Thi-sen, his partner's father, and requested his help in securing a safe house. Thi-sen knew of a hunting lodge that was vacant and told Sejong he'd check with the owner and get back to him. Ever the resourceful diplomat, Thi-sen soon had the keys in hand for an eight-room hunting lodge in the Lorn-Ti Forest just forty miles from Pyongyang. Sejong called Kylo with the good news and gave him the directions to the lodge, saying that he'd meet him there with the keys.

11

Judy was pulling an all-nighter in her trailer, at the controls of an autonomous F-15 fighter aircraft conducting a training exercise in the mid-Atlantic some three hundred miles east of Washington, DC. Creech Air Force Base was three hours behind DC, where it was six a.m. The weather was clear, visibility was ten miles, and the winds off the Atlantic were twenty-eight knots. Staying five thousand feet above the water was comfortably below the commercial aircraft that were coming and going from the local airports. Ostensibly the training exercise was under the control of the Fifth Air Tactical Command stationed at the Wilson Air Force Base in Delaware; however, the air traffic controllers at Reagan International Airport kept a mindful eye on the F-15 fighter on their monitors.

Judy, figuring that she'd spent enough time fighting the twenty-eight-knot crosswinds at five thousand feet, requested permission to climb to ten thousand. She was curtly denied.

'You got to soldier on,' she thought to herself as she pushed the stick to the left, compensating for the bird's drift to port in order to stay on course, knowing that every move she made was recorded and evaluated by her instructors. If there was anything constant that factored into her training, it was that every move, no matter how minor, was scrutinized by Air Force professionals who had flown hundreds of hours in F-15 fighter planes during war and peace. Judy knew that whatever criticism she received from the brass was for her own good, and she took it with the respect these men and women deserved. Judy dreamed that one day she would be monitoring men and women like herself with one goal in mind: to use everything at her disposal to make her charges the best pilots in the sky.

"How ya doing, 717?" asked the flight instructor at the Fifth ATC.

"A-OK, sir," Judy responded. She was so shocked to hear her instructor's question that she almost stood at attention and saluted her speaker box.

"Good. New heading: turn to 330 degrees, come to an altitude of 7,500 feet, and increase air speed to 375 mph. Confirm, 717," said the instructor.

Judy quickly and confidently confirmed her new instructions. Looking at the overlay of her new course, she recognized landmarks and realized that they were taking her home to Wilson Air Force Base. She had just twenty minutes to touchdown.

Glancing at her watch, Judy heard the door opening and her CO, Colonel Prescott, entering the trailer. 'What the hell is he doing here at this hour?' she thought as she leveled off at 7,500 feet and increased her speed.

"How's my little soldier?" Prescott said, slurring his words as he approached her from behind.

"I'm in the middle of a training exercise outside of Washington, DC," Judy responded, not looking back at the colonel approaching her flight console. The next thing she felt was Prescott's hand on her shoulder and the smell of Jack Daniels on his breath.

"Come on, Prescott, I've got a fully armed bird at 7,500 feet, traveling 375 mph, over a populated area east of DC. Now's not the time to fuck around."

Judy cried out as Prescott buried his head on her shoulder and began biting her neck and fondling her breasts.

"Get the fuck off me!" she shouted, fumbling for the mace cannister in her bottom drawer that Rose had given her for just this situation. Taking her hands off the controls, Judy clawed at Prescott's face, but it only caused Prescott to get more excited. He humped the back of her seat until he came in his pants. Proud of his conquest, Prescott let go of Judy's chair and promptly fell to the floor, where he squirmed in delight and fell asleep. Judy, angry at herself for not using the mace on the bastard, grabbed hold of the controls and began preparing the bird for landing at Wilson. However, when she requested a fly-by-wire landing, to let the bird fly itself home, she was denied. She surmised that they wanted to test her ability to land her bird after her mission. Judy acknowledged their command and switched off the autopilot and lined up her bird for a north-by-northeast landing on runway T188. Slowing the bird to 240 mph, she banked to line up with the runway, lowered her landing gear until it locked, and raised her flaps to two-thirds.

"Easy does it," she said to herself as she reduced her speed to 180 and began her approach. Once in the crosshairs, it was just a matter of extending her flaps to the full position and raising the plane's nose, and after a few moments gliding her home, she floated to the ground with a perfect three-point landing. The two wing landing gears simultaneously hit paydirt, followed by the nose wheel gently lowering to the runway.

"Voilà," she shouted to the screen as she engaged the brakes and brought the F-15 to a complete stop. The rest was up to the ground crew, who would tow the F-15 to its hangar. Glancing over her shoulder she spied Prescott getting to his feet and retreating to the trailer's bathroom. Judy sat there for a moment contemplating why she didn't mace the bastard but decided to grab her things and get home to have a drink and take a long, hot shower.

12

Central Intelligence Agency
Langley, Virginia
Annex Room M-3668

E lizabeth Kleinshure was sitting at her desk holding a yellow flyswatter in one hand and a cup of coffee in her other hand when Sal, one of her staff, knocked, then abruptly entered her office in a huff.

"We're in big trouble," he exclaimed, collapsing into a chair in front of Kleinshure's desk.

"Careful, he's somewhere behind the curtains and—"

"Fuck the fly!" Sal shouted. "Our guy in Seoul is in an American military hospital."

"What's he doing there?" Kleinshure asked, nervously tapping the flyswatter on her desk.

"From what I was told, when the hotel chamber-maid went to clean his room, he was unconscious on the floor," Sal said as if she knew what he was talking about.

"So, why an American military hospital?" she asked, checking out the curtains.

Sal wanted to say, "Listen, you dumb shit, he's carrying a fake passport," but instead said, "He's carrying a fake United States diplomatic passport."

"Well, that's not good."

Sal had little doubt that most, if not everything, he told Kleinshure went in one ear and out the other, passing through a brainless skull.

"If he talks, we're all in trouble, serious trouble. Jail trouble... or maybe they-make-us-disappear trouble," Sal said, wondering if that warm feeling in his pants was piss.

"Can we terminate him?" she asked.

Dumbfounded, Sal just said no with his head.

"Too bad, it would solve everything," she said, raising the flyswatter to strike the curtains, but the elusive insect was not there. Changing the subject, she asked, "Are there any countries that don't have insects?"

"I don't know. Why?" Sal said, checking his pants.

"OK then, it's time for a shredder party," Kleinshure announced. "Get every file, note, phone conversation, report, et cetera of the Korean operation and feed 'em to the shredder."

After Sal left, Kleinshure wondered if it was time to

do a runner. She'd accomplished a great many things at the agency—I mean, who could have almost assassinated Kim Jong-un, the president of North Korea, with the idiots she had working for her? From the very beginning, they had all bought in to the scenario of a preemptive strike at North Korea's nuclear facilities; it was brilliant. It struck a nerve at the highest level of North Korea's military, none other than the eminent General Zoko. He, among others, was salivating at the idea of taking over the government from a childish dictator who lacked the knowledge and experience to defend the country from foreign intervention. The rest was all who to pay and how much. Thankfully, she had done her homework, and over the years she'd amassed millions of dollars using shell companies as repositories of CIA employees' and contractors' expenses. It was textbook money laundering, and in an organization that prides itself on secrecy, it was child's play. However, before packing her bags, she had some items she needed to attend to.

'OK,' she said to herself, 'my agent in the US military hospital in Seoul will probably be dead in a few days. That leaves his partner in South Korea, whatever his name was, to get rid of. I'll get Sal to track him down using the people we paid to be our middlemen, that South Korean gang. They have the resources on the ground to find him and dispose of him. Yep, it's all coming together, severing loose ends, so to speak. Yes,' she thought, 'it's time to find a hospitable place to retire... naturally a place without those pesky insects.'

13

At their customary noon meeting, Kylo was briefed regarding the whereabouts of Si Woo's daughter, Neeku, and was told that she was in a South Korean hospital undergoing bone marrow transplants. Si Woo's mother-in-law and five-year-old daughter, Leia, were being billeted at an undisclosed location. In addition, a wiretap of General Zoko's staff had uncovered that his orderly had been receiving encrypted messages from a burner phone. Attempts had been made to observe his movements but had failed. Reports had also been received that their agents had located the Black Hand's base of operations in a warehouse in the seaport city of Makpo. Makpo had long been known as a major port of entry into South Korea for drugs and contraband from abroad. Kylo was searching for evidence that the Black Hand had played a role as an intermediary between the CIA and General Zoko in the attempted assassination of North Korea's Supreme Leader. He got what he was hoping for by way of a text message intercepted from a member of the Black Hand to General Zoko, who purported to be holding a CIA agent in the south who was responsible for the attempted assassination. The message was short and to the point.

We have CIA agent who paid you to kill Kim Jong-un.

You want him, pay 2 million dollars.

Say yes to 01288259066; say no we sell to CIA.

Kylo asked his men how long it would take to organize a commando raid on the location where the Black Hand was holding the CIA agent. Most thought it would take at least three weeks to select and train the men, assuming that the Black Hand was not moving the agent from one safe house to another. Just to use the commandos brought into play that Zoko would get wind of the operation since the commandoes were composed of military men under, if not directly, associates of General Zoko. In the end, most believed that if the ransom was genuine, they should wait and intercept the CIA agent's transfer to Zoko.

The meeting then turned to the recent activity at Zoko's compound and the comings and goings of the conspirators.

"Are they planning a coup?" one of the detectives asked.

"Have you identified these conspirators?" Kylo asked angrily.

"Yes, except for one or two drivers, we have identified these eleven officers," one of the detectives answered, placing a box of files on the conference table.

"How long have you been sitting on these?" Kylo said, thumbing through the papers.

"They came in from the field this morning, sir," the detective murmured.

To this, Kylo merely nodded and leered at the detective.

Standing, he summarized where they stood vis-à-vis the attack on the Supreme Leader, the ransom demand from the Black Hand, and the possible coup attempt from General Zoko. Getting their hands on the CIA agent responsible for the attack was paramount to their case, but the fact that the CIA agent was in South Korea complicated matters. If they sent in their North Korean Tactical Police to get the agent, the Black Hand would undoubtedly kill him. On the other hand, if the Black Hand tried to negotiate a price for the agent directly with the CIA, the CIA would probably dispatch a team to South Korea to kill their own agent and sweep everything under a cloud of disinformation. One course of action not discussed was whether some of the conspirators were getting cold feet and exploring asylum in the west. After all, Dr. Hyeon had disappeared, and the police had been mute as to any developments in the search for who put Si Woo up to killing the Supreme Leader. Now, with the ransom demand from The Black Hand, Zoko's position was becoming precarious. With everything up in the air, Kylo needed a confidant of American and British intelligence and once again turned to Sejong to employ Thi-sen.

"Where are you?" Kylo said to Sejong by phone, praying his calls were not being monitored by the conspirators.

"I'm in town," Sejong replied.

"Good, I'm hungry. Stop by HQ and I'll treat you to dim sum," Kylo said.

Sejong immediately got the drift of what Kylo meant by offering a Chinese meal usually prepared on a Sunday on a Wednesday.

"Call Thi-sen," Kylo said to Sejong as he entered the director's office.

"Certainly, but what do you want me to say to him?" Sejong asked as he speed-dialed Thi-sen on his mobile.

"We have to meet with him. I need his help... I'll explain," Kylo said nervously.

Seeing Kylo upset was disconcerting to Sejong, who had always imagined the revered chief as a rock able to weather the storms of police life, especially from the top.

"When he answers tell him you're with me and I wish to see him immediately," Kylo instructed.

Sejong spoke to Thi-sen and found that he was packing for a trip to Hong Kong later that day.

Changing his mind, Kylo reached for the phone. "Excellent, let me speak with him.

"Thi-sen, forgive the theatrics. What time is your flight?" Kylo asked.

Thi-sen told him it was at six thirty, some four hours from the current time.

"Excellent. Sejong and I will meet you at the security desk at the airport at five."

After he disconnected the call, he directed several of his personal security men to bring around two black, unmarked cars with tinted glass and a team of heavily armed tactical officers to take him and Sejong to the airport. While en route, Kylo reserved a VIP conference room at the airport for their meeting and arranged for Thi-sen to be escorted to the room when he arrived. The meeting room was set up with a self-service bar at one end and a silver tea cart on the other. Laid out in the center of the table were hot and cold hors d'oeuvres.

"Let's have a drink, gentlemen," Kylo suggested pouring himself a stiff scotch with a splash of water. Thi-sen found an unopened bottle of vodka and poured three fingers of the elixir over ice. Sejong poured himself a glass of Chardonnay.

Fortified, Kylo began the meeting by emphasizing the importance of secrecy. "Trust no one. What we say here today must go no farther than this room. General Zoko has many friends in high places, people who owe him and will look the other way in his defense." Taking another drink, Kylo continued. "Zoko has received a demand from the Black Hand in the south regarding a CIA agent they are holding hostage. They claim this agent paid them to act as an intermediary between the CIA and General Zoko to assassinate our Supreme Leader. I suspect that the Black Hand may be shopping for the best price they can get for this CIA agent and will probably up the ante as soon as Zoko agrees to their demands. In that case, Zoko and the conspirators will probably flee the country." He picked up a tooth-pick and speared an olive.

"How much are they asking?" Sejong asked.

"Two million USD," Kylo replied.

"What can I do to help?" Thi-sen asked.

"I need to know if any of the traitors have reached out to the west for asylum."

"Easy enough. What's your timeframe?" Thi-sen asked.

"They may be already on the run. I don't know the extent of the conspiracy," Kylo said in frustration.

"Can you close the borders?" Sejong asked.

"That may cause more harm than good. It will look like we've ordered martial law."

"I will be in Hong Kong tonight, dining with Sir Malcolm Weatherbee, the British trade commissioner," Thi-sen said. "I will see what he knows, or better yet, what he can find out on our behest. As soon as I get in-formation, I will contact you."

"Excellent, I couldn't ask for anything more. How-ever, we must use a secure method of communication," Kylo said, handing a leather case to Thi-sen. "Inside the case is special mobile device. Looks like a real cell phone, doesn't it? However, this phone can only call me. Let me show you; even I can use it and I'm no IT guy," Kylo said, taking the device out of its case.

"If you have two bars or more, you're in range of a tower and can send a message. Then you can type in your message, which will be encrypted in an unbreakable code and sent to me... only me. It's that simple."

"Can you send me messages?" Thi-sen asked.

"No. This version is only for sending, not receiving." With that, the men finished their drinks and made their farewells.

14

"Where is she?" Sal asked, glancing around Kleinshure's office.

"Where else? Gone for a smoke," a voice replied from the office pool.

"The usual place?" Sal said, heading for the door.

He exited the building and headed for the employee parking lot, looking for a black SUV with its engine running and a driver engulfed in smoke. Spying Kleinshure's car, Sal knocked on the driver's side window and shouted at the occupant, "Open up."

No response.

"I must speak to you."

"Go away," the occupant responded.

Frustrated, Sal began banging on the window and tugging on the driver's door handle. Finally, Kleinshure rolled down the window, allowing some of the smoke to escape the car, and replied angrily to her midday smoke's interruption.

"What in the hell do you want?"

"Something's come up that requires your immediate attention," Sal softly said.

"Well, in that case, it will just have to wait," Kleinshure said, taking a drag on her cigarette while attempting to raise her window. Sal forced the window open with his hand.

"Goddammit, it can't wait, and what are you smoking in there?" he said, recognizing the sweet, funky smell of cannabis.

"That's none of your business. Now get lost," she said through a cough. When he didn't, she said, "Well, if it can't wait, get in the car and tell me."

"Not in that gas chamber, lady," he shouted, trying to get his hand into the car to open her door from within.

Kleinshure slapped his hand and screamed, "Will you get the hell out of here?" alerting a woman in a nearby car.

"Are you in trouble, dear?" the woman rolled down her window to ask.

"Yeah, big trouble," Sal replied.

"Do you want me to call security?" she asked Kleinshure.

"No, it's OK," Kleinshure told the Good Samaritan. "He's one of my subordinates and can't take no for an answer... you know what I mean." Kleinshure exited the car, dropping a bag of potato chips to the ground and kicking it under her car.

Once in the private confines of her office, Sal broke the news that they'd just received an ultimatum from the Black Hand. They had their agent and wanted two million for his return or they'd sell him to the North Koreans, where he would be tortured until he told of his involvement in the assassination of Kim Jong-un, at which time they'd unceremoniously put him to death.

Examining the message, Kleinshure's only remark was, "I would have thought they'd ask for more money."

"Did you read the message? They've got Mark, and they will probably offer him to North Korea, who will pay anything to get their hands on him. I can see it now, the North Koreans will conduct a 'show trial' for all the world to see how stupid we were to try and kill a world leader."

"Don't worry, it will never get to that," Kleinshure reassured him.

"Don't worry my ass! I'll tell you what's going to happen. Mark will spill the beans about us—you, me, and the others; then our bosses will drag us to the employee parking lot and in front of thousands of CIA employees hang us by the neck until we're dead as a reminder that 'stupidity is not an excuse at the CIA.'" But the stark reality of what Sal said did not impress

Kleinshure; she was in her own world of when and where to run when the shit hit the fan.

"Call a meeting. We'll discuss our response to this message." Kleinshure thought that with some delays, she might make her exit from the sticky situation and set up a bug-free life in some remote corner of the world, but where was still on her mind. She also came to the realization that a non-extradition country would not be an option since the CIA would and could track her down and eliminate her in a host of horrible ways.

"Two million, huh?" Kleinshure said to no one in particular. Her team was assembled in the conference room.

"It sounds like they tendered the same number to the North Koreans," Sal said.

"Well, just ask them if he's still alive and well... what do they call it?" Kleinshure asked.

"Proof of life," Someone blurted out.

"Yes, that's it. We'll ask for that... it will give us time to plan our next move," Kleinshure said.

"Next move, my ass. We ought to say, 'Yes, two million dollars? OK, where and when do you want the money?' Why fuck around at this point? We should pay up and cut our losses," Sal said angrily.

"NO! Ask for proof of life first. Now I've got an important call," Kleinshure said, leaving the room.

15

I t was one of those rare weekends where Judy had the day off from her duties and thought it would be a good idea to spend some quality time with her younger brother, Joey. She felt guilty spending all her waking time in her trailer at the base, sitting at her console, staring at her monitors, with one hand on the stick that controlled her F-15 fighter plane some several thousand miles away on mock missions, communicating with a host of air controllers both on the ground and in the air. The most critical part of her missions involved ducking and weaving around populated areas filled with private and commercial aircraft. The wrong altitude, course, or speed could result in disaster. Compounding the task was the knowledge that her F-15 fighter plane was just that, a mean motherfucker armed to the teeth with two 20mm cannons that could fire off five hundred lethal projectiles in a matter of seconds, as well as two air-to-ground, laser-guided Tomahawk missiles that could destroy anything she wanted obliterated. If the mission was two or three hours long, Judy was pumped, sitting on the edge of her seat, glued to her screens, sweating, staring, and praying from takeoff to landing that she didn't screw up. Yeah, a day off with her bro should be a walk in the park, and she knew the very place to take him: the Barbecue Spit. Their baked and grilled baby-back ribs were to die for, especially with their special smoked, honey-glazed sauce. Her mouth watered just thinking about it. Supposedly the chef honed the art of barbecuing ribs in North Carolina and won several awards at county fairs before moving to the godforsaken town of Indian Springs.

"How about some ribs tonight?" Judy asked her brother as he quickly put on his clothes to get to work at the Piggly Wiggly in town. Joey wanted to make a good impression now that they'd moved him from his warehouse duties to working in the store. They were training him how to stock the shelves on aisles four and five. Aisle four was bread on one side and crackers on the other, and aisle five was water on one side and soda on the other.

"What? I didn't hear you," Joey said, rushing around, dressing.

"Joey, I asked you if you wanted to go out for barbecue tonight," Judy said, repeating her invitation.

"I can't tonight," Joey said, tucking in his shirt.

"Since when?" Judy teased.

"Going to Pamela's for dinner." Joey brought his bike out of their trailer and down the steps to the street.

Judy watched her brother ride off down the gravel path to the street, wondering since when did Joey have a girlfriend. She brought her now-cold cup of coffee to the sink. She wasn't sure where she had been mentally not to see what was going on in her own home. She'd been so protective of Joey's life for so long, more a mother than a sister so that the roles got blurred. But she couldn't shake it. "Joey's got a girlfriend?" She thought they were just coworkers at a supermarket, but now they had a dinner date? Maybe she was making a mountain out of a mole hill. Full of energy, Judy decided that her place looked dull and dingy; a good spiffing up would bring some life to her place, but she decided to wait until tomorrow. She called Rose to see what she was up to and got her answering machine.

With nothing to do, Judy got in her car and decided to check out homes for rent in North Las Vegas, just forty minutes from the base. In fact, seventy-five percent of the base personnel lived in or near North Vegas. It would cost more to rent a place there, but her trailer was too small, and with Joey now a lady's man, and at his age, privacy became an issue.

After a forty-minute drive Judy took the first exit off Route 95 and started down a row of houses on postage-stamp lots. When she got to an interesting HOUSE

FOR RENT sign, she'd stop and Zillow the specs. Most were pastel-colored ranchers with gravel lawns. The first house was a three-bedroom, two-bath, 1,467-square-foot rental for $1,525 a month—which was approximately twice her current rent. Scanning the photos of the rooms, she saw a bright, colorful layout with enough room to entertain the Fifth Army. After driving around checking out the dozens of listings, Judy realized that the owners were all using the same playbook, which was about one dollar per square foot. Dejected but not deterred, Judy decided a milkshake would brighten her outlook, so she stopped at a McDonald's and ordered a black-and-white shake to the young clerk's confusion.

"Say, what's a black-and-white?" she asked.

Judy smiled since she'd been asked the same question wherever she went. "Well, I see you're not from the land of milk and honey. A black-and-white shake is chocolate syrup, a cup of whole milk, and two scoops of vanilla ice cream whipped up in a blender till it's rich and thick."

"Right, I got it, but"—the young woman paused for effect—"out here in the Badlands we have soft-serve chocolate and vanilla. How 'bout I mix them together with some milk and blend it?"

"In that case, yes, yes, yes," Judy replied, proceeding to the take-out window to pay and collect her concoction. Judy decided that she'd better run the numbers before attempting to rent new digs that cost twice as much as she was currently paying. All she knew was that her annual army salary was sixty-two and a half thou before taxes, and that after taxes, food, insurance, her auto loan, and Joey's medical payments, she was just getting by. Deciding that North Las Vegas should probably wait till she could get a better handle on her finances, Judy lowered her windows and took Route 95 back to Indian Springs. She enjoyed the wind whipping through the car as she pretended to be in the cockpit of her F-15 fighter jet, racing through the sky at twice the speed of sound when she was actually just over one hundred miles per hour in her car. Even at that speed, the car buffeted and moaned and groaned; it was exhilarating and scary, bringing to mind the pressure real fighter pilots must feel when reaching speeds that defy human endurance. She wondered if she could take nine or ten g-forces without losing it and blacking out. Once home, Judy explored the contents of her freezer for something for dinner. Since it was just her, she was thinking she could experiment and be creative when Joey called her excitedly.

"You're invited for dinner tonight! Say yes."

"Where?" Judy asked.

"At Pamela's house."

"Is this OK with her dad?"

"Of course, sis; he's the one that invited you," Joey said incredulously.

"Yes, OK, but where do they live and what time? And what's Pamela's last name?" Judy asked, fumbling for a pencil and paper.

"Six p.m., 54 Canyon Road, North Las Vegas," Joey

said. "And Pam's last name is Navarro, so be there or be square."

Oh God, it was so good to hear the happiness in his voice as Judy sat at her Formica-and-chrome kitchen table. Looking at the note in her hand, she wondered how far she had been from Pamela's house that afternoon. "Fuckin' déjà vu," Judy murmured to herself. It wasn't the first time she felt like she'd lived through something before.

Looking at her cell phone, Judy realized that this was the first time Joey had called her sis. It felt good; it gave her a warm and loving feeling that her brother was man enough to consider her his sis. She had seen and spoken with Pamela at the supermarket but this, tonight, was a social engagement.

Judy knew nothing of Pamela's father other than that his last name was Navarro. "Well, it's time for a little fact-checking," she said to herself, putting on her baseball cap and pretending it was a Sherlock Holmes deerstalker. First Sherlock would confirm Pam's address by googling the White Pages. There she found a Derek Navarro at the address Joey gave her on Canyon Road. Next she googled "Derek Navarro" and found he was a roofing contractor with offices in Indian Springs and Las Vegas, doing business under the name of Sunshine Roofing, Inc. "OK, Mr. Navarro you've passed the smell test," Judy said to herself, removing her baseball cap.

She began looking for something to wear; after all she was attending an important dinner engagement. After going through several outfits Judy decided country casual was apropos; a cowgirl shirt, blue jeans, and western boots should do just fine. Sitting and congratulating herself on her accomplishment, the no-hassle approach to what to wear, Judy realized that she was neglecting to pick up something for her hosts. Checking the time, she called Mae's Bake Shop to see when they closed and was told if she hurried, they'd wait for her. That was the great thing about living in a small town; people were so accommodating. After perusing the pies and cakes on display she selected a frosted carrot cake. Then it was home to shower, dress, and prepare for the gala event. Out to her car with her hair still wet she raced, popped in a CD, opened her windows, stepped on the gas, turned up the volume, and sang along with The Sons Of The Pioneers' rendition of the classic "Tumbling Tumbleweeds," remembering, as her bro said, to "be there or be square."

16

Sejong's Estate

Sejong was relaxing on his veranda, sipping an iced tea as he waited for Amor to arrive.

She was in the kitchen organizing some finger food for them when Sejong noticed a large bird circling the house. With each revolution it seemed that the bird was either looking for prey or—no, no, no, the bird was choosing a spot to land. With great flourish he spread his enormous wings; bending them against the breeze to reduce his speed, he came to land on a tree branch not twenty feet from where Sejong sat. Sejong's first thought was this was the largest bird he'd ever seen in the wild. The wingspan was easily eight or nine feet, and based on its coloring he knew it was a male raptor.

"What are you doing so far away from home?" he

asked the mighty bird as Amor walked onto the veranda holding a tray of food. "Isn't he magnificent?" Sejong said, pointing to the bird.

"Oh, Sejong, what kind of bird is he?" she asked, not believing her eyes.

"He's a raptor, a hunting bird, but his kind are very rare… he's a golden eagle from Mongolia," Sejong said with a smile.

"He does have an aura about him," Amor said, placing the tray on the table. "Well, should we invite him for dinner?"

"I don't think he'd accept our invitation; golden eagles prefer freshly killed game."

Then the strangest thing either one had ever seen happened: the eagle moved from side to side on the branch, singing a song they'd never heard before. He seemed to bow bowing his head in time with his song; then stretching his wings to their full extent, he gracefully dropped from the branch. With his noble head turned to the sky, he flew away with great, powerful strokes of his wings.

Speechless, Amor and Sejong looked at each other in acknowledgement that they had just witnessed a once-in-a-lifetime experience. However, secretly Amor took it as an omen of things to come. From the first time she met him, the man who carried the name of the fifteenth-century king of Korea, Sejong the Great, she was mesmerized by his intelligence and kindness. Theirs was a great love in body and soul. There was nothing she wouldn't do to make him happy. When he went off to university in Europe with his brother, she had patiently waited for him. She told her father, Thi-sen, that her life was on hold until Sejong returned. He only smiled and hoped she was right, for she was the sun in the morning and the stars at night.

She was the mirror image of Thi-sen's late wife, a woman of incredible Eurasian beauty. There was nothing a doting father would not do for his princess: she attended the finest finishing schools in India and China; he took her with him when he visited world capitals in Europe, Africa, and Asia on business.

"My dear, let's enjoy a smoke," Sejong said, offering his hand to Amor.

Taking it, she said, "Yes, my love, let me just tell Asu-ra that we are through with dinner and she can clear the table." She headed for the kitchen.

With wine glass in hand, Sejong collected a small, wooden box containing a few ounces of weed, a pipe, and a gold lighter. It was now Sejong planned to tell Amor how he was going to revenge the massacre of the Korean people during the Korean War and the assassination attempt on his brother Kim Jong-u. But first, to soften the impact and the extent of the upcoming endeavor...it was good to put Amor in the proper frame of mind. Yes, he was preparing to tell her of the plan but not necessarily all the details. Just an overview should do, he said to himself.

.   .   .

After a few intoxicating rounds of cannabis, Sejong briefly outlined his plan. Omitting the finer details, he gave Amor the rationale for his need to act now before the US attacked North Korea: that the CIA was responsible for Kim's attack as a preamble to an all-out strike on North Korea's nuclear facilities. By the time Sejong was through with his presentation, he was more convinced that his cause was just and right; that no matter what North Korea did to appease the colonial powers, they would still destroy North Korea because they could. The same analogy could be found in the story of the frog and the scorpion.

A scorpion, which cannot swim, asks a frog to carry him across a river on his back. The frog hesitates, afraid of being stung by the scorpion, but the scorpion argues that if he did that, they would both drown. The frog considers this argument sensible and agrees to transport the scorpion. Midway across the river, the scorpion stings the frog anyway, dooming them both. The dying frog asks the scorpion why it stung him despite knowing the consequences, to which the scorpion replies, "I couldn't help it. It's in my nature."

The next morning Amor slept late. The first thing Sejong did was call Admiral Shumi-un, the chief procurement officer in the North Korean Navy. If there was anything he needed, the admiral knew where it was and, more importantly, how to get it.

"Admiral, this is Sejong, Kin Jong-un's brother. I

wish to see you on an important matter." Sejong held his breath. He knew that enlisting a man like Shumi-un to his cause was critical to its success.

"And what is this in reference to?" the admiral responded.

"It is of the utmost importance that I see you in person, but I'm not at liberty to disclose the details on an unsecured line. Do you understand me?" Sejong replied.

"I understand perfectly," the admiral responded as if speaking to his superior officer.

"Fine. Please come to my home and tell no one of my call or where you are going," Sejong said, giving the admiral his address and cell phone number. The admiral and Sejong agreed that two o'clock was convenient for both parties.

Sejong then spoke to his staff and told them to prepare the private dining room for a VIP. He told them what to serve and when. Assuming Admiral Shumi-un would be dressed in his uniform, Sejong decided he would also dress for the occasion in a formal attire. He went to his study to prepare his notes for his presentation. He had a list of items that he needed, and at the top of his list was a ship that could carry men and materials across the Pacific, through the Panama Canal, around the state of Florida, and up the Eastern Seaboard to the waters off the mid-Atlantic coast.

Sejong wanted to use an American freighter that was captured during the Korean War as a symbol, and an American Victory ship was precisely what he wanted. After preparing a brief outline for discussion purposes, he left room to address comments he anticipated the admiral would make. He did not want to steal the show but didn't want to look like a novice either.

At precisely two o'clock, a chauffeur-driven black sedan arrived at Sejong's home. The driver, dressed in an ensign's uniform, exited the car and, holding open the rear passenger's door, saluted the admiral as he got out. As Sejong had imagined, the admiral was dressed in his white uniform with blue striping; he looked magnificent in his regalia. Sejong moved to shake the admiral's hand and welcome him to his home. The admiral was considerably shorter than Sejong but carried himself as if he were ten feet tall. Passing through the entryway, the men stopped to greet Amor. The admiral graciously kissed her hand to the surprise of both Sejong and Amor, who bowed to the admiral's show of chivalry. Taking her leave, Sejong escorted Shumi-un into his study, where the gentlemen sat facing each other on overstuffed, butter-soft leather armchairs.

"Sejong, tell me. Why the secrecy?" the admiral asked with a smile.

"Admiral, our nation is on the verge of attack, nuclear attack, from the United States. We discovered, after the assassination attempt on my brother, that members of our own military, in conjunction with and under the encouragement of the CIA, were responsible for the attack," Sejong said, letting the admiral absorb his statement.

"Our own military?" Shumi-un asked in shock.

"If I tell you who the leader is, can I have your assurance that you will not betray my trust?" Sejong pressed.

"As an officer of the Korean Navy I will hold everything you tell me in strict confidence," the admiral assured him.

"The traitor is none other than General Zoko," Sejong said.

The admiral was speechless; sitting back in his chair he merely nodded his disbelief. Taking a deep breath, he asked, "And you are certain it's Zoko?" with tears building in his eyes.

"Yes. Multiple sources have confirmed his involvement in the plot."

"It's hard to believe that a man I've worked with for over forty years could conceivably be the leader of plot to overthrow our country," the admiral said sadly.

"I realize this may put you in a difficult position, so I ask you… can you work with us knowing that we will bring Zoko and his conspirators to justice?" Sejong asked, knowing in his heart that the admiral would put his country first.

"I promise you my love for my country now and always comes first."

"Good. I'm confident that we can work together at this critical time to stop, once and for all, the destruction of our beloved country by the American war machine. History has taught us that appeasement brings nothing when we act meek and everything when we are strong. Our cemeteries are filled with men, women, and children who cry out from their graves for us to revenge the massacre brought about during the Korean War.

"Now, let me share with you our plan of attack," Sejong theatrically said.

Unrolling a large sheet of paper, he placed it on a coffee table between their chairs. "It begins with securing an American freighter, a Victory ship used in the Korean War, from our inventory and making it seaworthy. This is our way of symbolically bringing the war to them. Next would be selecting a captain, his officers, and crew. We'd need to update navigation, engines, stabilizers, crew quarters, and galley. Since our mode of attack will be cruise missiles with atomic warheads, they must be sequestered below decks in a lead-lined container under layers of cargo before we transit the Panama Canal. In addition, we must have all the paperwork to pass through the canal unchallenged. I will establish the funds necessary through a series of international banks to pay for our endeavor. My question to you is, how long will it take you, assuming I can deliver the missiles to the ship in two weeks, to accomplish these tasks?" Sejong said, handing a copy of the plan to the admiral.

Making some notes on a small pad, the admiral said, "Tell me more about where you plan to secure operational cruise missiles."

"Kim told me some time ago that he purchased four advanced cruise missiles from Iran."

"And the installation of nuclear warheads in these missiles?" the admiral continued in the same vein.

"I'm assuming that our nuclear scientists can modify a nuclear warhead, given that the request to expedite the process comes from the highest member of the government."

"I think that I should assume the responsibility of securing the missiles and fitting the nuclear warheads to them," the admiral suggested.

"In hindsight, it would probably be prudent for you to assume the responsibility for these weapons," Sejong humbly admitted.

"It can be somewhat complicated dealing with these various agencies," the admiral said. "Assuming the Victory ship can be towed to a dry dock and proves seaworthy, it shouldn't take more than two weeks to secure the missiles."

"Excellent. And when can you start?" Sejong asked, eager to conclude the meeting.

"When I get back to my office today. Is that soon enough?" the admiral replied with a smile.

"I couldn't ask for more. Are you free to dine with us tonight?" Sejong asked.

"I have a previous engagement with my granddaughter this evening; it's her recital and I gave her my promise," the admiral said as Sejong escorted him to his car.

"My best to Amor," the admiral said. Then he was gone.

17

National Police Headquarters
Pyongyang, North Korea

Fearing that General Zoko might pay the ransom and get the CIA agent from the Black Hand, Kylo decided to organize a raid to grab the CIA agent before he was delivered to Zoko. Assembling a team of experienced counterintelligence officers, he posed the question of how and when to extract the agent. The officers agreed with the premise but doubted the successful outcome of the mission. Some said that at the first inkling of an attack on their base, the Black Hand would kill the agent; others believed that too many lives would be lost on both sides to justify the operation. Sitting on one's hands did not seem appropriate to Kylo, though, since with every passing hour their window of opportunity was closing. So, throwing caution to the wind, Kylo decided to act and began assembling a raiding party to enter South Korea at night by boat.

The next meeting Kylo had was with experienced men who had conducted similar operations in the past. They pointed out the difficulty they had had logistically entering and exiting South Korea, especially the home base of the Black Hand. Undeterred, Kylo reached out to sleeper cells in South Korea to secure a van and proceed to Makpo to find a safe house for the team. They were then to photograph the warehouse holding the CIA agent and the streets around the warehouse from all angles. Next, they were tasked to peruse the shoreline within one mile of the town for a secluded inlet for Kylo's team to land their Zodiac boat. The files were then to be transmitted via an encoded satellite link to headquarters for analysis.

Next Kylo met with his director of tactical operations. After reviewing what information they had on hand, Kylo asked him to choose six men to carry out the extraction. They were to acquire a ship capable of transporting the men and materials quickly and silently through uncharted, shallow waters off Makpo, where a Zodiac would bring the team ashore. From there, they would rendezvous with a van, which would take them to a safe house to prepare for the assault on the warehouse.

"When do you plan to carry out the mission?" Kylo's DTO asked.

"How long do you think it will take to be ready?" Kylo said, quickly ducking his question.

"I would prefer to have more details so that I can give you a realistic answer."

"No. A week, a month, what?" Kylo said, getting uncharacteristically irritated.

Both men took a long breath and decided that it would be prudent to revisit their discussion after they had more information in order to avoid biting each other's heads off. In the interim, the DTO was to investigate a naval vessel that could transport the team hopefully to the site and back. He would acquire charts of the route, the tides, the projected weather, weapons, explosives, and whether they would need to build a mockup of the warehouse to rehearse the CIA agent's apprehension.

Privately, Kylo hoped he could launch the operation within two weeks. With a map of the Korean peninsula in front of him, he wondered if an amphibian route was the safest way to land his men and attack the warehouse or if approaching by helicopter would be better. The distance from a takeoff point in North Korea to Makpo and back was approximately five hundred miles —well within the range of their police helicopters. However, that would call for the helicopter to fly as the crow flies, over populated cities and towns in South Korea where radar would undoubtedly detect their movements and dispatch fighter jets to intercept them. No, the only realistic chance of success was by sea, and using that scenario, everything needed to be perfect to avoid disaster.

A day later the DTO called, requesting a follow-up meeting with Kylo.

"I've received the information you sent me, the safe house, warehouse photos, the neighborhood around the warehouse, and several locations to land our Zodiac," the DTO said.

"Excellent, I'll have my team here within the hour. Will that give you enough time?" Kylo said, amazed he could come up with a plan on such short notice.

"Yes, and I'll bring my team leader with me to answer questions."

That afternoon, after adding a few chairs to the conference room, the DTO began his presentation.

"We will transport the team on a sixty-five-foot fishing trawler. It will depart from the southwest city of Nampo and travel south around Changwon into the Yellow Sea, staying forty miles off the western coast of South Korea until it reaches the island of Jaeundo. From there, the ship heads closer to the coast, zigzagging around several small islands until it sees a blinking light on shore and then deploys the Zodiac and follows the light beaching on the shore. The team then transfers to a van, where they will be taken to a safe house in Makpo, arriving at three a.m.

"At seven a.m., two members of the team will be taken by van to reconnoiter the warehouse and possible points of entry. That being done, a plan of entry to the warehouse will be undertaken to extract the CIA agent without casualties on each side. Then we will make our escape back to the beach and our trawler. If all goes according to plan the trawler should be in international waters heading due north and back to Nampo in twelve hours. Any questions?" the DOT said.

"What about the South Korean Navy?" one of the attendees asked.

"There are many trawlers traveling in all directions on the Yellow Sea at that time of night. I doubt a small fishing vessel will be challenged and boarded."

"But there's the possibility?" the man asked.

"Yes, that's true, but the odds are in our favor based on the lackadaisical attitude of the South Korean Navy toward small fishing boats, especially late at night."

"Aren't you being a little cavalier regarding the extraction of the CIA agent from a fortified warehouse when we are six and they... who knows how many guards are defending the warehouse?" another attendee stated.

"We have the element of surprise on our side, and at that hour, I doubt most would be willing to give their lives for someone they're selling to the highest bidder. In other words, what do they have to gain?" the DOT replied.

The questions and answers went on for a little over an hour until Kylo summed it up.

"In every operation of this kind there is always the lingering doubt that we have not done our homework and covered each and every eventuality. However, in this situation we don't have the luxury of time. There is no time to answer all the pros and cons of this endeavor. 'What if this' and 'what if that' can go on forever, and what are you left with? Paralysis, that's what. That's why we employ professionals, men who can think on their feet and act appropriately in the face of danger... and make the right decisions with the blink of an eye." He slammed the table for effect, knowing in his heart that the plan had little to no chance of success.

Directly after the meeting, an aide told Kylo he'd been called to the hospital.

"What's it all about?" asked Kylo, hurrying to his car.

"They wouldn't say, but it sounded serious," the aide replied, biting his lip.

It took only minutes to get from police headquarters to the hospital, where a detective hurried him to the hospital director's conference room. There Kylo saw a group of doctors in white coats with worried looks on their faces. It didn't take a rocket scientist to figure out that something was wrong... terribly wrong. Once Kylo was seated, the chief of neurology began to explain why he was there.

"Director Kylo, you've been asked to join us to hear

a very painful development in our Supreme Leader's condition. Upon the resuscitation of our Great Leader, we have determined that he has suffered brain damage to his cerebral cortex. The cause is still under evaluation, but this damage has resulted in diminished brain function and our Leader is in a state of amnesia. He has no memory of who he is and is confused when asked questions about his life.

Clearly, we are trying our best to not upset him, but we doubt we can keep his condition secret for very long here in the hospital. That's why we've asked you to meet with us. We seek your guidance in this matter."

"When you say secret here at the hospital, how many people know of his condition?" Kylo asked hesitantly.

"That's the problem. Many departments shared information about the patient's condition leading up to the diagnosis," the doctor reported.

"I see. And has Ri Sol-ju been told?" Kylo asked.

"Of course. It was impossible to keep anything from her. She's been his greatest advocate, questioning everything we did and why. She's a wonderful woman and we have great affection for her, but the damage done by the poison, the polonium, was devastating to our Leader's ability to circulate oxygenated blood to his brain and"—at this point, the doctor hesitated, took a tissue out of his pocket, and dried his eyes—"the damage was done."

"And it's irreversible?" Kylo asked in a whisper.

"Yes," the doctor said.

"Can he be cared for at the palace, in his quarters?" Kylo asked.

"Yes, we can replicate the conditions here at the palace," the doctor said, realizing that being around his wife and children was a good idea for both Kim and his family.

"Then why don't we do so. Meet with Ri and ask her. If she agrees, organize what is needed at the palace and have it installed. The National Police Force will provide security at the palace for our Leader and his family," Kylo said, rising from his chair and shaking the doctor's hand.

Leaving the hospital Kylo called Sejong and left a message. Then came the hard part: reporting to his superior, Pak Thae-bok, the chairman of the Supreme People's Assembly, on the recent developments.

18

Pamela's House
North Las Vegas, Nevada

Arriving a little after the appointed hour of six p.m., Judy parked behind a Ford F-150 pickup truck in a driveway filled with asphalt shingles. Glancing in her rearview mirror, she decided that what they saw was what they got. 'Anyway,' she thought, 'you can't improve on natural beauty.' However, halfway to the door, she forgot to take the carrot cake and had to retrieve it from her back seat, mumbling to herself that she should have left it beside her on the front seat.

"Hello," Pamela said, opening the door.

"Hi, I'm Joey's sister," Judy said, thinking to herself that Pamela already knew that.

"Hey, sis," Joey said, coming up behind Pamela.

"Let me take that," Pamela said, offering to take the cake.

But the string on the box had become curled around a button on Judy's cowboy shirt, and it was an account of give and take to free the box. Meanwhile, watching the comedy of errors was Derek, Pamela's father, who seemed to be wondering if it had been a good thing to invite these people in the first place.

"Hi, I'm Judy," Judy said, extending her hand to Derek. He had a hamburger patty in his right hand, so they shook each other's left hands as Judy smiled and thought to herself, 'If I make another faux pas, I'll fuckin' kill myself.'

"I hope you like burgers?" Derek said, lightening up the conversation.

"Burgers are great," Judy responded, thinking about how she had just gone to McDonald's and wondering if Derek would offer milkshakes.

"Can I get you something to drink?" Derek asked Judy, hoping she wouldn't request a mixed drink.

"Ah, beer would go nice with burgers," Judy said.

"I've got Coors. Is that OK?" Derek asked, praying she wouldn't ask for an imported brand like Stella.

Meanwhile Joey and Pam had grabbed Cokes and were outside sitting around a large, blazing firepit.

"Why don't we join the kids?" Derek said, leading the way.

Once seated by the firepit, both took long drags on their beers for courage and began making small talk.

"So, you're a pilot, Joey mentioned," Derek said.

"I fly autonomous F-15 jet fighters," Judy said, clarifying that she wasn't exactly in the cockpit.

"What's the difference?" Derek asked, taking another swig of his Coors and wondering who she reminded him of.

"I control the F-15 from a video console in a trailer," Judy said.

"Like a video game?" Derek said, pleased with himself.

"Yes, it's like a sophisticated video game... just that this one fires Tomahawk missiles."

'So there,' Judy thought. ...it's not a fucken game...I blow the shit out of things too.

"What do you do...for work?" Judy asked knowing full well that Derek was a roofing contractor.

"I install roofs." he said, keeping it simple just to be safe.

'I know who she looks like,' he thought. 'She was in *Norma Rae*, short, sandy-haired, used to go out with that actor... he used to drive hotrods?'

"What do you do for fun?" Judy asked, changing the subject.

"Outdoor things... camping, fly fishing, rock climbing," he said, though he'd just started climbing and only because his last girlfriend got him interested.

"Where do you go camping?" Judy asked, seemingly interested in something she might try.

"Over by Lake Mead."

"Oh, we've never been there. Is it user friendly?"

"What do you mean, 'user friendly'?" Derek asked, not knowing the term.

"Does it have restrooms?" Judy replied.

"Yes, they have those Porta Potties," Derek said.

With that out of the way, Derek lit the gas grill and began cooking the burgers while the kids brought trays of rolls, coleslaw, baked beans, and potato salad and placed them on a picnic table. Dinner was served. With food in their mouths, the tension was off from making small talk and they could focus on what was for dessert.

"Do you want any ice cream with your cake?" Pamela asked, wondering if you could top carrot cake with vanilla ice cream.

"No, thanks, Pam," Judy said.

"I'll try some," Joey said in support of Pam's idea.

"Me too!" Derek said, raising his hand as if he were in kindergarten.

After the table was cleared and the leftovers returned to the fridge, Pam and Joey retired to the living room to watch television while Judy and Derek took seats next together by the firepit.

"That was a great cookout," Judy said with the taste of raw chop meat in her mouth. She thought about how she should have told Derek to burn the living daylights out of that meat that passed for hamburger patties.

"So, where did you learn how to fly a fighter jet?" Derek asked now on his third beer and feeling good all over.

"In the army. Actually I started flying drones in Afghanistan," Judy said, getting interested in the hulk sitting next to her.

'Who knows?' she thought. 'Maybe he has potential.'

"You were in Afghanistan?" Derek asked.

"Yep, for God and country... two tours killing the Taliban," Judy said proudly. It gave her a good feeling reminiscing about the best years of her life. She recognized in Derek's eyes what an impression she made on him. She was a hero in his eyes, more than a woman—a warrior.

"I often thought that I wanted to serve, but life, Pamela came first. After my wife left us, I had to be a mom and dad to my baby, and with the help of my dad we were able to raise a beautiful girl. I got to tell you, my poor baby had a lot of problems—sicknesses, fevers, hospital visits... we didn't think she'd survive sometimes, but by the grace of God she persevered."

"I know what you mean," Judy said, sadly thinking about Joey and the operations he's had over the years to correct what God got wrong in his development.

"Where are you from?" Derek asked, knowing Judy was from Michigan.

"The asshole of the country: Flint, Michigan, where you can't find work and you can't drink the water," Judy said, nodding.

"Well, my father brought me here from New Jersey as a baby after my mother died from some sickness," Derek said.

"But why Nevada?" Judy asked.

"My uncle, my father's brother, was a stone mason and was working on the Strip building the hotels, and there was good money then in construction. So, my father learned the roofing business, and the rest is who I am today: a laborer banging nails in people's roofs."

"No, you're a man supporting your family in the only way you know how. I'm proud of you. You could have cut and run, but you stayed and raised a loving young lady," Judy said, grasping Derek's hand.

It was at that moment that these two strangers felt a bond, a connection to each other surpassing all the faint and flimsy connections they had had in the past. Sometimes it's said that life can change in the wink of an eye; for some inexplicable reason something inside the two of them connected and they began to look at each other as soul mates. And as they hugged each other, they cried in the delight of a new tomorrow.

19

The Information and Technology Center
Pyongyang, North Korea

I t came as a shock to Sejong when Kylo rang to tell him of his brother's condition.

"And it's irreversible?" Sejong asked, choking on his words. He was in his car, and he gripped the steering wheel for support.

"Yes," replied Kylo.

After a few moments, Kylo continued, saying, "I'm awaiting instructions from the hospital for when we can transfer Kim to the Palace."

"When do you expect that might happen?" Sejong asked.

"As soon as his residence is prepared for his return. The hospital is organizing the preparations so that he can be monitored and attended to whenever necessary.

He will have twenty-four-hour medical attention at the palace," Kylo said.

"Good, I trust you'll keep me informed as to when I can visit my brother?" Sejong said sadly.

"Absolutely. I will protect our Sovereign Leader with my life," Kylo said emphatically. After a few moments of silence both men signed off.

Sejong then pulled over to call Amor to tell her the bad news. He asked her to visit Ri Sol-Ju and console her in this time of pain and doubt. She replied that she would visit her as soon as possible and be with her until he could join them.

"Tell her this: our hearts are broken by the news, but we are family and united by our bond to always be there for each other," Sejong said, bursting into tears.

"I will, my love, now and forever," Amor said, beginning to cry.

Sejong looked at himself in his rearview mirror and said to his reflection, "My dear brother, we will revenge the actions of these traitors."

Moving his Mercedes-Benz into traffic, he checked his GPS for directions to the Information and Technology Center. The GPS directed him through a somewhat unsavory neighborhood of rundown and dilapidated buildings. 'This must be a mistake,' he thought. 'The ITC can't be around here.' Stopping on a side street, Sejong voided his GPS setting and reset the directions to the ITC. They came up with the same directions. So, with doubts in his mind, he soldiered along, wary what may come of his venture, when he came to an old four-story building and was told by the computerized voice, in no uncertain terms: "YOU HAVE ARRIVED."

"Can't be," he said to his GPS.

Since parking in and around the building was difficult, Sejong found a spot in an alley a couple of streets away. Locking his Benz, Sejong hoped it wouldn't be stripped by the time he came back. He passed the rear of the building, which contained two dumpsters filled to capacity with bags of rubbish and empty food containers from takeout restaurants, as well as a small parking area for employees' cars, and was shocked to find a dozen late-model European sports cars. There were a couple of MGs, a Jaguar, three Triumphs, four Porsches, an Alfa Romeo, and, of all things, a new, fire-red Ferrari. One might think this place was an outlet for the Colombian drug cartel, but he knew Amor's father, Thi-sen, was the major drug dealer in North Korea. Turning the corner, Sejong proceeded to what he assumed was the entrance to the building, a large, rusted steel door. Above the door were three video cameras pointing in different directions, and mounted alongside the door was a callbox with a red button and speaker. Pressing the button, Sejong stepped back and made himself known to whoever was monitoring the front door. Nothing. Once again Sejong pressed the button without a response.

Finally, on his third try, a voice said briskly, "State your business."

"I am Sejong, and I recently spoke to someone regarding an important government matter," Sejong said to the box.

"There is no access to this building without a confirmed appointment," the voice said.

Having had enough of the voice's insolence, Sejong pushed the red button again until the voice said, "Yes, what now? Didn't you get the message the first time?"

"Listen, since I'll only say this once. I am Sejong, the brother of our Supreme Leader, Kim Jong-un, here on state business. If I am not allowed into this building to meet with the director of the ITC immediately, I will call Kylo-Ren, the director of the National Police, who will send a group of commandoes to break down this door and put all of you into vans to be transferred to prison. Do I make myself clear?"

"OK, OK," the voice said quickly as Sejong heard the electric door rotors disengaging the locks.

Sejong opened the door as a boy came running down a flight of stairs to properly greet a VIP of the first magnitude, saying, "Forgive my impertinence. I had no idea of whom I was speaking to," as he bowed to Sejong.

"Take me to the director," Sejong demanded.

As the two of them mounted the stairs to the next level, the boy persisted in his dribble, explaining his inexcusable behavior by pointing out that many people came to the building asking for things, food mostly, because they picked over food in the dumpsters and expected that they could get scraps of leftovers.

"I've had enough of this. Keep your mouth shut unless I speak to you," Sejong said in disgust. "Now where is the director's office?"

"He's in a meeting," the boy sputtered out.

"I didn't ask you that. I said where is his office?" Sejong said, grabbing the boy by his shirt and pulling him frighteningly close.

The boy, now as white as a sheet, pointed to a door at the end of a long hallway, saying, "That one, that's the director's office, but no one's allowed in."

With that, Sejong cautioned the boy to say nothing to anyone and to return to his duties. Sejong swiftly marched to the director's office, passing open rooms filled with computers and young men dressed in western clothes—T-shirts with peace signs, jeans with holes in them, Mickey Mouse shirts—drinking cans of beer and smoking, from the smell, large quantities of weed. This wasn't a government building doing scientific work; it was a frat house. Upon reaching the door the boy had pointed out, Sejong found that instead of saying the director's name and title, it read:

———

Darth Vader
No Light Swords Allowed

———

Not seeing the humor, Sejong unceremoniously opened the door to find a stout, little man dressed in a silk Chinese robe with a joint dangling from his mouth, staring at an oversize monitor of two women having intercourse with an enormous dildo.

"Sorry to break up your meeting, but I have business to attend to," he said to the horrified little man, who was busy closing his robe.

"Who are you and who let you in?" the little man sputtered out.

"I am Sejong, the brother of Kim Jong-un, our Supreme Leader and President of North Korea. Now, who are you? The director of the ITC or some pervert?"

"I am Tano-Sun, the director of the Information and Technology Center, and what you've witnessed is not what you think. Actually, it is our job to monitor Western sex fantasies so that we can get the enemies' attention turned to our propaganda."

"Really. And you think I'm going to believe this self-serving excuse? Save the bullshit for your staff. We need to talk. Now close your robe and shut the monitor," Sejong said, pulling over an office chair.

Recognizing that he couldn't pull the wool over Sejong's eyes, the director let his hair down and spoke without pretense. Sejong explained in a somewhat roundabout way that he needed malware inserted into US and Russian military command and control systems.

"To what end? When do you need this done?" the director asked, lighting up a joint and passing it to Sejong, who took a drag.

"The Fourth of July," Sejong said.

"And what is the significance of this date?" the director asked.

"A very important date to those in the US," Sejong said, assuming the director would Google it after he left. "Now what do you really do here?"

"You don't know?" the director took a drag and passed the joint back to Sejong.

"No. Tell me," Sejong said, holding the smoke in his lungs for maximum effect.

"We separate obscenely rich American oligarchs from their ill-gotten money that's laundered through offshore banks," the man said proudly.

"You what?" Sejong said in disbelief.

"Listen, our economy in North Korea is dependent on the generosity of American thieves. Where do you think we get the funds to run our way of life? We don't produce anything of value except weapons, and there are plenty of other nations who produce weapons better and cheaper."

"And what are we talking about moneywise? How much do we siphon off these unsuspecting American thieves?" Sejong asked, getting interested.

"In some cases, ten to twenty percent from *one* of their accounts," the director said.

"In dollars and cents, how much does it amount to... from one of their accounts?" Sejong asked, looking for a number.

"As an example, last week we relieved a major American thief of four billion dollars," he said, looking at Sejong to see how he took the information.

"Well, how much money is out there in offshore banks to plunder?" Sejong asked.

"The World Bank published a white paper some years ago and estimated that there were between fifty and one hundred trillion dollars in offshore accounts," the director said to Sejong, who sat there, speechless.

"Look, in the USA, the rich, I mean the filthy rich, rip off their government to the tune of fifty trillion dollars by establishing thousands of shell companies for the sole purpose of laundering money without paying taxes... and the government knows exactly what they're doing. You ask why? Because the rich run the country for their own welfare."

Sejong sat there, thinking about how sanctimonious American politicians were when talking about their so-called democracy in light of the inequity between the rich and poor; when their government, by design, allowed the rich to defraud the people of a fair, graduated tax system.

"Very enlightening," Sejong said taking his last drag on the joint.

Both men, now in Never-Never Land, pondered the stupidity of mankind and how easily they could be manipulated by unscrupulous people.

"And our economy is dependent on the generosity of American thieves?"

Sejong asked in dismay.

"Yep," said the director, turning the monitor back on as Sejong left his office.

20

Virginia Beach, Virginia

As Elizabeth Kleinshure sat on the deck of her beachfront house, she marveled at all that would happen in just two days.

In two days, Elizabeth would fake her death and begin her journey to another life far, far away—away from the chaos of the CIA to a land she'd never been to, with a different culture, language, food, weather—well, just about everything would be different: North Africa. Morocco, to be specific. Why Morocco? Because of the mild weather, proximity to the ocean, affordable beachfront housing, servants, exotic foods, a community of likeminded expatriates all escaping the tax man, and most important, no extradition treaty with the US.

But first things first, she said to herself. In preparation for this auspicious day, Elizabeth had rented a car from Avis with the intension of leaving it at Newark International Airport on her first leg into the unknown. She had issued herself three official diplomatic US passports and driver's licenses from three different states under the names of Allison Brant, Sara Murphy, and Grace Hayworth. She also established credit cards for these aliases from banks that helped her launder the money she stole from the CIA during her tenure as the go-to person for clandestine travel arrangements. Over the years, Elizabeth had siphoned off thirty-seven million dollars from hundreds of agents' expense accounts, and no one was the wiser, nor would they care if they were.

With these documents and these bank-issued credit cards, she could go anywhere and do anything. Citibank was also helpful in getting her some pocket money—four thousand euros and four thousand dollars' worth of dirhams, which she carried in a hidden money belt under her clothing. So, when she rented the car from Avis, she used the driver's license and credit card issued to Allison Brant; the same was true for her Delta ticket to Lisbon. She knew enough to purchase a roundtrip ticket. A one-way ticket would raise a red flag at the port of debarkation; a diplomat never travels one way.

Taking out her newly purchased Louis Vuitton carry-on suitcase, she selected three lightweight travel outfits, one to wear and two to pack. "Nothing flashy, one doesn't want to attract attention to oneself when one's on the lam," she said to herself, smiling. She felt excited and invigorated, thinking that she finally was cutting the leash from her neck and playing a ditsy fool at the CIA.

"Now, how shall we make them think we killed ourselves?" she said.

Elizabeth had put some thought into it and had decided it would be drowning at sea. Yes, there was something permanent about walking into the sea. 'We came from the sea, and we ultimately return to the sea, the circle of life. How fuckin' poetic,' she thought. In her suicide letter, she wrote,

> To whom it may concern:
> I, Elizabeth Kleinshure, being of sound mind and faculties, have decided to leave this miserable world and, in doing so, leave all my worldly possessions to the families of the men and women of the CIA, who gave their lives to make this world a better place to live.
> In addition, regarding my role in the attempted assassination of Kim Jong-un, the President of North Korea, I had to do it, and I take full responsibility for my actions. I organized and directed the plot to kill him to revenge the murder of my father, Sergeant Benjamin Kleinshure, and the men of the First Marine Division who were taken prisoner during the Korean War. My father and fifty-two of his men were taken to a field, made to dig their own graves, had their hands tied behind their backs, and were shot in the

back of their head. MY ONLY REGRET IS THAT
THE S.O.B. IS STILL ALIVE.
Elizabeth Kleinshure

With that done, Elizabeth needed a drink, a vodka
on the rocks. Retrieving a notepad from her desk, she
reviewed what she'd done and took a sip, then reviewed
what was still on her to-do list. Finishing her drink,
Elizabeth felt a little antsy; that note describing what
happened to her father really upset her. Those bastards
had deprived her of a father, and her mother, her dear,
lonely mother, had never recovered from his death.

Elizabeth had to get out of the house, and so she decided to take a walk on her beach. Slipping on her san-
dals and grabbing her hat, she looked out at a deserted
beach with soft, white waves washing the shoreline.
Small, white birds raced up and down, checking what, if
anything, the waves brought in to eat. Far out at sea
she glimpsed the outline of a container ship on the
horizon, traveling to a faraway land, like her. Looking
back at her house she had a tingling feeling—maybe of
remorse, maybe doubt. This place, this beach house,
had been very therapeutic for her. She hoped her new
home would afford her the same comforts. Fighting off
the melancholia of the moment, Elizabeth threw herself
into finishing her plans, knowing hordes of investigators would be over every inch of her house, office, car,
bank accounts, private life, family history, loves, travels,
hobbies, and friends.

To-Do List

1. Ask the agent to have the property inspected by a reputable pest and mold control company... and have problems corrected immediately.
2. Ask the agent to have my servants, Mohammad and his wife, move into the villa and prepare for my arrival. (Instructions to follow.)
3. Ask the agent to inspect the kitchen appliances and replace with new, top-of-the-line Bosch appliances.
4. Ask the agent to inspect electrical service and increase service to the equivalent of 400 US amps.
5. Ask the agent to contact the Mercedes-Benz dealer in Marrakesh and have my car delivered to the villa.
6. Ask agent to have HVAC inspected and replace whatever is necessary. In addition, have window screens installed on all windows.
7. Ask agent to test drinking water for contaminants. If over recommended standards, install a reverse-osmosis water filtration system for drinking water.
8. Ask agent to have Maroc Telecom install a satellite dish and service contract for cable television and high-speed internet service.

9. Ask agent to install a Generac backup propane generator with spare propane tanks.
10. Ask agent to replace water heater with new high-capacity unit.
11. Ask agent to check Mohammad's driver's license and add liability insurance for servants on my lease car.

Hoping she had covered all her bases pertaining to her residence, she sent her message to her agent in Morocco, bouncing it around the internet through a variety of secret, untraceable intermediaries unknown to most of the world's intelligence community.

She turned her attention to her disguise. Since her appearance would only be recorded at airports, she decided that a hat, wig, scarf, and sunglasses might do the trick. It was a chance she'd have to take since a transatlantic voyage was too slow and would expose her to thousands of passengers' inquisitive eyes. She also considered having the sniffles and using a handkerchief to periodically wipe her nose, especially when facing a camera. That was a possibility, especially if her eyes were teary. She found a handkerchief in her drawer and rehearsed in front of her mirror. "That just might work," she said to herself. "Just don't overdo it."

Next, she turned her attention to staging the suicide. She had a bottle of sleeping pills she'd recently refilled in her medicine cabinet. Her "plan" was to wash the pills down on the beach with vodka before walking into the ocean. The mixture of ninety-proof vodka and sleeping pills was a perfect recipe for doing away with one's life, so she would be sure to put both props in view on the sand. The props on the beach would be placed just before she left for the airport, and all the doors to the house and car would be left open for investigators. She even went as far as to leave seven thousand dollars in cash in her wall safe with her personal papers, reinforcing the appearance that money had no value to her where she was going.

Elizabeth was excited like a little girl on the night of her departure. She laid out a conservative, black outfit to wear on the first leg of her journey, plus a new pair of comfortable designer shoes. Quickly dressing, applying just the right touch of makeup, she was ready for what she referred to as "Act One." After strapping her money belt under her blouse, she slipped on her blazer and looked at herself in the mirror. "Break a leg," she said to her reflection. Collecting her things, she grabbed the Avis car keys; placed the suicide note on the kitchen table; and stuffed her handbag with Allison Brant's diplomatic passport, driver's license, credit cards, airline tickets to Lisbon, Avis rental car papers, and eleven hundred dollars. She quietly turned off the lights and made her way to the rental car, where she placed her suitcase in the trunk, started the car, and, taking one last look at her house, backed out of the driveway and drove away, never to look back again.

21

The Apache Watering Hole

Colonel Prescott's favorite saloon was The Apache Watering Hole in Indian Springs.

Legend had it that the saloon rested on the very spot Geronimo once pitched his teepee. Whether it was true or not was debatable, but the building was certainly old enough, and based on its decor and hand-made furnishings, it breathed nostalgia for a time when Native Americans ruled the West.

"What are you drinking?" Prescott asked his old buddy Moe Shorthair, a genuine, seventh-generation Apache, as he pulled up a chair.

"Spring water from the State of Maine," Moe said, holding up the bottle as proof.

"You pussy," Prescott said going to the bar to get a

Coors. "You got my love-making pills?" he asked when he returned to the table.

"Where do you get the time and energy for all that mischief?" Moe asked, taking out a small, plastic bag with a few red pills in it.

"What's this?" Prescott asked, examining the bag.

"They didn't have the blue ones. Anyway, these are stronger… one hundred milligrams. Just take one, you'll see," Moe advised.

Moe worked at the warehouse at the base and had been getting things for Prescott and other friends for a long, long time.

"Who you got in mind this time?" Moe inquired.

"That little one in reception," Prescott said with a broad smile.

"Blonde bombshell who chews bubblegum?" Moe said.

"It's good exercise for her lips, you know what I mean?" Prescott said with a smirk.

"When and where, white man?" Moe asked.

"Gotta go, Kemosabe," Prescott said putting a twenty on the table, and as he strolled out, he tipped his hat to the bartender, western style.

Once in his Jeep Wrangler, Prescott took out a wrinkled slip of paper that held his next victim's details: *Betty Ann Monroe. 26 Cherry Lane. 709-1221.* But before running off, he remembered the old Boy Scout motto and popped two red pills into his mouth. Saluting his rearview mirror, he said, "Be prepared," and stepped on the gas. Off he went into the night, zigzagging his way to satisfy his thirst for women lucky enough to be on his list. Although he thought he knew the way, he made several wrong turns due to, as he would later say, "fuckin' bad street signs," but eventually found 26 Cherry Lane and drove up the driveway. Happy as a jay-bird, he celebrated by taking a swig from the bottle of Jack Daniels he kept stowed under his seat. He shouted to the house, "I'm home."

Meanwhile, inside the split-level house at 26 Cherry Lane, Betty was busy fetching "a cold one" for her hubby, Dominic, while he was engrossed in watching two gorillas trying to separate their opponent's heads from their respective bodies. This sport was conducted under the auspices of the AIBYHOS, an acronym of the "American I'll Bite Your Head Off Society," in a twenty-foot, circular cage in front of spectators downing beer and devouring homemade blood sausages.

"Where's my beer?" the lady of the house heard from her hubby.

Her cell phone rang just as she was depositing the "cold one" on a side table next to his Serta adjustable lounger, where he could grab it without missing any of the death-defying action of the now-bloodied combatants on his eighty-four-inch high-definition TV.

"Hello, who is calling?" she said as a professional receptionist.

"Betty, Betty, can you hear me?" Prescott asked.

"Who's calling?" she asked again, retreating to the kitchen.

"Betty, I'm here. I want to see you," Prescott said, unzipping his pants and checking if his pecker was at attention and ready for combat.

"I can't come out now," Betty said in a low voice.

"Betty, I said come out right now. This is Colonel Prescott speaking."

Frightened, Betty weighed her options. Either she could deny an order and maybe lose her job or pretend she didn't hear his command.

"Betty..." he began to say when Betty said, "I'll be right out." And holding her cell phone, slipped into her flip flops, Betty stole out of the house to appease the colonel.

When she got to the driver's side window of the strange car in her driveway, she looked in to see the smiling face of Colonel Prescott motioning for her to get in.

Betty, hesitant to follow his instructions, shook her head, saying, "No, no, I can't. My husband—"

"Get in right now. I have something for you," he demanded.

Those must have been the magic words. It must have brought out the little girl in Betty because she couldn't wait to see what is was. She whipped around the car and popped into the passenger seat, eager to see her new toy. Prescott took no time to present his pecker to her as he grabbed her by the hair and stuffed her head in his groin, rubbing her face against his Viagra-laced engorgement. Like a dog in heat, Prescott whooped and whistled in ecstasy.

"Kiss it… make nice… he loves it," he cooed as he bounced up and down in his seat.

Back in his castle, the real man of the house, took a time-out from the action as ambulance drivers collected the bloody remains of the losing contestant while the audience watched a commercial for a pest control company. This was time enough for Dominic to drain his dragon while calling out for his little darling to fetch him some chips and dip. All that action brings on the hungry horrors in a man.

"Betty! Betty, where the hell are you?" he shouted without getting a response.

He ventured into the kitchen. Not seeing her there, he roamed around the house looking for her. She was not in the bedroom, not in the spare bathroom… nowhere. Going into the seldom-used living room, he glanced out the window to see the headlights of a car in his driveway. Out the front door he sprang to see who had invaded his turf, until he came face to face with the driver, who was busy jumping up and down with some babe in the front seat… someone wearing his wife's bathrobe.

'Oh shit, it's Betty,' he realized. Grabbing the locked door handle, he pounded on the driver's window to no avail. Finally, he grabbed a paving stone from his driveway and wildly smashed the window until it broke. This didn't seem to stop the man's wild activity, so Dominic began on striking him in the head with the stone until he got the message.

Sensing that it was time to make her escape, Betty extracted herself from Prescott's grip and flew like a banshee from the car to the protection of her home. Several neighbors came to see what the ruckus was all about, which was Prescott's opportunity to say adieu to 26 Cherry Lane. Throwing the car into reverse, he stepped on the gas while an old lady attempted get out of his way. He swerved to miss her, and the car went over a gravel lawn. After running over a lawn statue of Mother Teresa, he smashed into a house and ended up with one of his tires spinning in the air. Seeing this, bystanders called 911 and jammed the incoming lines to the police station. Luckily, Officer Brenda fielded the call and was out in her car with lights flashing, siren screaming, on the way to the scene of the crime. In a matter of minutes she was looking at the bloody face of Colonel Aloysius Prescott.

"Are you in any pain, colonel?" Officer Brenda asked calmly only to be met by a nonresponsive Colonel Prescott. She reached in and turned the car engine off and took the keys with her.

"I'll be right back, colonel." Officer Brenda hustled back to her patrol car where she put in a Code 705, Passenger Car Accident, Driver in Critical Condition... Ambulance and Tow Truck... STAT. She opened her trunk, retrieved her first aid kit, and ran back to attend to Prescott's injuries. Blood covered his head and face, so the best she could do without moving him was to carefully dress his wounds, mindful of the fact that there might be glass.

"You'll be all right, colonel. An ambulance will be here momentarily. Is there anyone I can call?" Officer Brenda asked while applying a clean dressing to his face. But the Colonel only smiled a sorrowful smile.

After the ambulance took Colonel Prescott to the base hospital's emergency room, Officer Brenda interviewed Betty and Dominic Monroe and some of their neighbors. With a good picture of what happened at 26 Cherry Lane, she went to the Creech Air Force Base Hospital to check on the colonel. Finding him still in the ER, she spoke to one of the hospital residents who told her his wounds were extensive.

"Fractured skull, left eye damaged, and glass fragments in face and neck. He needs to go to the University Medical Center in Las Vegas," he said.

"What's the delay?" Officer Brenda asked.

"Moving him," he replied.

"Don't you have a chopper here at the base?" Officer Brenda asked.

"We do, but it's regulations. Got to get approval first, and you know what I mean. You didn't hear that from me, right?" he said.

However, after the paperwork found a receptive general, an advanced Bell AH-1Z attack helicopter was fueled up and ready to fly the colonel to the University Medical Center in Las Vegas with its Tomahawk missiles still onboard.

22

Victory ship at Haeju dry dock

Sejong awoke to a nasty, rainy, cloudy day. It was a day that sent shivers up and down his spine. It was also the day he'd been waiting for. The victory ship was set to sail on the midnight tide.

He could hardly believe it. The ship had been quickly retrofitted; a crew chosen; the stores were stocked with food and supplies; the fuel tanks were filled; and most importantly, the cruise missiles with nuclear warheads were on board. It was just a matter of making a perfunctory final inspection and addressing the officers and crew of the importance of their mission, and of course, christening the ship. In Sejong's eyes, Admiral Shumi-un had done a yeoman's work in securing everything he asked for and more. Under his keen eye, the crew's living quarters had been updated for the first time in sixty years, along with the water tanks, kitchen, lifeboats, and the bridge, which had been modernized with up-to-date navigation instruments. He realized that this was a ship, a 445-foot American Victory ship, that plied the South Pacific during World War II, carrying men and supplies, dodging Japanese submarines and warplanes, and now it was taking the war to America. How sweet it was! It was finally "justice" for the Korean people.

When Sejong reached the town of Haeju, he saw on the waterfront a large, wooden structure with many trucks unloading crates and boxes and knew instinctively that his ship was inside. Sure enough, a contingent of naval police was checking everyone and everything entering the building. In fact, they stopped Sejong until they called Admiral Shumi-un who gave the OK for him to enter, attesting to the importance the admiral had for the mission and the secrecy required for its success.

Once inside the building, Sejong was impressed by the size of the ship out of the water. It was immense, like a huge, gray whale. To one side there was a series of staging frameworks with elevators that carried workers to various levels. Looking up, Sejong saw the admiral at the ship's railing, telling him to take the elevator to "Number Four." Once he was on board, the admiral proudly took Sejong around, pointing out the improvements they had made for the safety of the crew and the success of the mission. He took him to a vantage point from which they could peer down into the cargo hold, where the container with the missiles was located.

"In that lead-lined container, we've secured the four Iranian cruise missiles with nuclear warheads," the admiral said.

"Excellent. And how and when will we deploy them?" Sejong asked.

"After we cross the Panama Canal and are out at sea, under the cover of darkness, we will remove the pallets surrounding the container and unpack the missile launchers. From there, we'll fasten them to the deck at midships. We will then cover them with canvas until we're close enough to bring out the missiles and insert them in their tubes. Are you following me so far?" the admiral asked.

"Yes, but why not insert the missiles after installing the launchers?" Sejong asked.

"Good question. We can't install the missiles at that time because the missiles are not secure enough in their tubes. Let me put it this way: missiles are not like a bullet traveling down a gun barrel; they sit loosely in their tubes until an internal catapult sends them out a short distance and their propulsion system, an engine, takes over. So, if we install the missiles too soon, we are at the mercy of the vibrations caused by the pitching and rolling of the ship. This can damage the inner workings of the bomb. Mind you, it won't detonate, but it may shift the tolerances just so; it will not start the chain reaction."

"I see," Sejong said. "Then how do we fire the missiles?"

"That's done over here," the admiral said, leading Sejong to a console containing switches and buttons.

"These switches numbered one through four turn each missile on, like a power switch. Below each switch is a red button that arms the nuclear warhead. Below that is a green button that fires the missile. So, it's power, arm, and fire for each missile."

"And the guidance systems?" Sejong asked.

"Each missile is directed to its target by a prepro-grammed GPS setting."

"What are the targets?" Sejong asked.

"The seats of power: first target the White House, second target the Senate, third target the House of Representatives, fourth target the CIA," the admiral said.

"Excellent, I couldn't ask for better targets," Sejong said.

"Now I wish to introduce you to the captain of the ship, Captain Jawa-si." The admiral turned to a young man standing at the ship's wheel.

"Captain, please join us. I want to introduce you to Sejong," the admiral said, motioning for Jawa-si to come forward.

Jawa-si marched smartly forward to accept Sejong's extended hand, which he took after giving a low bow.

"Captain Jawa-si has commanded a naval destroyer for the past six years with honors, and his performance has been spotless. He is respected by both officers and crew and is the perfect captain for our newly christened ship.

"It is an honor to be the Captain of this ship. He said putting on a serious face.

"And we will sail tonight?" Sejong asked.

"We will begin flooding the containment compartment with seawater at seven o'clock tonight and expect to launch at high tide, 1:14 a.m.," Captain Jawa-si said.

"Excellent. Please show me the course you'll take tonight," Sejong said, leaning over a large map of the Korean peninsula as the admiral and Captain Jawa-si approached the chart table.

"I assume you have heard of the capture of our trawler by the South Korean Navy?" the admiral said.

"No, I haven't heard anything," Sejong replied, looking concerned.

"It seems that one of our fishing trawlers was intercepted last night by the SKN off Makpo. On board were ten heavily armed commandoes from our Tactical National Police Force. It is alleged that they were to rendezvous with another police unit in Makpo to kidnap an American citizen on vacation in South Korea," the admiral said, realizing how stupid it all sounded. At first, Sejong was startled by the news but then worried it might jeopardize his plans.

"Do you think they'll intercept our ship?" he asked, staring at the map.

"No, the trawler was foolishly well within the territorial waters of South Korea, just asking to be captured," the admiral confessed. Jawa-si jumped in to point out the planned route for tonight.

"Here," Jawa-si said, pointing to the map. "Our course will take us due west, just north of the 38th Parallel, into the international waters of the Yellow Sea, passing Shanghai and entering the East China Sea, which is the gateway to the Pacific Ocean. From there, we will set our course to our predetermined refueling stops and then to the Panama Canal."

With that out of the way, and Sejong eager to see Kylo regarding the fiasco in the south, the admiral hastily organized the officers and crew for Sejong's pep talk.

Sejong took his leave, reminding Captain Jawa-si to confiscate all cell phones regardless of rank and lock them up in his safe. For security, the only communications to and from the ship would be through the ship-to-shore radio room.

In his car, Sejong called Kylo to set up a meeting but found Kylo was not accepting incoming calls. Sejong surmised that due to the failed mission of the other night, Kylo had a great deal to explain to the 'higher-ups.'

However, unbeknownst to anyone, Kylo had been ordered to the Supreme People's Assembly to explain the fiasco he had created between North and South Korea as result of his attempt to abduct an American citizen visiting South Korea. The meeting was held in the Senate chambers usually used for high-level hearings.

In attendance were several district managers, two judges of the National People's Court, the chairman and speaker of the Supreme Assembly, and high-ranking military leaders, which, coincidentally, included General Zoko.

The meeting began with a short statement from Speaker Pak Thae-bok. The speaker summarized the headlines in the national press and statements made by the South Korean government, which consisted of unsubstantiated facts and rumors.

"Director Kylo, I understand you have a statement you would like to read to the panel," the speaker said.

"Thank you, Mr. Speaker. I come before you today to accept sole responsibility for the raid to arrest a person, from here on referred to as Mr. X, to stand charges in the attempted assassination of our Supreme Leader, Kim Jong-un.

Our investigation uncovered a conspiracy to kill our Supreme Leader at the behest of the American Central Intelligence Agency. We claim in our indictment, attached to my statement, that Mr. X is actually a CIA agent who paid the notorious gang known as the Black Hand to find a group of dissidents eager for regime change in North Korea to assassinate our Supreme Leader. They did so by convincing a trusted member of the Presidential Guard to kill our leader by promising his daughter, who was suffering from a terminal disease, treatment in South Korea. After discovering that

Mr. X was being ransomed off to the highest bidder while he was a prisoner of the Black Hand in Makpo, we decided to strike before the conspirators here at home or the CIA had a chance to buy his freedom. I realize that the chances of capturing the CIA agent were remote, but I had to try. I couldn't let Mr. X slip away."

"Thank you, Director Kylo," the speaker said before suggesting they take a brief recess to confer with each other, which turned out to be put on the calendar for the following week.

23

Newark International Airport

By the time Elizabeth Kleinshure reached the Avis rental return kiosk at Newark International Airport, she was exhausted. It wasn't necessarily the six-hour drive from her home in Virginia Beach to the airport that had worn her out; it was the thought of what lay ahead. This portion of her "great escape," the next several hours, would be the deciding factor for whether she succeeded or failed... and failure meant ending up with a long stretch in federal prison or termination the quick and easy way. So, with her carry-on in tow and her trusty handbag slung over her shoulder, she marched into the terminal to get into the TSA security queue with her fellow travelers.

Glancing ahead of her she saw that the queue broke into two lanes, one in front of a young, male security guard, and the other in front of an elderly woman. Both viewed the oncoming passengers with stern looks on their faces, eager to find some irregularity in their paperwork. Which one should she choose, the young man or the nice, kindly, little old lady? The little old lady would probably smile at her when she showed her the US diplomatic passport.

"Oh, how nice to meet you your honor," she'd probably say, gushing upon meeting a dignitary. So, as both agents motioned for Elizabeth to come forward, she looked both ways and chose the young man. As she thought, he peeked at her passport and sent her to an official to take her through the security checkpoint unmolested.

'Well, I dodged the bullet that time,' she thought, looking for a place to have breakfast. Discouraged by the bill of fare, she inquired at a gate where the VIP lounge was.

"Oh my, you have to go back through the main concourse into Terminal B and up the escalator to a..." upon which she walked away, shaking her head, and went to McDonald's.

Finishing a meal that topped the scale in saturated fat, she moseyed over to her gate to await the call for boarding. Instinctively she took out her prepaid burner iPhone registered to Allison Brant and checked if the police in Virginia Beach were looking for her body. Nothing yet, she surmised. "Maybe it's too early," she said to herself while checking if her plane was leaving on time. Elizabeth was not noted for being a patient person. She often told people she was multitasking when she was really a nervous wreck.

Finally, the gate agents called for those in the first-class section to board, and Elizabeth was the first in line. Practically jogging down the jet bridge, she found aisle seven and took the seat by the window, praying the seat next to her would be unoccupied, which looked promising until, as the door was closing, a well-dressed gentleman rushed in to claim the seat next to her.

Panting, he stowed his carry-on in the overhead bin and then removed his suit jacket, asking the flight attendant to place it in the forward closet, which she did with a flirtatious smile. He then gently lowered himself into his seat. The first thing Elizabeth noticed as he sat beside her was the cologne he was wearing; she didn't know what it was, but the aroma was intoxicating. Besides, he was one of the most handsome men she'd ever seen. With a face that was fashioned from Italian marble, he carried the rest of himself like a nobleman. Honestly, when he turned to introduce himself, Elizabeth was speechless. She couldn't tell if his accent was Italian or Spanish or Greek, but he was stunning. Oh, if she could only tell him that she was a fugitive from the law, with an oceanside villa in Morocco and thirty-seven million dollars in the bank, looking for a handsome man to spend all her money on forever and forever.

So, gathering up her courage she blurted out, "I'm Elizabeth—" then froze.

'Shit, who am I today?'

"I'm Elizabeth Allison Brant," she said quickly, "but I go by 'Allison.'"

'And I'm a fuckin' idiot too,' she thought.

Mr. Handsome merely smiled an understanding smile.

'He's probably accustomed to his effect on women,' she thought.

He had reached up to press the red button to call the flight attendant when she noticed his solid-gold cufflinks in the shape of Don Quixote, The Man of La Mancha.

"Those are beautiful cufflinks," she said with a shy smile.

"Thank you. Would you care to join me in an aperitif?" he asked, and she noticed he had perfect teeth.

"A prosecco?" she asked.

"Excellent choice, but would you like to try our famous Spanish aperitif, Rosso?" he asked as the hostess came to take his order.

"Yes, thank you. I'm always game for something new," she said, thinking she might want to join the "Mile High Club" with him.

"Let me check," the hostess replied to the man's request for a Rosso.

When she returned with another brand of aperitif, a dry Chambery, they both smiled and accepted.

"Salud," he said, raising his glass.

"Salud," she said, clicking his glass with a smile.

After a couple of drinks she had the courage to ask what part of Spain he was from.

"Barcelona," he proudly replied.

"A beautiful city. Our cruise ship started and returned there, and the people were... the people were happy and full of life," she said, holding her breath.

"And where do you call home?" he asked, taking a sip.

"Me? Well, Langley, Virginia," she said, realizing she hadn't rehearsed what to say in a social situation.

"Isn't that the home of the CIA?"

"Yep, our intelligence agency," she said.

"And what do you do there?" he pressed.

"Oh me... I'm a spy," she said with a wide smile.

"Well, in that case, let's drink to you, my lady of mystery," he said.

After more schmoozing both were eager for a hot breakfast to give them the energy to continue their romantic jousting. Neither was sure where they were going emotionally, but a fire was certainly burning in Elizabeth's loins. Tapping him on his knee she bent over and asked him, "By the way, what is your name?"

"Are you ready?" he asked. "Well, my formal name is Juan Carlos de Todos de Borbon y de Grecia."

"And what do your friends call you?" she asked.

"Just Juan," he said as the hostess removed their trays.

"Care for a drink?" he asked.

"Certainly. What goes between breakfast and lunch?" she asked, touching his arm and leaving her hand there.

"A glass of Russian vodka on the rocks."

"Sounds delicious," she said, placing their order.

"Are you staying in Amsterdam?" he inquired.

"No, I connect to a flight to Madrid," she said, crossing her legs and giving him a glimpse of her firm and shapely thighs.

"I'm connecting to a flight to Frankfurt," he murmured as the hostess brought over two nips of Grey Goose and ice-filled tumblers.

They toasted to a new beginning and immediately felt the woes of the world escaping their psyches. The alcohol gave them a feeling of freedom and the desire to explore uncharted places and things. They looked at each other with passion in their hearts and minds, and they drifted hand in hand to the privacy of the restroom, where they made mad love on the lavatory sink. They lingered until reason got the better of them and, with the memory of that moment, retreated to their seats.

"I have an oceanfront villa in Morocco I want to share with you," she said, throwing caution to the wind.

"But you don't know who I am," he said, softly placing his hand on her thigh.

"I don't care. I want you... I need you," she confessed.

"But I have a shameful past," he whispered.

"I can afford to overlook your past if you can accept me for who I am and overlook my past," she said, beginning to choke up.

"Allison, we can't talk here," he began when she

said, "No, my name is Elizabeth... Elizabeth Kleinshure."

"I thought so," he said with a knowing smile.

"You show me your past and I'll show you mine," she offered.

"We don't have enough time... and you won't look at me the same way after you know," he said.

Scrambling for where they could go in and around the Amsterdam airport for their confessions, she asked how long he had to make his flight to Frankfurt.

"Not long. My travel agent cut it short; maybe an hour," he said. He considered getting a later flight but rejected the idea since his tickets were issued in such a way that they couldn't be changed. Besides, he might not be able to get a flight at the last minute, and he had to be in Frankfurt that evening.

"In the event we arrive on time, how long is your layover?" he asked.

"Oh, I have over two hours," she said.

"Good. You follow me to my gate, and we'll find a private place to discuss the rest of our lives," he said, making light of it. They snuggled together under a blanket and slept.

Arriving on time in Amsterdam, they walked hand in hand to his gate, where they found seats to talk in private.

"Tell me, my lady of mystery, what is so terrible that

you think it will drive you away from me?" he asked, taking her hand.

"I hunger for you, ...more than you can imagine." she began. Taking a long breath, she told him who she really was and what she'd done at the CIA.

"Bravo," he said when she'd finished telling him about siphoning off the CIA's income, "but what's so bad about sharing the wealth?"

"Oh, my love, there's more. About six months ago, I sent two members of my staff on a mission to kill Kim Jong-un, the president of North Korea." Taking a breath, she continued. "It was their task to pay a gang in South Korea, the Black Hand, to find North Korean dissidents to carry out the attack on Kim, which was unsuccessful. Kim survived. As a result of this act, one of my agents is in a hospital in South Korea dying, and the other is being detained by the Black Hand, who are holding him for ransom. It's only a matter of time before the agency discovers that I was responsible for the attack. In light of my impending arrest, before I left, I faked my suicide, which brings me here," she said, sitting back. She was happy to get it all off her chest.

"But with all that money, what possessed you to kill Kim?" Juan asked.

"Revenge. Revenge for the murder of my father and fifty-two of his men during the Korean War," she said without hesitation.

"But what happens in the fog of war is often buried with the victims," Juan said.

"Yes, I understand that, but this was a war crime

and murdering POWs is punishable by hanging," she said, sitting back as Juan nodded in agreement.

"My shame is not the magnitude you carry with you," he said. "Mine is more the tale of a man's inability to find a meaning to life. It isn't a story of one not reaching his potential, but rather an utter waste of his life in search of money at any cost, by using his looks and guile to separate elderly women from their money. Therefore, what you see before you is a well-dressed gigolo. I ask you, is this the type of man you would trust with your love? You shouldn't because lying and cheating are just part of the craft. I would do and say anything to get my hands on my victims' money, jewelry, and possessions. I have learned, over many years, to separate my feelings from the prize. I am a user of women because they are trusting and eager to please, because they think they can reform me, make me a better man. Elizabeth, don't waste your time and money on me; I'm not worth it. I've shattered too many lives. My advice to you is to walk away without looking back," he said as he rose to his feet to enter the queue to board his flight, but just before he could enter the jet bridge, Elizabeth rushed forward and gave him a kiss while stuffing an envelope in his pocket. Then, with tears streaming down her face, she rushed away.

24

Indian Springs High School Baseball Field

"Who called this meeting?" Judy asked Officer Brenda as she arrived at the baseball field in her newly washed police car.

"Not me," Officer Brenda replied, opening a can of Coors Lite.

"You on a diet?" Judy asked, pulling a Bud from her cooler.

"I'm always on a diet," Officer Brenda replied as the third member of the gang of usual suspects arrived at their usual meeting spot.

"I was in a hurry and left my cooler on the kitchen table. Does anyone have a cold one for me?" Rose pleaded.

"I have one." Judy tossed her a Bud. "But don't make it a habit," she said, rubbing it in.

"Well, did you see him?" she asked Officer Brenda.

"Yep."

"And?" Rose asked.

"He's in bad shape," Officer Brenda said.

"What do we have to do to get something out of you?" Judy asked in desperation.

"OK, besides a fractured skull and head and neck lacerations, not to mention unknown damage to his left eye, the colonel is up shit's creek and looking at 125 years in jail on a long list of charges: rape, kidnapping, leaving the scene of a crime, assault and battery, to name a few."

"But the newspapers didn't describe what he actually did," Judy said.

"It all started when he arrived at the Monrore's house on Cherry Lane. It's alleged that the colonel parked in their driveway and demanded by phone that Betty Monroe come out of her house and get into his car, where he forced her to perform oral sex. Upon witnessing his wife in his car, Dominic Monroe struck the colonel's window until it broke and continued striking the colonel until he tried to escape, backing his car across the street crashing into a neighbor's house.

"How's that for a blow-by-blow? Pardon the pun," Brenda said.

"No shit!" Rose exclaimed.

"That being said, I received a different slant to the saga of what makes Colonel Prescott tick," Officer Brenda said.

"From who? And cut the legal mumbo jumbo," Rose said.

"From his friend Moe Shorthair. He claims that Colonel Prescott is suffering from a psychological condition that compels him to attack and control women due to a mixture of alcohol and Viagra. This rage is compounded by his inability to find a meaningful relationship with women."

"That's bullshit. Pure, unadulterated bullshit," Judy said, spilling beer on her blouse.

"Whoa, my little fighter pilot," Officer Brenda said.

"Don't 'whoa' me! He didn't put his claws on your tits, Officer Law and Order," Judy cried, looking for where she hid her napkins.

"What if Moe's right? What if he's sick? What if he's actually a drug addict?" Rose said, throwing her thoughts on the table.

"Look at it this way. He's lying in a hospital receiving antibiotics to stave off an infection in his brain. Betty's husband fractured his skull. According to what I've heard, he'll probably lose his left eye. It took two hours to dig out the glass embedded in his face and neck. I don't think he knows where he is; I don't think he knows what he did and why he did it. So, we might want to take a second look at that crazy old man and ask what made him into a monster," Officer Brenda said.

With that, the women sat silently in their cars, sniffling and sipping their beers until Judy broke the ice with some good news: she'd found a man. To say there was surprise on her friends' faces would be an under-statement.

"You what?" shouted Rose in amazement.

"Who is he?" Officer Brenda inquired.

"A local man," Judy said.

"What does he do?" Rose asked.

"He's a roofing contractor."

"Is he still married? You know, like, separated?" Officer Brenda asked, speaking from experience.

"Nope, I think," Judy said hesitantly.

"Does he have kids? And do they live with him?" Rose inquired, also from experience.

"A girl, and yes, she lives with her father," Judy said.

"Where does he live?" Officer Brenda asked, wondering if he was in her jurisdiction.

"On a scale of one to ten, with ten being the highest, how would you rate his lovemaking?" Rose asked with a smirk.

"Eleven—no, fifteen. Approaching—" she started to say when Brenda interrupted her with a resounding "Oh, go fuck yourself! No one's worth anything greater than a seven in this part of the west, and I know from experience."

"Well, Officer Brenda, you think you know, but you don't know my Derek," Judy said, pounding her chest like she was Miss Queen Kong.

"OK, now let's get down to the nitty-gritty. How tall is he, and what size is his shoe?" Rose asked, pinning Judy down with the question that would answer forever whether Derek was a seven or better.

"Not fair!" Judy screamed.

"Uh-uh, my little fighter pilot. Either he is or isn't a size fifteen," the intuitive Officer Brenda said, hitting it on the head and putting it to rest.

With crocodile tears swelling up in her eyes, Judy conceded that they hadn't done the dirty yet.

"I know. You're a good girl and you're saving yourself for Mr. Right, but how would you know if you don't make whoopee?" Rose, an experienced woman of the world, said.

The women raised their beer cans to toast Judy, each thinking what they should do next.

Judy thought a get-together for drinks would be nice.

Rose thought a cookout at her place would be nice.

And naturally, Officer Brenda thought of how to get Derek's fingerprints.

25

Cryptic phone call from Kylo to Sejong

"Sorry for not getting back to you sooner, and yes, I'd be happy to have lunch with you and Amor at your home this afternoon. What time is convenient?" Kylo said, knowing that Sejong would correctly interpret the message as a guise to have a confidential conversation far from inquisitive ears and eyes.

"The pleasure is mine. Say one p.m.?" Sejong suggested.

"Excellent, one p.m.," Kylo said. Preparing to leave for Sejong's estate he called his trusted driver and personal bodyguard to bring his car around. Once in the car, Kylo asked if they were armed and was assured that they both were. He gave them instructions on where to take him and, after their arrival, to keep a watchful eye on the grounds for intruders.

"Sorry for the cryptic message, but as you'll soon learn I am under surveillance from within and without," Kylo said, shaking Sejong's hand and bowing to Amor.

"We have much to discuss," Sejong said, leading him into his study. The men took seats opposite each other in light-brown leather armchairs. Amor took their drink orders and asked her maid to prepare hors d'oeuvres for their guest. Once the formalities were attended to, the three of them prepared to share what they knew in the privacy that was necessary during these uncertain times.

"To you, my faithful comrades," Kylo said, raising his glass to toast Sejong and Amor.

"And to you, our faithful servant of our Supreme Leader and the sovereign nation of North Korea," Sejong said with a slow and meaningful bow.

Kylo looked at Amor. "I wish you to convey my appreciation to your father, for his assistance in determining if any of the conspirators were seeking asylum in the west. He found there weren't any, since there's no need to flee. There's a coup underway, and the army, under the leadership of General Zoko, will soon occupy the seat of power."

"It's gone that far?" Sejong asked, shaking his head.

"In addition, Thi-sen spoke to a reliable source who told him that the South Korean police have freed the CIA agent held by the Black Hand and interrogated him. The agent claims the CIA was not responsible for the attack on Kim Jong-un, that the attack was planned and financed by a rogue official in a minor agency for personal reasons. He further claims that the CIA was caught completely off guard.

The agent also said that there never was a preemptive strike planned against North Korea; it was only a talking point to enlist North Korean dissidents to join the cause for revolt against Kim Jong-un. And to put recent developments into perspective, I was called to the People's Assembly and asked to explain how our police commandos were captured off Makpo in a fishing trawler, and seated at the table, not five feet from me, was General Zoko, the person responsible for the attack on our Supreme Leader. I venture to say that Zoko has infiltrated our police department and knows everything we do. They, the South Korean Navy, were waiting for us in the waters off Makpo. We fell into a trap, and I feel I acted in haste before contemplating how Zoko would use it to his advantage to overthrow our government," Kylo said sadly.

Sitting back in his chair Sejong glanced over at his lovely partner, taking in the gravity of the events swirling behind the scenes and how it might affect his plan to finally destroy he United States. But first, he wanted to tell Kylo the sad news he had learned from the doctors about his brother's condition. Shaking his head, Sejong began.

"I spoke to the doctors attending to Jong-un, and ah, they said that Jong is suffering from a form of amnesia, and... and he will never be the same."

"It's a permanent form of amnesia?" Kylo asked.

"Yes, the damage to his brain is extensive, and he'll need constant nursing care. I've requested that he be transferred to the palace to be with his family. His wife is devastated."

"I fear what Zoko will do now that he has Kim in his clutches," Kylo said.

"What do you mean? He's not safe at the palace?" Sejong asked, sitting on the edge of his chair.

"You didn't know? The army has replaced my policemen and women and reestablished their security at the palace," Kylo told them to their surprise.

"They're coming at us from all sides," Sejong said in dismay. "And the People's Assembly, could we…"

"Could we what? They're all in bed with Zoko; it's too late. Soon the gates to the army base will open, and the tanks will roll out to proclaim martial law and seize all the news outlets, announcing they're saving the country from the South Korean boogeymen."

"But the people love Kim," Amor said.

"True, my dear, but they have him under lock and key," Sejong said.

"But they would come to his aid if they knew he's being held against his will."

"No, they have over one million soldiers at arms. Where will the loyal opposition come from? Our women and children?" Kylo said.

"I'm sorry if I'm reaching to the stars for an answer, but we're desperate,"

Amor said.

"Forgive me, dear Amor, if I sounded cavalier, but

believe me, I am terrified, too, at these developments and feel impotent in the face of the odds against us," Kylo said.

"Can we turn to Beijing for help?" she asked.

"At this point, I doubt they would enter the internal affairs of a trading partner unless there was a clear indication of who's in charge," Kylo responded.

"And how would they know that there's been a coup?" Amor asked.

"When they see the army firing at the people and the resulting carnage in the streets, it will be Tiananmen Square, Korean style."

"What if it precipitated a world war?" Sejong said, pulling a rabbit out of his hat.

"A world war between which nations?" Kylo asked, playing along with Sejong to see where he was going.

"The United States and North Korea."

"Because the United States struck our nuclear facilities?" Kylo asked.

"A preemptive strike by the United States was the sole reason Si Woo attacked our Supreme Leader," Sejong reminded Kylo.

"True, but it was without evidence of the fact."

"How do we know? How do we know it wasn't a page from the CIA handbook to measure our reaction to a nuclear threat? What if Thi-sen was misled and they were planning a preemptive strike and found that by faking it they could attain the same result, the denuclearization of our nation?" Sejong suggested, which took some time for Kylo to weigh.

"OK, continuing in the same vein, what if we could place nuclear weapons close enough to, let's say, Washington, DC? Nuclear weapons that could destroy the US capital in a matter of minutes. Would that deter them from a preemptive strike?" Sejong asked, seeing Kylo's reaction.

"In that case, how would it deter the coup?" Kylo asked.

"Because Zoko and the People's Assembly would think twice if it came to a showdown with the United States, that's why," Sejong said, putting the last nail in Zoko's coffin.

"That's all well and good, but..." Kylo began, but Sejong suddenly rose from his chair and said, "The bombs will be in position soon."

26

Hilton Hotel
Madrid Airport

Kleinshure's flight from Amsterdam to Madrid was uneventful without her handsome escort. She couldn't believe she had had an orgasm mounted on a sink in the first-class restroom. It must have been a dream, she mused. In real life, a romantic scene like that only existed in a mushy Harlequin novel.

Her room at the Hilton was quite large, with a living room, dining room, and bedroom with a king-size bed. Eager to relax before ordering dinner, she stripped and hopped into a hot shower. Standing there as the water poured over her body, she dreamed of what might have happened if Juan had taken her up on her offer, if he'd escaped with her into a new life, a new beginning for them both.

Turning the water temperature to cold brought Elizabeth back to reality and propelled her out of the shower to find a towel. Looking at herself in the mirror she found that she wasn't sad about losing Juan because she knew he would be in her dreams forever. What did that one actor say? "Happiness isn't something you experience; it's something you remember." Oh, how right he was. She could no longer contain herself, and so she sobbed and found comfort hugging her pillow. After a while she got out of bed and began drying her hair. We search for happiness all our lives and find it in the recesses of our minds, she thought. Why don't we recognize happiness when it's staring us in the eye?

"Are you hungry?" she asked herself, looking through the room service menu. "Should I try their traditional paella? Will it be too much to eat? But I'll pretend I'm eating with Juan. I'll tell them to bring two settings. What a marvelous idea. Now, what would Juan order to accompany our paella?" Google recommended a bottle of rioja. "Perfect," she said to herself as she ordered her dinner for two.

'Now, what should I wear?' she thought, examining her meager wardrobe. 'Something festive, the navy suit should be perfect to go with Juan's electric-blue eyes.' When she got close to him, she could see a world in his eyes, sometimes blue waves crashing on the rocks and other times the peacefulness of a blue sky.

Unfortunately, due to a lack of space in her carry-on, she couldn't fit the accessories to go with her navy outfit, so she had to make do with her comfortable black shoes and silver earrings.

"Music... what shall we play to accompany our dinner?" Guitar music, of course, and nothing better than Tony Mottola's rendition of "All The Way." God, that song brought back memories. Elizabeth was a freshman at Springfield College, and her roommate, from somewhere in Pennsylvania, used to sit on her bed and play the guitar while singing that song over and over again. She remembered some of the lyrics.

> *"When somebody loves you*
> *It's no good unless he loves you, all the way*
> *Happy to be near you*
> *When you need someone to cheer you, all the*
> *way."*

"Yep, that should set the mood. Then we'll let the magic of 'Clair de Lune' take us into the clouds, where we'll soar to the heights only the gods have seen."

As she sat at her dining room table, a knock on the door announced the arrival of her dinner for two. Opening the door, she saw a young man dressed in a black tuxedo with a cart carrying her order. The presentation was so elegant she was forced to control herself lest she laugh at the absurdity of a middle-aged woman pretending to be dining with her imaginary lover. But, still in that spell, she motioned for the waiter to set the table while she scurried to find her handbag for fifty euros to give him. Once the formalities were over and the waiter left, Elizabeth poured glasses of rioja for Juan and herself. Looking over at the empty seat opposite her she raised her glass to toast the only man she ever truly loved, a man a woman like her could only dream about.

The next morning Elizabeth was up early and in immediate need of a hot cup of coffee. Examining the dining room table she saw the remnants of her dinner with Juan. 'How in heaven's name did we finish that bottle of wine?' She laughed at the thought. "It must have been the conversation... no, it was the music... yes, the music.' Still walking on a cloud, she was startled by her cell phone ringing. 'Who has my number? Should I answer it?' Reaching into her bag she sat on her bed, took a long breath, and said, "Hello, who is calling?"

"It's me, Juan. Where are you?" he asked.

Elizabeth couldn't believe it was Juan. Her head started to spin. Was it really him?

"Juan, my love, it's me, Elizabeth. I'm in Spain. Where are you?" she asked, holding her breath.

"I'm in Frankfurt... at the airport. I'm leaving for Madrid to be with you," he said to a delirious Elizabeth.

"When will you be here?" she said, choking on her words.

"I arrive at nine thirty. Where are you staying?"

"I'm at the Hilton Hotel at the airport. I'm in room 767," she said, out of breath.

"Good, wait there. We'll be together soon."

"I'll wait for you forever, my love," she said holding back her tears of utter joy. "I love you."

"I love you too," he said and then boarded his flight.

She sat there at the dining room table, holding her cell phone in one hand and resting her head on her other. 'What just happened?' she thought, beginning to sniffle. 'What made him change his mind?' After a few minutes, without an answer, she rose and walked slowly into the bathroom to splash cold water on her face. Drying her face with a hand towel, she leaned on her sink and looked at herself in the mirror.

"Looks are what count," she said to no one in particular, "and by God, I've got to get my shit together before he arrives." The plain and simple answer of why he was back, to Elizabeth, was just that: he was back. The reason was not important.

'Go with the flow,' she thought. 'First, call housekeeping and have the room cleaned. Next, get an appointment at the spa to make me look and smell beautiful, if they can? Then tell the front desk that I'm staying another night. Oh yes, then change my airline reservations to tomorrow and add Juan to our flight to

Lanzarote. Last but not least, call my agent to adjust our departure to Rabat for the following day and let her know that there will be two passengers—but before I forget, have Mohammad collect us from the marina at the same time, just the next day. Anyway, I'll call him with updates when we're on board the yacht.' She did all this while making copious notes on the back of the room service menu.

Now that she had a plan, did she have enough time to peruse the boutique in the lobby for a new outfit? "Of course," she said to herself, grabbing her handbag and room key.

27

Indian Springs High School Baseball Field

"Where is she? Did you say ten?" Officer Brenda asked, checking her Mickey Mouse watch.

"She's been distracted since she's been schmoozing around with Derek,"

Rose replied.

"What'd she tell you?" Officer Brenda pressed on for an answer.

"'Bout what?" Rose said, looking around.

"You know," Officer Brenda said.

"You know her," Rose said.

"What!" Officer Brenda replied.

"Fine... just fine." Rose barked.

"Don't tell me... The thrill is gone," Officer Brenda stated for the record.

"No. It's getting serious," Rose shot back.

"In a good way?" Officer Brenda asked hesitantly.

"Nothing's easy," Rose said as Judy joined the gang.

"Sorry, had to do something for Derek," Judy said, getting into the back seat of Rose's car.

"What's more important than our clandestine meetings in the outfield?" Officer Brenda said.

"True," Judy and Rose said simultaneously.

"We want to know what's going on with you know who," Officer Brenda said.

"Is it getting serious?" Rose interrupted.

"Did I tell you we went to Lake Mead?" Judy asked.

"Don't change the subject," Officer Brenda shot back.

"No, we went as a family," Judy said proudly.

"And?" Rose asked.

"It felt good. It felt real, not staged. We're a family," Judy said watching her words resonating off her colleagues.

It was quiet for a while as each searched for a meaning, an outcome to what Judy had just told them.

"What are you trying to tell us in your usual roundabout way?" Officer Brenda asked.

"That it's real. I can feel it," Judy said.

"And it's not just the sex talking? I mean, you hardly know the guy," Rose said.

"No, I feel comfortable with him. I want to be part of him. I love him and Pamela. You know, they're good people, and in this crazy world, that's rare."

Without leaving any room for comment, Judy

changed the subject to tell them what she had heard through the grapevine about the Colonel Prescott saga.

"I heard he was transferred," Rose said.

"I understand the Monroe's dropped the criminal charges," Officer Brenda murmured .

"Well, you are both right. The brass found it better to bury the incident by having the colonel plead guilty to a battery charge punishable by a fine and a suspended sentence. In addition, the colonel was reduced in rank and transferred to a base on Guam, where he'll push a pencil for the next three years until his honorable discharge," Judy said.

"Oh, and I guess he'll then get his full retirement," Rose said.

"I guess so, but probably as a major, which is two paygrades below a colonel."

"What about Betty? Didn't she have a civil lawsuit out against him?" Rose asked.

"I heard the colonel settled out of court for an undisclosed amount," Officer Brenda said.

"All in all, he was a sick old man, as crazy as a hoot, and paid in spades for his crimes. Blind in one eye, fractured skull, and put out to pasture on a desolate island in the Pacific," Judy said.

"Amen!" Rose said.

The ladies, agreeing on the Colonel Prescott matter, returned to the implied but unmentioned matter of whether or not Judy would wed.

"So, our little fighter pilot, have you set a date?" Rose asked, catching Judy by surprise.

"What?" Judy squeaked out.

"Well, I got to know. I serve and protect the town of Indian Springs, and I must have advance notice to change my schedule," Officer Brenda said with much authority.

"Exactly. There are countless things that must be done before one of the most important social events of the year. When will the announcement appear in the Sunday Edition of the *New York Times*?" Rose asked.

"Did you know there are sharks in Lake Mead?" Judy interjected.

"Where do you get all this bullshit from?

"No, no, it's true. There's a sign by the lake to beware of the man-eating sharks. I mean, how can I make something like that up?" Judy said.

"Yeah, and there's a sign at the entrance to Roswell, New Mexico, to turn left on to Route 69 to get to a brothel named the 'Alien Cathouse,'" Officer Brenda added.

"OK, I want you both to know that Derek and I are planning on getting married as soon as we iron out some minor details," Judy confessed.

"Pray tell, what minor details?" Rose asked.

"It's a family matter," Judy said.

"Why? Does he have a big family?" Officer Brenda asked.

"No, but he wants to invite his brother and his father doesn't want anything to do with him," Judy said sadly.

"What happened?" Rose asked.

"No, I shouldn't... it's private," Judy said, trying to end the inquisition.

"Oh, fuck it. Just tell us. I swear it will go no further than the three of us," Officer Brenda said.

"You both swear to God?" Judy asked.

"We do," they both said, raising their hands in unison.

"OK, when Derek's mother was sick—eight, ten years ago—Derek's father pleaded with his son Brad to return home to be with her. He told him that his mother wanted to see him before she died, but they never heard from him again. From then on, they never mentioned Brad's name."

"And Derek thinks if Brad returns home there can be a reconciliation?" Officer Brenda suggested.

"I don't know, but my baby misses his brother. They were inseparable as children," Judy said.

"OK, there might be extenuating circumstances for why Brad didn't return home," Officer Brenda suggested.

"Could you find out why Brad didn't come home so many years ago?" Judy asked.

"I can try, but I'll have to use my own resources out-side of my official duties as a police officer. Do you understand? I can't access state and federal databases," Officer Brenda explained.

"I understand. What do you need from me?" Judy said.

"As much as you can get from Derek: Brad's full name and address; phone numbers; social security number; driver's license number; passport number; any photographs or physical description; hobbies, clubs, schools; friends' names, addresses, and phone numbers; tattoos; girlfriends' names, addresses, phone numbers; medical conditions; names of doctors and dentists with addresses and phone numbers; any and all prescription drugs; if he is or was a drug addict. I know it's a lot to get for me, but the more I know about who he is, the better we'll be able to find him. I'll write this all down for you and email it to you tonight, OK?"

Then, with a three amigos hug, they wished each other "hasta luego."

28

Chairman Pak Thae-bok's Office
Supreme People's Assembly

Kylo was at the chairman's office at precisely one p.m., the appointed time given to him by the chairman's aide. However, most likely by design, Kylo was kept waiting forty-five minutes in the reception area to cool his heels, to show Kylo that he was outranked in the political pecking order.

"The chairman will see you now," chirped the aide.

Slowly getting to his feet, Kylo opened the door to the chairman's office to see a pompous little man busing himself to look important.

"Chairman," Kylo said to a blank face.

"What was this meeting about?" the chairman said with the back of his manicured hand.

"You know precisely what's it about. It's about the

overthrow of our country by a group of military men headed by General Zoko," Kylo said, setting the tone and substance of the meeting.

"We've heard those scurrilous accusations before from you and—"

But he could reject Kylo's comments, Kylo placed a computer tablet on the chairman's desk and began a recording of Si Woo's confession.

"Wild allegations? Look at this," Kylo said as he moved the pad closer. "This is Palace Guard Si Woo, who stabbed our Supreme Leader Kim Jong-un. And this is the reason, the incentive, to murder our Leader: his three-year-old daughter was dying of a childhood form of leukemia. His doctor, Hyeon, told him he could smuggle his daughter to South Korea, where she could get the lifesaving treatments to cure her disease if Si Woo stabbed our Supreme Leader."

Kylo advanced the recording to Dr. Hyeon's confession. "And this is Dr. Hyeon, who instructed Si Woo to meet one of Zoko's men to get instructions to carry out the assassination. At this meeting Si Woo was also given a weapon coated with a radioactive substance, a poison that ultimately brought permanent damage to our Leader's brain and organs.

"Dr. Hyeon also told us of meetings he and many other conspirators attended at General Zoko's home," Kylo said, letting it all filter into the chairman's mind.

At first, Kylo didn't know if what he'd shown the chairman was new to him or of no importance since it didn't elicit any emotion or comment. They sat there, silently staring at the tablet. Kylo knew instinctively through years of training that the first one to speak loses, so he held his tongue, waiting for the chairman to say the first word. The chairman tapped his knuckles against his teeth as if trying to say something but then stopped to think.

'I can wait until hell freezes over,' Kylo thought to himself, feeling confident that he might have just broken through to the man.

Finally, the chairman put his hands together in a form of prayer and asked, "Who's seen these recordings?"

"My detectives."

"Leave it with me."

"My question to you is: Were you aware of General Zoko's role in the planning and facilitating the assassination of our Supreme Leader?" Kylo asked.

"What I know and don't know are irrelevant. I am not on trial," the chairman stated for the record, thinking quickly about how he could extricate himself from Kylo's interrogation.

"In addition," Kylo said forcefully, "we have just received information that the CIA agent, from now on known as Mr. X, responsible for the attack, has been freed and is in the custody of the South Korean authorities. According to reliable sources, he has told them that the attack on our Supreme Leader was a 'one-off' attempt to kill Kim Jong-un by a rogue agency employee for personal reasons. He also admitted that he paid the South Korean gang known as the Black Hand to act as an intermediary between the CIA and renegade forces under the control and direction of General Zoko seeking to overthrow our government and install a military dictatorship."

"How can I check the veracity of these charges?" the chairman, said squirming in his chair as if he'd just had a bowel movement.

"These"—Kylo held up a sheaf of papers—"are my notes taken from my source in South Korea. He received them from an individual who was part of the interrogation of the CIA agent, and I know for a fact that you have a back-channel way of checking the veracity of these statements," Kylo said, rhetorically twisting the blade into the chairman's spleen.

"It's highly impractical that they would share such sensitive and inflammatory information on their trading partner with their intelligence agency—" the chairman tried to say before Kylo lowered his next blow.

"Please spare me your high-minded excuses. I know who you speak to at the ministry in South Korea. Would you like me to refresh your memory? I have several recordings of your conversations here on my tablet; wait, I'll play them for you," Kylo said, grabbing his tablet and pretending to find the chairman's conversation with the South Korean minister.

"This doesn't change the fact that you directed an incursion into South Korea without the proper authority. Do you make our foreign policy, or does the People's Assembly?" the chairman said, attempting to change the subject.

"I would have, but could I trust you to do what was right for our country?

That is the question!" Kylo slammed his fist on the chairman's desk for effect.

"Do you know who you're talking to?" the chairman said, getting to his feet.

"From where I sit, a traitor—a man who brought another traitor to our meeting, General Zoko." Kylo smiled at the nervous chairman, and it was at that moment that he knew exactly how to play the coward opposite him.

"He was invited to hear your testimony as a courtesy to our military brothers—"

Kylo raised his hand and stood. "You can stop the act. I know what you did, and if you want to avoid the hangman's noose, you'll do exactly as I say. Do you hear me?"

Stunned, the chairman could not utter a sound.

"Do you hear me?" Kylo repeated himself, walking over to the frightened chairman and slapping him in the face.

"Sit," Kylo ordered the chairman as if he were merely talking to a criminal in his interrogation room. The chairman complied without a word.

"Now listen. I'm not going to repeat myself if you want to avoid the gallows," Kylo said slowly to the man whose life depended on following his next instructions.

29

"Yes, I assure you. My men have swept my office for bugs and haven't found any. I am of the opinion that the main source of confidential information pouring out of our department is the result of a mole," Kylo sadly said.

"And how do you plan to find this mole?" Sejong asked.

"I had thought of subjecting our staff to take a lie detector screening, but we have too many people and it would take too long."

"Then what do you plan to do?" Sejong asked.

"You set a trap to catch a rat," Kylo said with a smile.

"What will you use as bait?" Sejong asked.

"That's what I wanted to speak with you about. I had a very interesting meeting with Chairman Pak Thae-bok. I believe he might be of use to us in getting to General Zoko," Kylo said.

"In which way?" Sejong asked, getting excited by the thought of bringing Zoko to his knees.

"I'm planning on having the chairman invite Zoko to his office on the pretense of removing me as the director of the National Police."

"But will he do it?" Sejong asked.

"He will and I'll write the invitation."

"Why? Do you have something on the chairman?"

"I told him he'd hang for treason if he didn't follow my instructions," Kylo said.

"Excellent. When do you plan to do it?" Sejong asked.

"As soon as I get my ducks in a row," Kylo said. "Now tell me about the nuclear bombs you mentioned at our last meeting. Was it real?"

"Very real, and just days away from Washington, DC," Sejong said proudly.

"And the delivery system?" Kylo asked, assuming this was all conjecture and wishful thinking, not an actuality in the works.

"Cruise missiles with nuclear warheads, four of them," Sejong replied to a wide-eyed Kylo.

"You're not joking... or are you?" Kylo said, astonished at the thought.

"No. It has been my desire to revenge the massacre

of our people by the United States during the Korean War."

"What you say is true and it has been a part of us, a part that makes us a great nation," Kylo said. "Our history, the history of our people, goes back thousands of years. And you above all carry the name of our illustrious leader, King Sejong, who brought enlightenment and progress to our people by stressing education, science, humanity, love, and kindness to one another. When all around us were barbarians, we stood tall and resolute to the rule of law that King Sejong inscribed, laws that were passed on from one generation to the next."

"I am proud that my father, Kim Jong-il, chose me to carry forth the name of King Sejong, and I have spent every day trying to live up to his memory and his teachings. But there is a time for reflection and another time for action. We Koreans have lived under the boot of many tyrants—the Japanese, the Russians, and the Americans, who enslaved our people for their own strategic purposes. Our people have had enough of the whip, and call out for justice and revenge. That's why our ship carrying our nuclear weapons will be in striking distance in a matter of days."

"Sejong, you must call off the attack. We gain nothing by killing millions of innocent people. The last thing we need now is another world at war; that's why we must concentrate our efforts in bringing down General Zoko. He's the enemy. The Americans didn't send the CIA to kill our Supreme Leader; it was a madman bent on revenge. The Americans were shocked by this person's actions and are seeking to find the person responsible. All I know is that there is a connection, a connection to war crimes during The Korean War," Kylo said to a silent Sejong.

"It's too late," Sejong mumbled.

"Just tell them to return home," Kylo said softly.

"If they're attacked, they will launch their missiles."

"What do you mean by 'attacked'?" Kylo asked for clarification.

"Challenged by an American warship."

"They have the ability to launch that quickly?" Kylo asked.

"All the captain has to do is push some buttons."

"And how many missiles are they carrying?" Kylo asked.

"Four Iranian cruise missiles with nuclear warheads," Sejong replied automatically.

"If they're not told to stand down, when are you scheduled to fire?" Kylo asked.

"The Fourth of July," Sejong said, coming to realize that his dream, a dream of a destroying their archenemy, was a futile effort with no meaningful reason.

"At what time on July fourth were you planning to attack?" Kylo said, making notes of Sejong's remarks.

"Nine p.m. Eastern Standard Time, when their capital is ablaze with fireworks."

"OK, this what we must do before they get any closer to their launch site. Wait—where is the launch site?"

"Two hundred miles off the coast of Virginia, in international waters."

"And one last question: What type of ship is carrying the missiles?" Kylo asked, jotting down every detail in his notepad.

"An American Victory ship from World War II, the same ships that invaded our country during the Korean War."

"Sejong, do you have a way of contacting the ship?" Kylo said, holding his breath.

"Yes, I do."

"Wonderful," Kylo said, taking a deep breath of relief. "Now listen to me; we're going to a special room here at headquarters to contact the ship. You will tell the captain to proceed to deep water and throw the missiles into the sea. He is then to return home to his port from which he departed. Is that clear?"

"Drop the missiles into the sea?" Sejong said, realizing that it was all over.

30

Hilton Hotel
Madrid Airport

Finding they had nothing that fit her in the hotel boutique—Kleinshure decided everyone in Spain was a size four—she returned to her suite to find the maid cleaning up last night's dinner for two.

"Maravilloso," she said to the maid, motioning for her to join her in the bedroom, where she removed the sheets and told her, in a sort of sign language, to make the bed with fresh sheets. This confused the poor girl, who did not customarily change the sheets each day, until Elizabeth presented her with a crisp twenty-euro note. After all, everything had to be just right for Juan.

'He should be here by ten thirty at the latest,' she mused to herself while filing her nails.

Holding her hands out to inspect her nails, she thought they needed something; a ring, not too ostentatious, might add the right touch. She rose and went to the room safe in her closet and tapped in her usual numbers, 2020. Taking out her small jewelry bag, she poured the contents on the bed. Looking down on the assorted rings, pins, bracelets, and mementos, she felt saddened. Was this the sum and substance of her life? Would any of this junk make an impression on Juan? She thought not.

'Am I fooling myself into thinking that I can compete with the crème de la crème? He'll be here soon, and I'm filled with doubts instead of joy.

'Get over it,' she coached herself. 'I'll screw him as he's never been screwed before. I'll shove a firecracker up his ass and sing "I'm a Yankee Doodle Dandy." In retrospect, maybe I won't sing. I'll take this little gold ring for luck,' she said to herself as she slipped it on her finger. 'A boy I was going steady with in high school gave it to me a hundred years ago. I don't remember his name, but he had such a pretty face and long, blonde hair,' she thought, twisting the ring around on her finger.

"Now I'm ready," she said standing in front of the bathroom mirror. "My motto from now on is, 'You can't improve on perfection.'"

Juan arrived just as predicted, at ten thirty a.m. on the dot, carrying two elegant Montblanc suitcases. Pushing them into the room he embraced Elizabeth and spun her around like a ragdoll until the room was filled with the love and laughter others merely dream about.

"Good flight?" Elizabeth asked as he put her down.

"Take your clothes off," he demanded as he removed his shirt.

Like two lovers in heat, they ripped each other's clothes from their bodies and folded their bodies into each other. First they moved slowly, in a melodic way; then, as the music of passion found its tempo, they crescendo to a wild dance of colors that flashed inside their minds as they clenched and shook and wrung each other out. Spent, they settled into a shared embrace and slept.

As they arose some hours later, they lay there, looking at the ceiling and wondering if the other was hungry. Fearful of breaking the wonderful mood, Juan asked, "Is it too late for breakfast? If not breakfast, maybe they'll serve a brunch?"

Elizabeth agreed, food was necessary, so they took a quick shower together and, putting on casual outfits, quickly made their way to the dining room. There they enjoyed brunch with a fine white wine and double espressos. Bringing their coffee and cookies with them to a poolside table, they discussed their agenda for the trip to Morocco. Elizabeth went over the arrangements she'd made to add Juan to her plans; her attention to detail and succinct answers to his questions impressed him.

"Wonderful, I can't wait to see our villa," he said, giving her a warm feeling in her heart.

"I do hope it lives up to its photos." Elizabeth said, showing him an aerial shot on her cell phone.

"Oh, that's so majestic, situated above the city. Bravo, my dear."

Since their flight to Lanzarote in the Canary Islands was early the next morning, they decided on a light dinner of local fish and a salad in their room. Juan spent the next several hours on paperwork that entailed reams of bank statements; joining Elizabeth in bed, he showed her a sheet full of figures that she couldn't read since she needed her glasses and was too tired to get out of bed to find them.

"I'll need one hundred thousand euros transferred into this account tomorrow," he told her, waving a sheet of paper.

"I'll attend to it in the morning, dear," she said, turning her bed lamp off without realizing that she had just agreed to give him one hundred and twelve thousand nine hundred and fifteen dollars. And that was just the beginning.

The flight from Madrid to Lanzarote was only two and a half hours and almost completely empty. Added to that, the flight attendant, a flirtatious young woman, invited them to choose, with the wave of her arm, to sit wherever they wished. Juan immediately thanked the young waif with a twenty-euro gratuity and asked to see the cocktail menu. Elizabeth observed for the first time, up close, how women were attracted to Juan and felt proud that, if only for the moment, he shared her bed.

Their flight, which was smooth as silk, took them over the Rock of Gibraltar and the northern tip of Morocco, where Elizabeth tried in vain to point out where their villa was in Tangier, but low-lying clouds blocked their view. After a few cocktails she gained enough courage to ask Juan how he had gravitated into the life of a gigolo.

"I was at a resort on the island of Majorca, off the coast of Spain, on a holiday. When I arrived by ferry, I hadn't booked a reservation, so I asked the taxi driver to take to me to a nice villa for the night. He took me to the Cala d'Or in what's called the Old Town. It was just beautiful... steps from the water with breathtaking views of the beach and shops, restaurants, and hotels.

"Well, it just so happens that a woman, an American woman from, let me think—yes, South Carolina— was dining alone and asked, naturally through the waiter, if I cared to join her. Taking my drink in hand, I joined her, and as it turns out she was a recent widow on her first visit to Europe. For that matter, it was her first time anywhere outside the United States. After we spent the night talking, drinking, and enjoying each other's company, we finished off the night in her room.

"The next morning, over breakfast on the patio, she asked me to stay with her and be her guide while she visited Majorca. She said that she'd pay for everything and that I could name my price for my services. At first I refused to take her money, but she insisted and gave me one thousand euros in advance from her handbag, saying that the last night was the first time she had enjoyed making love. So, after breakfast we returned to her room and continued our lovemaking. During one of our walks on the beach, I told her I'd like to show her where I lived, Barcelona, so the next day we took the ferry to Barcelona and I introduced her to my city. She just loved it.

"'Are they all so young?' she asked me while strolling the streets one night.

"'In Barcelona, even the old are young. It's the Shangri-La of Europe. Did you know we live forever?' I said.

"'No, I didn't know. So tell me, how old are you?' she asked me.

"'Me, I'll be eighty-one in November,' I told her.

"'Really, you don't look older than—' she tried to say, but then I kissed her."

"Then you never gave her your real age, did you?" Elizabeth asked.

"Why? Is that important?" Juan asked.

"No, I'm a romantic and life's too short to dwell on tomorrows," Elizabeth said, squeezing his hand. "So what happened to your 'Lady of Spain'?"

"I'm not boring you, am I?" Juan asked.

"No, not at all. I'd hope that you left her gracefully?" Elizabeth asked.

"Who said I left her?" Juan said.

"But you said it happened years ago?" Elizabeth said, confused.

"True, but there is more to the story," Juan said with a wink of his eye. "As I said, she was a widow and had inherited her late husband's business, a large group of mills employing several thousand people throughout the state of South Carolina. I also told her I attended but did not graduate from university and that I majored in business and finance."

"Why didn't you graduate?" Elizabeth asked.

"That's irrelevant to my story. So, as I was about to say, she invited me to return with her to South Carolina and help her modernize the mill, which I accepted, and she installed me, so to speak, in her twenty-six-room mansion on a five-hundred-acre estate. I mean, it was a *Gone With the Wind* mansion, and I was the Rhett Butler to her Scarlett O'Hara, according to the chitter-chatter in town.

"It didn't take me long to discover that several of her key executives at the mill had set up bogus vendors who were fleecing the mill out of millions of dollars. From there on these men were charged by the state of South Carolina with grand larceny and a dozen other crimes and after a plea deal were sentenced to twenty years in jail and several hundred thousands of dollars in fines. She in turn took the course of leniency due to their long history at the mill, and after the men sold their homes and auctioned off their valuables as restitution, the charges were dropped. All in all, we felt satisfied that justice was done, and I left with enough money to continue my education. She will forever be a memory to cherish," Juan said, tearing up, at which point, Elizabeth reached over and kissed him.

31

Indian Springs High School Baseball Field

The next time they met at the high school baseball field, the sky was dark and foreboding, with intermittent thunder and lightning, as the three amigos huddled together in Rose's car. Officer Brenda had called the meeting to discuss what she'd found regarding the disappearance of Derek's brother, Brad.

"Do any of you want to share my coffee?" Rose asked.

"Is it black?" Officer Brenda asked with a sniffle.

"Do you have a cold?" Rose asked her.

"Just allergies," Officer Brenda replied with a sniffle.

"Never mind. Better safe than sorry," Rose said, sipping her coffee.

"Ladies, are we going to discuss Derek's brother or what?" Judy barked.

"Yes, I called this meeting because I know where Derek's brother has been," Officer Brenda said.

"Where?" Judy asked excitedly.

"He's in prison in Susanville, California."

"You're joking. Is there such a place as Susanville?" Rose asked.

"Yep, and it's only five hours west of us. It's above Sacramento," Officer Brenda said.

"How'd you find him so fast?" Rose asked.

"I'm not at liberty to disclose that."

"Oh, bullshit, Brenda. How'd you find him?" Judy asked, irritated by the irrelevant disclaimer.

"Googled public records," Officer Brenda admitted.

"What's he in for?" Judy asked.

"OK, here's the bad part. He's incarcerated at the California Correctional Center. He was convicted on vehicular manslaughter and is serving an eleven-year

Sentence," Officer Brenda said, checking her notes.

"What'd he do?" Judy asked.

"He caused an accident that killed a passenger in his car while he was on drugs," Brenda said.

"Was he injured in the accident too?" Judy asked.

"Walked away without a scratch."

"Who was the passenger that was killed?" Rose asked.

"A hitchhiker, a sixteen-year-old girl bumming a ride home at night," Officer Brenda sadly said.

"You mean Brad couldn't return home to be with his

dying mother and now can't attend his brother's wedding?" Judy said.

"Yep," Officer Brenda said.

"Is there anything we can do?" Judy asked.

"I doubt it."

"Could he get a pass, you know, just to attend the wedding?" Judy asked.

"I doubt it," Officer Brenda reiterated.

"Then there's nothing we can do?" Rose asked.

"You got it," Officer Brenda said.

With that bitter pill to take, the ladies sat, silently pondering their next move—if there even was one to make.

"Did anyone think that maybe Brad wouldn't want to attend his brother's wedding?" Officer Brenda asked.

"Why not?" Judy asked.

"He may not want to see his family. Look, he's been in jail for, I don't know, seven, eight years and never reached out to them."

"There can be other reasons. Like he was embarrassed or feels like a failure or he's just given up or he's a loner," Judy said, throwing everything she could think of against the wall to see what stuck.

"Assuming he can get a pass, shouldn't we ask him?" Rose suggested.

"Wouldn't that needlessly get his hopes up if he can't get out?" Officer Brenda interjected.

"OK, assuming, just hypothetically speaking, that Derek is OK with us attempting to get Brad a pass to attend your wedding, what's our next step?" Rose asked Judy.

"It's a little good and bad, so to speak. On the one hand we now know why Brad never came home to be with his dying mother, and on the other hand, why he might not be able to attend our wedding."

"But you'll discuss it with your fiancé, right?" Rose asked, noticing a perk in Judy's demeanor with the acknowledgement that Derek was her betrothed.

"Of course, but how should I break the news?" Judy asked her friends.

"You've got to be honest with him from the get-go. Like Brad, you can't promise something you can't deliver," Office Brenda advised.

"Right, but who is the point person, the decider, on who gets a pass and who doesn't?" Judy asked.

"The fuckin' governor?" Rose suggested.

"No, most likely the warden," Office Brenda said.

"How do we approach him?" Judy asked.

"Personally, I don't think we can. I think we need an intermediary, a person to plead our case."

"Where do you get this guy?" Rose asked.

"You buy one. They cost big bucks, and to compound that, they should be a local," Officer Brenda said.

"I'm confused. Who are these people you're talking about that can approach the warden on our behalf?" Judy asked, cutting to the chase.

"A shyster, a lawyer who knows the warden. Probably goes to church with him or they belong to the same county club or the same political party, that's who," Officer Brenda said, explaining to her naive friends how things are done in the real world.

"Oh, that seems hopeless," Rose said in despair.

"We don't have the juice, the connections, or, for that matter, the money to hire a person that fills the bill," Officer Brenda stated for the record.

"I'll have to tell Derek the bad news and let him decide what we should do," Judy said.

"That's the best course of action for now. Anything else is just pissing in the wind," Rose said, grabbing Judy in a bear hug.

"I love you, my dear amigos… till later," Judy said, leaving the car.

As the sun broke through the clouds, she stopped and looked up at the sky, praying that the storm inside her was gone, too, and that tomorrow would be a better day.

32

Senate Conference Room 107
People's Assembly Center
Pyongyang, North Korea

THE SOVEREIGN NATION OF NORTH KOREA
for the

Southern District of Pyongyang

The Government of North Korea) Case No. 4Y88317

)

V.)

)
)
General Ri Zoko
Defendant

ARREST WARRANT

You are commanded to arrest and bring before a
North Korean magistrate judge for the District of
Pyongyang without delay the above referenced
defendant who is accused of TREASON.

Count 1: The defendant did willfully instruct
others to assassinate the president of North Korea, Kim Jong-un.

Magistrate Judge: Pava-Lo

———

CONFIDENTIAL

To: General Ri Zoko
From: Chairman Pak Thae-bok

DRAFT INVITATION
It is my honor to request your attendance at the
People's Assembly to discuss the replacement of
our current director of the National Police, Kylo

Ren. We have found that Kylo Ren was responsible for the disastrous incursion into South Korean waters in a vain attempt to kidnap an
American citizen. This ill-conceived attack has
caused our nation grave international consequences. In light of these matters we would also
appreciate your guidance in choosing a new director of the National Police. Please respond by a
secure messenger directly to me with a date and
time that is convenient for you.

Respectfully,

Chairman Pak Thae-bok
The Supreme People's Assembly

Kylo returned to police headquarters after meeting with the chairman. He'd given him a copy of an arrest warrant and a draft of an invitation to send to General Zoko to lure him from the safety of his army base to the People's Assembly, where Kylo's men could arrest him.

Once in the confines of his office, Kylo outlined a timetable for how and when to carry out his plan. He knew that Zoko was a cunning adversary and that one small detail could jeopardize the outcome of the en-deavor. He also knew that Zoko would jump at the op-portunity to replace him as the director of the National Police with one of his stooges, which was one of the reasons Pak Thae-bok would give for their meeting. Another was the North Korean police commandos being held during the aborted incursion into South Korea to kidnap a CIA agent. Kylo had left it up to the chairman if he wished to include a trade the South Koreans couldn't refuse. Zoko would give them the man responsible for the incursion, Director Kylo, for the North Korean commandoes being held in a South Korean jail: a win-win for both sides.

Kylo realized that capturing General Zoko would be a challenging task. Assuming he'd take the bait and travel to the People's Assembly, how many guards would he take for protection? Kylo thought that most likely Zoko would travel by car with two armed soldiers and be followed by a chase car containing three or four more. From there, Zoko would probably be escorted into the building by three or four guards until he entered the room set aside for their meeting. In Kylo's mind's eye he saw what the room would look like; Zoko would enter flanked by two soldiers for appearance. He'd then shake hands with the chairman and other dignitaries while his guards took strategic positions around the room. Now a late-to-the-meeting senator would enter the room, causing a momentary distraction; the guards would take their eyes off Zoko for the blink of an eye, and when they looked back, they'd be staring at men aiming their guns at them. The so-called dignitaries would be revealed to actually be Kylo's policemen, all over the age of sixty, with gray hair, dressed in business suits. The policemen would quickly disarm the guards and have them invite their colleagues out-side the room in to join them so that they might also be disarmed. Throughout the execution of the plan, Gen-eral Zoko would sit calmly, watching his men surrender to the overwhelming manpower and professionalism of the police. In a way, he would admire how quickly the police engaged the guards and disarmed them. From there, the police would march the prisoners through the basement of the People's Assembly to three white vans parked by the building's loading dock. The pris-oners would be placed in one van and General Zoko in another between two of Kylo's detectives, who would formally advise the general that he was under arrest and charged with treason. The mock senators would be loaded into the third van to provide an escort to police headquarters. Later, Zoko's soldiers in front of the building would be advised to return to their base.

Kylo did not have to wait long for the vision in his mind's eye to become reality. When he heard the good news by phone, Kylo was delirious with happiness at the bloodless outcome of a very dangerous mission. He made up his mind that he would personally congratu-late each man on a job well done and bestow on each of them the Medal of Honor, the highest honor bestowed on a member of the National Police.

But what to do with Zoko before his trial? That was the question, a question Kylo was afraid to ask himself for fear that it might turn out to be another Makpo blunder. A city jail was out of the question with a mole still at lodge in the police headquarters. They'd have to squirrel him away, where no one could find him, and for the time being, Zoko was put under a twenty-four-hour watch in a holding cell in the basement of police headquarters.

33

Lanzarote Airport
Canary Islands

Clearing Immigration and Customs to enter Lanzarote was a breeze for Elizabeth, who was now known as Sara Murphy, effectively breaking the link to Allison Brant. The next link, and hopefully Elizabeth's last to the United States, would break when she reached Morocco, where she'd be known as Grace Hayworth, residing in Tangier. The authorities in Morocco would have no idea that Ms. Hayworth had entered their country without clearing immigration or customs. She would arrive from the Canary Islands by private yacht, and no one would know or care where she came from.

Wasn't it marvelous? she thought as she and Juan boarded their private yacht for the twenty-four-hour journey to the port of Rabat. It was a sleek, seventy-five-foot, oceangoing motored yacht with a crew of four who would ensure that their passengers navigated the waters between the Canary Islands and the coast of Morocco in luxury. Included in their passage were meals served either on deck or in a private dining room, a stateroom with a king-size bed and private bathroom, a lounge for cocktails and television, and an area on deck for sunbathing. All in all, not bad for one thousand euros each.

After a tour of the ship by the captain, they decide to get some sun and relaxed on deck with glasses of a sweet white wine and a hummus dip with toasted pita slices. After watching the island of Lanzarote disappear on the horizon, they decided to break in their king-size bed with a midday romp, followed by a lazy bubble bath for two, which, with the gentle rocking of the ship, put them to sleep in each other's arms. Awaking some time later, they toweled each other off and, lying in bed together, spoke of what lay ahead and how happy they felt at that moment. Elizabeth prayed that she would be as happy in future as she was right here and now.

Slipping into the marina in Rabat some twenty-four hours later, they were met at the dock by a slight, gray-haired man in a black suit and tie. He introduced himself as Mohammad Sucson, their chauffeur and the man about the villa, as he collected their cases and led them to their Mercedes-Benz, which was parked in the marina's Members Only lot.

"Mohammad, how long of a trip is it to the villa?" Juan asked.

"From Rabat to the villa is 251 kilometers, two hours and forty-eight minutes of travel time," Mohammad replied.

"Thank you, Mohammad," Elizabeth said.

For the remainder of the ride, Juan and Elizabeth discussed the sights they passed and places they may wish to visit later. It was exciting to see both how quaint and exotic the neighborhoods were between Rabat, which was modern, and Tangier, which struck them as old world, but as they drew closer to the villa, the neighborhood changed into a vibrant and opulent scene with villas dotting the hills here and there. Then, finally, at the crest of the hill was their sprawling villa, with breathtaking views of the Mediterranean on one side and the Atlantic Ocean on the other. The villa and its vistas literally took the new inhabitants' breath away, and after Mohammad quickly went around to open the car doors for the new owners, Elizabeth and Juan wandered to a vantage point to take in the utter beauty of their new surroundings.

"It's more than I expected," Elizabeth whispered to Juan.

However, after meeting Mohammad's wife, Salma, a tour of the villa and its furnishings revealed that a remodeling was in order. Elizabeth and Juan's belongings were brought to their rooms; Mohammad and Salma put their clothes away as instructed and took their suitcases to a closet meant for travel purposes. They then met for tea in the dining room to discuss some of the things they wanted done to make life comfortable for the four of them living under the same roof.

"Are you comfortable with your rooms in the villa?" Juan asked to the shock of Mohammad, who had never heard an employer ask him such a personal question. He was always addressed and treated as a servant, nothing more; his comfort was of no importance to the master of the house.

"Thank you for asking, my lord. Our accommodations are excellent, and I pray you'll enjoy living in your new villa," Mohammad said in perfect English.

"We thank you for preparing our villa, and with your help, we expect to improve some of the furnishings," Elizabeth said gracefully.

Mohammad and Salma nodded that they understood.

"We will make a list of what we expect you to accomplish over the next few days, weeks, and months. However, we will be mindful that in some instances we will bring in contractors to assist you in accomplishing many of the changes," Juan said, trying to ease their doubts.

"Thank you, my lord. We will follow your instructions and look forward to serving you," Mohammad said as Elizabeth dismissed them.

.   .   .

Later, relaxing on their veranda overlooking the sea, Elizabeth and Juan discussed the challenges and opportunities that lay ahead as they turned the villa into what they envisioned: a home for the two of them and possibly a home to safely host new friends.

As they spoke of a new life together, men and women of the CIA were at Elizabeth's house in Virginia Beach, investigating her disappearance. In the days since her disappearance, rumors had spread within her department and in human resources as to why a twenty-plus-year employee would walk away without a letter of resignation. The CIA lived on paperwork, and without the right form, it just wasn't done. So, when word filtered back that Elizabeth had ended her life, questions were raised about her suicide note. It sounded bizarre and like a woman completely out of her mind. That couldn't be Elizabeth Klcinshure; something made her do it, but since there were no signs to contradict the preliminary findings, what was done was done, under the rug for the time being until the inquest by the state of Virginia, whenever that would be.

Had Elizabeth, now using the name Grace Hayworth, known how cavalierly the agency was regarding her disappearance and faked suicide, she might have taken a less circuitous path to Morocco. But, after checking the internet for any news of her suicide, the results came up blank, as if it wasn't worthy of note, not even in the *Virginian-Pilot*.

'Maybe it's too early,' she thought, 'or maybe the agency finds it prudent not to disclose sensitive material that might be contrary to the announcements from the White House about how close they are to disarming North Korea.' So, for the moment, Elizabeth's mantra was, "Keep your head down and trust no one."

34

"They don't answer?" Sejong asked the communications tech.

"Are you sure it's the right call number?" Kylo asked Sejong.

"Yes, look," Sejong said, handing his cell phone to Kylo to see.

"Try it again," Kylo instructed the tech.

"Still nothing," the tech replied.

"Maybe they are being blocked by something," Sejong hypothesized.

"Let me check the weather. What is their location?" the tech inquired.

"He should be close to the Cuba by this time," Sejong said.

"Then I hope he's on the leeward side of the island. A hurricane is bearing down on Cuba from the Atlantic Ocean," the tech said, checking the area's weather forecast.

"Will that block his receiving our calls?" Kylo asked.

"I don't know, but he might be saving his batteries," the tech speculated.

"We'll try later," Kylo said, thanking his tech and asking him to try reaching the ship every hour on the hour.

"If you contact them, call me," he said, tapping the tech on his shoulder.

"Smart boy," Sejong said.

"If anyone can contact them, he's the one," Kylo said.

Later, while Kylo and Sejong relaxed, sipping tea, Kylo asked Sejong, "How many people know about the ship and its mission?"

"A number of people, but Admiral Shumi-un was the person who handled most of the delicate matters."

"Specifically, what delicate matters?" Kylo asked.

"Well, he acquired the ship, the missiles, the installation of the nuclear warheads, and the captain and crew," Sejong said, rattling off some of the details.

"Is there anyone else in North Korea who doesn't know about your secret mission to destroy the world?" Kylo said sarcastically.

"Yes, there are..." Sejong began to say when Kylo

raised his hand and said, "First and foremost, we must recall the ship or destroy it. Are you sure there is no other way to contact them? How about by cell phone?"

"I had the captain confiscate all the cell phones. Anyway, they'd probably be out of range," Sejong said.

"Assuming they're at anchor somewhere off Cuba, we must calculate how long it will take them to reach their launch site," Kylo said.

"We need someone with maritime experience, preferably in navigation and fuel consumption," Sejong said.

"Someone in the naval department or—I know! The university. Yes, best to avoid anyone who knows Admiral Shumi-un," Kylo said.

"Do you know anyone that fits that description?" Sejong asked.

"No, but I'll ask one of my bright young detectives to find the right person," Kylo said, picking up his intercom. "Lama Su, get me Clu-tra."

"Is Clu-tra one of those bright young detectives?" Sejong asked.

"He's so bright he frightens me," Kylo admitted.

A few moments later Kylo received a call from his communications tech asking to see Kylo on a very important matter. Kylo immediately granted the request.

"Did you reach the ship?" he asked his communications tech.

"No, but I have something else to discuss with you… in private, please."

"In case you didn't know, this is Sejong, Kim Jong-un's brother. I think we can trust his discretion," Kylo said before asking the tech to sit with them.

"Well, I have been tasked to download and transcribe the phone numbers that were called and received on this phone, as well as the text messages," the tech said.

"Whose phone is it?" Kylo asked as the tech handed him a transparent evidence bag.

As soon as Kylo noticed the name on the bag, his demeanor changed from restful to elated.

"Is it there?" he asked.

"Yes!" the tech cried, showing Kylo a printout with one name highlighted in yellow.

Kylo took the paper and instantly knew who the mole, the spy, the traitor within his department was—a man trusted with the nation's secrets; a man revered by his colleagues: Major Ketsu-onyo.

"Whose phone was it?" Sejong asked.

"General Zoko's, that's who!" Kylo said, shaking his head in disgust. "Thank you. Forgive me, what is your name?"

"My name is Cato," the boy said with a smile followed by a slight bow.

"Well, Cato, you've discovered who was passing confidential information to the enemies of our great nation, and for that, we bow to you." Kylo and Sejong rose and bowed to the astonished Cato, who burst into tears and left the room to return to his duties.

"We do have some very talented people here," Kylo remarked.

As they each poured another cup of tea, the phone rang with news that Clu-tra was on the line.

"Clu-Tra, I have a job for you," Kylo said. "Find me someone at the university versed in naval matters. We're tracking a freighter somewhere off Cuba, sailing to the East Coast of the United States. I wish to know when that freighter is set to arrive in the vicinity of Washington, DC. In addition, there's a Category 4 hurricane currently bearing down on Cuba, and the ship is 414 feet long and does fifteen knots. Do you think you can do it?"

"Yes sir, I'll get right on it."

"He's a good boy and can probably do the math in his head, but let's see who he gets just to be safe, yes?" Kylo took a sip of his tea.

"But tell me, how did you get your hands on General Zoko's cell phone?" Sejong asked.

"Sit, my young colleague, and I'll tell you about one of my rare accomplishments," Kylo said with a broad smile.

"Tell me. What have I missed?" Sejong urged him.

"My men arrested Zoko when he went to the People's Assembly to meet with Chairman Pak Thae-bok. It was a classic 'now you see him, now you don't,' perfect timing, perfect execution. They were in and out in less than ten minutes... and without firing a shot."

"And what about the other conspirators? Are they still at large?" Sejong asked.

"Not for long. We've identified all seventeen—yes, there were only seventeen that we know of—and they're being rounded up. From what I was recently told, only three are still at large." Kylo nodded.

"Excellent. Our nation owes you a great deal for arresting the traitors planning the overthrow, and now you must help me recall the Victory ship carrying my foolhardy attempt to revenge the massacre of our people during the Korean War."

"We will try, but you must be prepared to destroy the ship if it's the only way to stop it."

"Oh, one last question: Where is General Zoko being held?" Sejong asked.

"In the police HQ basement, of course," Kylo said with a coy smile.

35

California Correctional Center
Susanville, California

"Honey, I've got to pee," Judy stated for the fourth time.

"Can you wait till we get to—" Derek began to say.

"No, please. This gas station," Judy said as Derek pulled over to the restrooms on the side of the gas station.

Judy got out and rushed to the restroom. In a moment she was back by the car, shaking her legs in distress. "The door's broken," she said. "Can you ask the attendant for the key to the men's room?"

Derek ran into the gas station and brought out a key on a long chain attached to a chunk of two-by-four.

"Guard the door. I'll be right out," Judy said.

"Here's the key," she said when she returned from the men's room.

"Next time we go anywhere, no coffee. Nothing to drink for you, baby,"

Derek said, putting the pickup truck in gear and burning rubber reentering Route A1 to the Susanville Correction Center. They had a nine o'clock appointment with the prison counselor and a good fifty miles to go. It was now a little after eight.

Their first impression of the place was that it reminded them of army barracks surrounded by an eight-foot chain-link fence. On one end was a two-story, white building with a wooden sign out front signifying that it was the administration building and that they were at the visitors' entrance. Parking in a visitor spot they entered the building and passed through a security check like in an airport and were sent to a receptionist who gave them an application to complete. When they returned the application, the receptionist asked for their driver's licenses, which she scanned in a small device. They were then directed to take the application with them and give it to the prison counselor in Room 119.

Entering a small, dusty office, they saw a bulky man with a bulbous, red nose and mustard-colored teeth, sitting in an oversize, black Naugahyde desk chair, circa 1956, sporting a short-sleeve, purple shirt opened at the neck.

"Sit," he said to them and took their application.

"You're here to see Brad Navarro?" he asked.

"Yes, sir," Derek replied.

"I see you've never been here before, is that right?" he asked, looking up from the application.

"Yes, sir," Derek replied.

"Why?" The man folded his chubby hands on his desk.

"It's a long story," Derek responded as he was instructed by Judy to keep his answers short.

"Well then, make it quick," the man said.

"What?" Derek asked, confused.

"Why you didn't visit sooner? He's your brother, right?"

"Yes, but I never visited him because..." And then, against Judy's instructions, he replayed the sad story of his mother's illness and their plea for Brad to be by her side; how when she died without seeing him, they disowned him, not realizing until just recently that he had been in prison at the time they sought his help. He shared how he and Judy desperately wanted to reconcile with Brad because they want to invite him to their wedding.

"We don't cater to frivolous requests from guilt-ridden family members. You should have brought him into your hearts long ago. I know Brad, and he's a good and sensitive boy, and what he did many years ago was wrong, but to cast him aside when he needed you? Well, that's just as wrong," he said to a silent Derek and Judy. "When are you getting married?"

"As soon as we make the arrangements," Judy said.

"Where are you getting married?"

"The Candlelight Wedding Chapel in Las Vegas," Judy said.

"I know the place," he said with a mustard-colored smile.

"You know the place?" Derek asked.

"Yes, but it's a long story." The prison counselor leaned forward on his elbows. "OK, now listen carefully. I'll allow it on three conditions. One, that Brad is OK with it. Two, that you pay all the costs to hire a videographer to broadcast Brad via Skype live to the venue. And three, that you make a wholehearted reconciliation with this boy who will need all your love when he gets out. Do you understand?"

"Yes! Yes, thank you," Derek said. "We will."

They hugged each other in joy.

The Prison Counselor escorted them back to reception, where they shook hands and waited for an orderly to take them to the visitors' reception center to see Brad. The center was a large room divided by wooden tables with one chair on one side for the inmate and two on the other side for visitors. At the end of each row was a guard on what resembled a lifeguard chair, looking down at the tables. Signs were on the walls, reminding the inmates and visitors of the rules: "No Shouting, No Eating or Drinking, No Smoking, No Fighting."

When they entered the room, they took a seat and waited for Brad to join them.

Inmates and visitors came and went. It seemed that the rules for touching were relaxed since many embraced and touched, holding hands; some tables even had children at them.

After a few tense minutes, Brad entered the room and spotted his brother. As Derek saw Brad approaching, he rose to his feet and, with tears streaming down his face, embraced his brother, burying his head in his chest. They rocked back in forth, crying for a long moment, until a guard, using a clicker, asked them to please be seated, which they did as they took a good, long look at each other.

"I missed you, kid," Derek said, wiping his nose with his fingers.

"It's been a long time."

"This is Judy," Derek said by way of introduction.

"Nice to meet you." Brad smiled at her.

"It's nice to meet you too," Judy said with a warm smile and a sniffle. "We just saw the counselor, and he said that you can be Derek's best man at our wedding… if you want to be?"

"Of course I would! He's my big brother," Brad said, upon which Judy lost it and broke down and cried with delight. Derek put his arm around his bride-to-be, and he, too, began to cry. On cue, Brad joined them in a family cry fest. They discussed their plans for the big event and how Brad would be part of it, but most importantly Derek begged his brother to forgive him. Brad reciprocated, saying that he was sorry for his actions that had contributed to the death of a young girl. Over the years he'd written the girl's family asking for their forgiveness. After a while, they forgave him and prayed that God would forgive him for his sins. Brad felt that with that knowledge, he could return to society a better person.

"I have to make it up to Dad for not being there for Mom," he admitted sadly.

"He understands now and is awaiting your return home, as is my daughter, Pamela. She's in the wedding party as a bridesmaid," Derek said.

"When we get back, we're taking her out to buy her dress," Judy said.

For the next twenty-five minutes that they were allowed in the visitors' reception center, they brought Brad up to date on what they'd done to their house in preparation for his temporary return home, the recent trip they had taken to Lake Mead, and what it was like to have an F-15 fighter pilot as part of the family. Judy blushed, admitting that she actually wasn't in the cockpit but controlled the plane from a trailer at the base. However, Derek made sure to mention that the F-15 fighter plane was just that: a fully armed tactical weapon that could engage bad guys on land, sea, and in the air.

"Awesome," Brad said, giving Judy a high five.

Leaving was harder than coming. They lingered, hugging Brad and telling him how much they loved him and longed for his return to the fold, only to ultimately say goodbye. But fate had an additional wrinkle for the story of a boy convicted of involuntary manslaughter nine years ago.

The prison counselor waylaid Derek and Judy as they headed out to the parking lot.

"I have something for you," the man gasped, handing Derek a manila envelope. "When Brad got here nine years ago, he wouldn't talk to me, but later on, after he started trusting me, he told me what happened the night of the accident."

"This is yours to keep? What's in here?" Derek asked.

"Read it, read my notes, you'll understand. One last thing…" He seemed to be searching for the right words.

"Tell us. What?" Derek asked, hoping he wouldn't change his mind.

"Don't let Brad drive at night," the counselor said, looking into Derek's eyes to emphasize the point.

"Why?" Derek asked, puzzled.

"Read the file and have a joyous wedding."

He walked back to his office.

36

Villa Roche
Tangier, Morocco

It was after a sumptuous dinner of Moroccan-style baked lamb and couscous that Juan explained why they had to sell the villa.

"My dear, I'm afraid that living in a lavish villa in Tangier is like waving a red flag at the local authorities," he said.

"What do you mean by 'local authorities'?" Elizabeth asked before sipping her pinot noir.

"Police, tax men, con men, immigration, newspapers, you name it," Juan replied, lighting a hashish waterpipe.

"Yes, but I just love it," she said regretfully.

"I know, my dear, and I love it, too, but we're on the lam and this is not what I'd call a hideout."

"If not here, where would you suggest?" she asked, letting him decide.

"A venue where we can come and go without restrictions or notice."

"What would that be?" Elizabeth asked.

"I got the idea while sailing from the Canary Islands to Morocco."

"A ship?" she said.

"Exactly. An oceangoing yacht, but larger. One hundred twenty-five feet should be adequate."

"I like the idea, but where would we call home?"

"The Mediterranean. Barcelona, Majorca, Tangier, Cannes, Monaco, to name a few," he said, feeling the drug affect his speech.

"Let's start looking tomorrow."

She downed her wine and invited him to bed.

The next morning, after some bedroom gymnastics and a hot shower, they sat down to a breakfast of fruit, nuts, and grains in a creamy yogurt followed by a rich Turkish coffee and baklava.

Their estate agent in Marrakech advised them of the thirty-day rule when buying property in Morocco: you can cancel the deal and receive ninety percent back or purchase another property within thirty days and use one hundred percent of the original price toward the purchase of a new property. Hearing their options, they decided to start looking for a smaller villa and split the difference toward buying a yacht.

Now, with the quest to find a less ostentatious villa in and around Tangier, their agent emailed them a list of available properties in the one-million-euro range, offering to arrange showings of the properties of interest. Several were quite nice but lacked the views they sought, but then again, they were a fraction of the price they spent on their current villa. In the end, they selected three that looked promising and asked their agent to make the arrangements and call them if they could be seen in the next few days. In the meanwhile, Juan was perusing the internet for yacht broker listings of thirty-five-meter yachts and found four listings in the three-million-euro range that, on the surface, looked spectacular, but that would depend upon a survey by a naval expert. Again, Juan reached out to his agent to make the arrangements to inspect the ships that were within 100 miles of Tangier.

They strolled out onto their patio overlooking the Rock of Gibraltar and sat under an umbrella, sipping their cocktails and talking about how fast things change when one's on the run. But Elizabeth understood that running was far better than sitting in a prison cell staring at steel bars.

"You know, I've often dreamed about what it would be like living on a yacht," Juan admitted.

"If it's like our passage from the Canary Islands to Rabat, I'd take it every day," Elizabeth mused.

"That was a lovely yacht," Juan said. "Anything going on in Virginia Beach?"

"No, and I'm surprised. I thought that I'd at least

have a mention in the home paper," she said, feigning her disappointment.

"What if they pocketed the suicide note?" Juan suggested.

"Why would they do that?"

"To control the narrative. What the local yokels don't know is in the agency's favor."

"You might be right," Elizabeth said.

"The less they know, the better."

"So, after we buy a new villa and buy or lease a yacht, where should we go?" she asked.

"That's a good idea," he said.

"What?"

"Leasing the yacht. It might work out—how should I put it?—cleaner," he said.

"In which way?"

"Well, when you lease, it's their ship. They own it, they service it, they maintain it, they insure it, they store it, they handle the paperwork, and there's no depreciation."

"Yes, that might be a better option than laying out millions of euros. What would the lease of a million-dollar yacht cost?"

"That would depend on several variables: the cost of the yacht, the interest rates, whether it's a lease-to-purchase or straight lease, the lease period in years, and other factors. My guess is ten thousand a month."

"Then we can try it for a year and see how we like it," she added.

"I agree. You lose when you buy on impulse and then end up selling for whatever you can get."

"Oh, before I forget, I transferred one hundred thousand euros into the account you wanted," she said in a matter-of-fact way.

"Thank you. It should cover some of my debts, plus leave a reserve for forthcoming statements."

"I'd feel better if you checked that you received the funds since it was the first time I used the bank's 'transfer funds' feature," she said.

"I will," he assured her.

The next day, they received a call from their agent that he had lined up two villas for them to inspect. Both were in the Marshan neighborhood of Tangier. A four-bedroom, three-bath house with kitchen, living room, den, and patio, with ocean views, was listed for 1.5 million euros. The another was on several levels with five bedrooms, each with its own bathroom; three terraces; courtyard patio; Moroccan living room; and two kitchens overlooking the Strait of Gibraltar listed for 1.2 million euros.

"That didn't take long," Elizabeth said.

"I'm checking out the Marshan neighborhood," Juan said reviewing street shots on Google.

"What's does it look like?"

"A modern section of Tangier."

"At least it's in the right price range."

"The list price is just that. But no one pays list price in North Africa, especially in Morocco," he reminded her.

"OK, you do the bargaining, my dear. I'm a notoriously bad shopper."

37

Office of Kylo-Ren, National Director of Police
Pyongyang

"Any word from the ship?" Sejong asked as he entered Kylo's office.

"Please sit. As of this morning, we still have not reached the ship, and if we are to intercept it, it must be soon," Kylo said.

"I know, and I'm preparing to leave to organize a search for the ship."

"Tell me, have you ever done something like this before?" Kylo asked his naïve, young friend.

"No, but who else can go without compromising the secrecy of the mission?" Sejong reminded Kylo.

"Secrecy is one thing; nuclear annihilation is another," Kylo stated without a retort from Sejong, who knew it was his fault that his nation and the world were in crisis mode.

"Sejong, I have no problem with you going forth to slay the dragon, but you must bring experienced men to do the searching. Men who have done this before, who, as the Americans say, 'It's not their first rodeo.'" Kylo tried to make light of the task for Sejong's sake.

"I've asked some of my trusted colleagues to meet with us after lunch in my conference room to discuss the matter. You will be there, yes?" Kylo said.

"Yes, of course."

"I'll see you then." Kylo gave Sejong a reassuring handshake as if to say that they would find a way out of this nightmare together.

Two men from each of the branches of the armed services gathered around a table in Kylo's conference room that afternoon. After a brief greeting and introduction of the military men to Sejong, Kylo passed out folders containing information on their topic of conversation, then got down to business.

"Gentlemen, we are gathered here this afternoon to save the world," Kylo said to the shock and disbelief of everyone in the room.

"You're not serious?" an army colonel asked.

"I wish it were only a bad dream, but gentlemen, we have sent a ship laden with nuclear weapons bent on the destruction of Washington, DC, and we don't know where it is."

"But… but why?" a naval captain asked.

"The why's are not important at this point in time; how to stop the ship before it gets into position to launch its nuclear warheads is."

"All right, you've got our attention. Now give us the good news," the air force commandant said.

"This is what I know in a nutshell. The ship, let's call it *Justice*, is an old four-hundred-fifty-five-foot American Victory ship. It's under the command of Admiral Shumi-un; its captain is Jawa-Si; plus officers and crew, it has a complement of about thirty-four men." There was some murmur at the mention of the admiral's name. Kylo waited until they quieted to continue. "It has oil-fired boilers driving a steam engine, a single screw, a twenty-eight-foot draft, and makes fifteen to seventeen knots."

"Assuming you don't know precisely where it is, based on when it departed and its speed, course, and final destination, where should it be now?" one of the naval officers asked.

"We calculated its transit through the Panama Canal a few days ago, and it may be sheltering from an Atlantic hurricane on the southwestern side of Cuba. Models predict the storm will veer north into the Gulf of Mexico. From here on, the models differ. One shows the storm crossing the US state of Florida out into the Atlantic Ocean before heading north. The other model shows the storm coming ashore in Alabama, then heading east through Georgia and South Carolina before entering the Atlantic and ultimately heading north."

"In any event, the ship must come around the Florida Keys to get to Washington," the naval officer said.

"Yes, that's true."

"What if we positioned a picket line of ships in the path of the *Justice*? Couldn't we intercept them?" Sejong speculated.

"That would take hundreds of ships," the naval officer told him.

"Then what do you suggest?" Sejong snapped back.

"A naval blockade is useless unless we know how far off land the ship will travel, especially if it's dodging a hurricane. It may seek calm waters hundreds of miles offshore. In that case we'd need thousands of ships, not hundreds," the naval officer said.

"OK, before we go too far afield, we are still trying, every hour on the hour, to contact the ship to no avail. My question to you is: Why have they not responded to our calls?" Kylo asked.

"There may be several reasons: their equipment is inoperable; no one is manning the radio; they are beyond the limits of their bandwidth; the antenna broke in high winds… or they are running silent," the other naval officer suggested.

"Why run silent?" Sejong asked.

"So they're not detected, especially if they haven't got a transponder. Look, all commercial ships over a certain size must have a transponder on board. It allows the country whose territorial waters they are in to track their location, heading, speed, and other factors like air traffic controllers to avoid collisions.

It's entirely possible that the ship is travelling without a transponder to avoid detection; ergo, radio silence."

"Well, I think we must close in on the ship now before it gets too close to its launch site," Sejong emphasized.

"True. However, have we explored all the tactics a seasoned sailor may take to conceal the ship's movements?" an air force officer asked.

"There's one very obvious tactic the admiral might have introduced—and probably has being an old salt: traveling at night," one of the naval officers said.

"Clarify that for a landlubber," Kylo requested.

"If I wanted to avoid the US Coast Guard, I'd quietly travel a few miles offshore from sunset to sunrise," the naval officer said.

"What do you mean by 'quietly'?"

"Well, I'd avoid looking like a Christmas tree, with lights and music blazing."

"Point taken. Anyone else?" Kylo asked.

"One last point I'd like to make is that it's not easy to track a ship in unpredictable weather, especially using aircraft, much less in the midst of a hurricane with hundred-forty-mile-per-hour winds and torrential rains," an air force colonel stated.

"Point well taken," Kylo said.

"Well, I've listened to my learned colleagues, and it's my opinion that we may not have sufficient resources, nor time, in that part of the world to conduct a fruitful search," the army captain stated.

"I agree with my army colleague that conducting a comprehensive search some twelve thousand miles away without the men, resources, or time to find a ship in enemy waters may be fruitless," the naval officer stated.

"I guess I'm the last one to put his two bits into the mix, and not to be redundant, I wholeheartedly agree that even considering finding a ship in a haystack is unlikely, if not impossible, under the aforementioned conditions.

I say nay to any operation and suggest working out something with the United States before the mushroom clouds engulf the world," the air force officer stated.

"Thank you, gentlemen, for your insightful knowledge and comments. Needless to say, we are faced with a 'damned if you do, damned if you don't' situation. That being said, I request that we refrain from speaking about this outside this room. And if there is nothing else—" Kylo began to say when he was asked about another pressing matter.

"We hear that General Zoko is under arrest. Is that true?" one of the army officers asked.

"Yes, that is true, but until we present our case to the prosecutors, I'm not at liberty to discuss it," Kylo said, ducking the question.

"But from what I hear from the rumor mill, he's charged with treason. Is that true?"

"Yes, that is the charge, but again, other than what I've just told you, I must in fairness refrain from divulging the circumstances," Kylo said, closing the meeting.

38

Judy & Derek
Driving Home

As soon as Judy and Derek got in their pickup, Judy opened the folder the prison counselor had handed to Derek and began reading its contents.

"What's in the folder?" Derek asked.

"Keep your eyes on the road or we'll have an accident too," Judy reminded him.

"Well, if you find something, you'll tell me, right?" Derek pleaded.

"Of course, my dear. You'll be the first to know."

However, what Judy did was review several pages at a time and then give Derek the gist of what they said.

"You're not going to believe this, but what Brad told his mock lawyer and what the policeman wrote on the citation are completely different," Judy said.

"What do you mean by 'mock lawyer'?" Brad asked.

"I don't want to skip around, but it seems Brad was appointed a public defender to represent him pro bono, but in California the public defender can appoint an aide, someone who works in his office, to handle the case, thereby freeing the public defender to handle paying clients and still be the lawyer of record. Do you understand me? Brad got a bogus, mock, make-believe lawyer. Someone who files paper in the office and pretends to know something of the law," she said in disgust.

"So what did Brad say and what did the arresting office write on his citation?" Derek asked.

"Listen, Brad told his mock lawyer that he picked up a hitchhiker around nine p.m., and about twenty minutes later he saw a pickup truck approaching him in his lane, flashing his high beams, then shutting off his lights, followed by flashing his high beams again, coming right at him. His passenger, the young girl, began screaming, and at the last moment he turned off the road and went down an embankment and hit a tree. He said that the pickup truck never made any effort to turn back into his own lane; he said he was playing chicken with him," Judy said angrily.

"And what did the cop write?" Derek asked.

"He wrote that after determining the girl was dead, he handcuffed Brad and put him in the back of the police car. He stated he gave Brad a breathalyzer test, but it was inconclusive. It was only several days later that a blood test found traces of an amphetamine in his blood. Well, it seems the arresting officer amended his report some time later, saying Brad was 'under the influence of a mind-altering substance.'

"Anyway, there was no trial, and by the way, what I'm telling you is from the actual transcripts with notes in the margin from our friend, the prison counselor," Judy said, shaking her head at how they had twisted the facts to get a conviction.

"I understand everything, but, but no trial?" Derek asked.

"Oh baby, they gave him a plea deal. 'Plead guilty and get ten years, or go to trial and get fifteen to twenty or whatever the judge feels appropriate to appease the girl's grieving family.'"

Judy continued to read the materials, but Derek was too upset to hear more about how his kid brother was railroaded into spending ten years in prison because he didn't know how the system works for people of color, the young, and the indigent. Judy promised Derek that when she got home, she'd meet with her friends and give them the file for their input. The rest of the ride was filled with the sad knowledge that during Brad's incarceration Derek's family had done nothing to help him. They had turned their backs on him; the cruelest cut of all was to be cast away with the trash.

. . .

As promised, Judy called a meeting of the three amigos the very next day. The baseball field was too wet for cars, so Rose invited them to her home, a small ranch-style house near the base.

"Greetings and salutations," Rose said, welcoming Officer Brenda and Judy to her humble abode.

"How'd it go in Susanville?" Officer Brenda asked, accepting a cold one from her host.

"Good and bad," Judy said, looking for a chair.

"You relax and let it all pour out. You're home now, and we want to help," Rose said reassuringly.

"I don't know where to start." Judy produced Brad's documents.

"What's that?" Officer Brenda asked.

"These are Brad's files; they were given to us by the prison counselor because he wanted us know what really happened."

"Let me see them," Officer Brenda demanded, reaching for the files.

"Go on. What was he like… Brad?" Rose asked.

"Oh, if I tell you, I'll cry," Judy said with a sniffle.

"Tell me. I'll supply the tissues," Rose said, going to find a box of Kleenex.

"Well, he's the spitting image of his older brother, just a little shorter and quieter."

"When does he get out?" Rose asked.

"Sometime next year, I think," Judy said, looking at Officer Brenda, who was eagerly poring over Brad's file.

"This kid, from what I've just read, was fucked over by his lawyer, the local police, and the state… without a goodbye kiss," Officer Brenda said.

"But where is his head at after all the injustice he's faced?" Rose asked.

"He's made it this far without the love of his family, and that's been devastating for Derek because he did nothing to reach out to his younger brother when Brad needed him most. I feel he'd do anything to undo his mistake. He's full of remorse, and I don't know how to comfort him," Judy said.

"What we can do is marshal our forces and bring justice to your brother-in-law," Officer Brenda forcefully said, seeking a three-amigos hug.

The three friends stood and embraced, feeling a determination to make things right for Brad Navarro, a soon-to-be member of the family.

With that done, they turned their attention to the forthcoming event of the season, the gala wedding of Judy Sluzac and Derek Navarro.

"Now, did we decide on a date?" Rose asked, taking out a notebook.

"Sometime in July," Judy said, wiping her nose.

"Well, everything depends on the date, so let's set a date so that we can book the Candlelight Wedding Chapel, the restaurant for the wedding dinner, hotel rooms for guests, and the wedding photographer. Did I forget anything?" Rose asked.

"We have to hire a videographer to Skype Brad in to the chapel since he's the best man," Judy said.

"OK, if you're both unable and unwilling to set a date, I will. Saturday, July seventh. All those in favor say yes," Rose said without allowing anyone to say no, thus settling the impasse.

"Oh, one more thing, business-wise," Judy said. "I might be unable to attend some of our forthcoming meetings. They're refitting my F-15 with a new, super-duper X1A1 missile. It's a laser-guided missile that, according to Raytheon, could destroy a battleship... if there were any more left."

"Well, let us know, and we will advise everyone around Maryland and Virginia that owns battleships to be on the lookout for you and your super-duper bomb," Officer Brenda said.

"No, there are only a handful of F-15s that have the missile, and I'll be testing them here, blowing the shit out of targets in the desert," Judy said.

"Sounds like fun. Can we watch?" Rose asked.

"I'll let you know," Judy said.

"But getting back to the here and now, how'd you get the prison to grant your request?" Officer Brenda asked.

"That's the amazing part. When I first saw the prison counselor, I thought he was a good ol' boy and we were dead in the water, but I was wrong, so very wrong. He turned out to be a wise man who put his trust in his quest to help and rehabilitate his charges. He's the one who documented the wrongful acts the system uses to incarcerate those without the financial means to avoid jail time," she said.

"Well said, my little fighter pilot. We'll take the fight to undo the wrong from here on out and bring justice to Brad, as God is our judge," said Officer Brenda.

39

Elizabeth and Juan
A test of their relationship.

Juan received a cryptic email from one Mrs. Romano, requesting his attendance at a meeting next week in Milan. Mrs. Romano was a major client when Juan first started his consultancy practice and had been a very generous sponsor over the years as well as a reference within her circle of friends.

Mrs. Romano was the heir to the R&R Distillery and a director of the Bank of Milan, with forty-six branches throughout Italy and Sicily. She also owned twenty-eight boutiques in Michelin three-star hotels throughout Europe. Her net worth was not disclosed, but some estimates were in the range of three to four billion euros. Needless to say, when the lady called, Juan dropped everything and went.

Juan's problem now was how to convince Elizbeth that his attendance in Milan was strictly business. In their short time together, Elizabeth had not asked about his relationships with female clients, mostly because she'd rather not know. However, the trip to Milan required a certain amount of trust on both parts if their relationship was to continue and flourish.

History: Mrs. Romano's late husband, Salvatore, was a powerful figure in the Milanese underworld by consolidating his illegal activities with legal businesses.

When Sal suddenly died of lead poisoning, Mrs. Romano inherited a fortune and the associated problems of running a vast enterprise. This was where Juan, after a short dalliance with the widow, stepped in to guide her on how and where she should store her surplus cash. Over the years, Mrs. Romano had introduced Juan to several of her wealthy friends who also required his services, both in the boudoir and in sheltering their extra cash where it could grow exponentially without the knowledge of the tax man. In doing so, Juan was rewarded in kind with a percentage of the profits and a generous retainer on forthcoming services and advice.

"Can I help you pack?" Elizabeth inquired.

"No, thank you, my love. It's a few days at the most," Juan said, taking two white dress shirts out of the wardrobe.

"Can you get away with one suit?"

"Yes, probably the blue one with a matching tie and cufflinks," he said.

"I assume you have roundtrip tickets?" she asked.

"Love, sit down beside me on the bed," he requested, patting a space next to where he was seated. "As I've said, Mrs. Romano was and still is a valued client who was instrumental in my consultancy, and my trip is just and only that: she needs my advice. She wouldn't reach out to me if it were a minor matter. I sense that something precipitated the call, something serious."

"Forgive me, my darling; it's my nature. I worry," she said, putting her arms around him.

"Did you tell Mohammad to take me to the airport?" Juan said, standing up and closing his bag.

"Yes, he's waiting to take your bags."

She followed Juan to their car.

"Call me?" she asked.

"Tonight," he reassured her.

After taking a flight from Tangier to Rome, Juan caught a connecting flight to Milan, the financial center of Italy. From there, he took a taxi to Mrs. Romano's villa in the Basiglio section. As the taxi drove up to the iron gates, the guard announced to the housekeeper that Mister Juan had arrived. Waiting by the front door in a silk robe was the unofficial countess of Milan, the Lady Romano. Hugging and kissing on both cheeks, they stole into the villa, hand in hand.

"You're as beautiful as the last time we were together," Juan said, squeezing her hand.

"Oh God, have I missed you," she said with a shiver.

"I could use a drink," he said.

"Anything you want, including me."

"A glass of white wine for starters."

He followed her to the living room bar, where she poured two glasses of wine.

Once she was relaxing by his side on a loveseat, Mrs. Romano toasted him: "To better days."

"What's wrong?" Juan asked.

"My son Joseph came home to tell me that he and his brother, Michael, were abducted outside a nightclub in Milan, taken blindfolded to a farmhouse, and Joseph was set free in order to demand five million euros for the safe return of his brother."

"Where is Joseph now?" Juan asked.

"He's here, in his bedroom."

"Have you called the Carabinieri?"

"No. The kidnappers said if we do, they'll kill Michael." She bit her lip.

"Can I speak with him?" Juan asked.

"Of course. I told him that a friend of mine was coming and that he'd help us," she said, going to get Joseph.

A few moments later, Mrs. Romano and Joseph entered the room. After the introductions, Juan expressed his sadness to learn what had happened to Joseph and

Michael, and asked if he could discuss the events of the night before.

"Yes. What do you want to know beyond what my mother has already told you?" Joseph said defensively, perking Juan's sense that the boy was hiding something.

"Tell me something about the nightclub," Juan started with a softball.

"What can I say? It's a nightclub," he said, seemingly annoyed by the question.

"No. I need more detail than that, Joseph. It tells me if they knew in advance that you frequented that nightclub and would be there on that particular night," Juan said, giving the boy a reason for the question.

Seeing the rationale, the boy thought about how he should respond. "We go there every so often. No specific times because the band is always the same."

"And do you meet people that you know there... and, for that matter, who know you?" Juan asked, giving him less wiggle room.

"Some people know us, and... there are some people we know."

"Do they do drugs there?" Juan said, looking directly at Joseph for his response.

"Some do and some don't," he said honestly.

"Tell me, did you stand at the bar or sit at a table last night?" Juan asked quickly to get him off center.

"We stood at the bar," he shot back.

"What did you drink?" Juan asked, not giving Joseph time to prepare an answer.

"Vodka."

"On the rocks or straight up?" Juan asked.

"Why does it matter?" he said, looking to his mother for help, which to Juan was a "tell" indicative of his inner turmoil.

"How many drinks did you have? How did you pay for them?"

"I don't remember," he said, exasperated.

"Did anyone follow you out of the bar?"

"I don't remember," he said, indicating for Juan that his answers would now be limited by his lack of memory. From here on, he'd use his lapse of memory as an excuse.

"OK, then what happened?" Juan asked, allowing him to use the story he gave his mother.

"A van, a white van, came alongside us. Its door opened, and two men sprang out and grabbed us and threw us into the van," he said, staying on script.

"Did you recognize them?" Juan asked.

"No, they were wearing masks."

"What type of masks?" Juan asked.

"You know, the ones you wear over your head with holes for your eyes and mouth."

"And this was all done in front of the nightclub with customers coming and going?" Juan asked.

"There was no one there," he said.

"I thought you said you didn't remember?" Juan pressed.

"I didn't say that," Joseph said angrily.

"Forgive me, I thought you said you didn't remember," Juan said. "And were there seats in the back of the van?"

"Yes, of course," he said.

"So, when they threw you in the van, you landed on the seats?" Juan speculated.

"Yes, on the seats," he said, getting confused.

"And did you and your brother fight back or sit there like good little children?" Juan asked, belittling Joseph's version of what had happened... if it ever did. He quickly followed up, since Joseph avoided the question.

"Now, when did they blindfold you?" Juan asked.

"When we got in the van." He sounded tired. Juan could tell he was close to shattering.

"Is that before or after they tied your hands?"

"Can we take a break? I'm tired of these questions," he said.

"Certainly... I have one last question before we do, though. When did you and your brother concoct this ridiculous story, and why?" he asked the dumbfounded boy.

"I'm sorry, I'm so sorry! We had no choice. They said that unless we get them the money, they'd kill us." He got on his knees and buried his head in his mother's lap.

40

The People's Assembly

"Thank you for seeing me on such short notice, but I must share with you a very serious development, one that will change our constitution and form of governance," Kylo said.

"Does this have to do with the arrest of General Zoko?" the chairman asked.

"Yes and no."

"Do we need members of the People's Advisory Council in attendance?" the chairman asked, thinking of the division of responsibilities within the Assembly and of what the Council's reaction would be to him usurping his position.

"Not at this stage. Let's call our discussion an exploratory meeting to see if we're on the same page regarding the future of our nation," Kylo said, taking out some notes. "To begin, there are rumors—at all levels, civilian, military, political, industrial, international, I can go on and on—regarding the status and health of our Supreme Leader. I say to you that the Kim Dynasty as we know it is at an end."

The quiet and sober chairman knew very well that Kylo was correct in his assessment.

"This is what I respectfully submit the Advisory Council should meet to discuss: a future role for our Supreme Leader, one in which his role is symbolic, not autocratic. A sovereign without a crown."

"Coincidentally, there have been several meetings within the Council regarding that very subject," the chairman admitted.

"Excellent. Now let me address governance. In lieu of a Supreme Leader, I suggest that the People's Assembly should be the governing body, similar to our partners in Beijing. Further, to enter the world of nations, I recommend assenting to the demands of the United Nations to denuclearize and, in doing so, transfer our nuclear weapons to China and enter a treaty with them for the mutual defense of our great nations."

"I see you've thought this through." The chairman smiled.

"The current atmosphere demands a restructuring of our nation to avoid a military coup as was planned by General Zoko," Kylo said, noticing the chairman nodding ever so slightly in agreement.

"What's Zoko's status?" the chairman asked.

"We plan to put him and his band of conspirators on trial soon. They're all pleading for lighter sentences for their testimony," Kylo said with a smirk.

"Excellent. Keep me informed," the chairman said, bringing the meeting to an end. He walked around his desk to shake hands with his new ally.

Leaving the room, Kylo had a pang of regret that he couldn't address the subject that was driving him crazy: how to contact the *Justice* and order them to deep-six the missiles and return home. Unbeknownst to him, another scenario was unfolding thousands of miles away in the port of Santiago de Cuba. By fate or by design, the *Justice*, having damaged its prop, found a safe haven in the only nation in the western hemisphere that shared a normative solidarity with North Korea.

With a hurricane bearing down on Cuba from the Atlantic and the *Justice* dead in the water some six miles from land, its ship-to-shore radio broken, they shot red distress flares into the sky in a desperate attempt to get the attention of someone, anyone, that there was a ship out there in distress. Luckily, an elderly woman walking her dog spotted the fireworks in the sky and called the police, who in turn called the coast guard, who sent a cutter out to investigate. The cutter saw that the *Justice* was floundering, and two tugboats were dispatched to the scene.

With lines set fore and aft, the tugs pushed and

shoved and towed the *Justice* through heavy seas to the sheltered harbor of Santiago, where they had the men and materials to repair the prop and replace a defective ship-to-shore radio. Once the port authorities realized that the ship was from North Korea, they encouraged the admiral and his crew, like visiting dignitaries, to shelter at hotels and private homes to ride out the storm. Before dispersing the crew, the admiral told everyone, including the authorities, not to disclose their whereabouts for fear of American sanctions. But good news is difficult to suppress, and people shared the excitement of saving the crew of a North Korean cargo ship and hosting them in their homes and hotels. Cell phone pictures flooded the internet... and especially got the attention of the Cubans' friends and relatives in Miami.

Awoken by a late-night phone call, Kylo was advised of the news from the United States regarding the "Miracle of Santiago de Cuba." He learned that, while Cuba braced itself for the onslaught of a category 4 hurricane, the crews of two small tugboats put their lives on the line to rescue a North Korean ship off the coast. The townspeople claimed that God sent the ship, called *Justice*, to the only port in the world where they would be accepted as brothers.

Soon, the media in the United States was on the case, and newspapers and television networks were sending reporters to Miami to collect stories and photos from the Cuban community. The photos were a goldmine to a community starved for good news from their homeland. They showed a town ablaze with celebrations as the *Justice* departed; the people lined the harbor, waving Cuban flags while water cannons shot high into the air and ship horns blasted a farewell. The *Justice*, with all hands on deck, was gliding out to sea.

After checking the veracity of the news on the internet, Kylo called Sejong to share it with him.

"They had to use red flares to send their mayday. Their radio was broken," he said.

"I knew there must have been a reason they didn't answer."

"They've reached celebrity status on the internet. We must contact them to get rid of the missiles before they are detained by the US Coast Guard."

"True, let me think. What constitutes international waters in North America?"

"I don't know, but I can find out," Kylo said.

"To be on the safe side, let's tell them to skirt the United States by, say, two hundred miles and dispose of the missiles as soon as possible," Sejong said.

"Agreed. Meet me at my office. We have to think of ways we can play this stroke of luck," Kylo said.

"I'll be there within the hour, and if I reach the admiral, I'll give him the instructions."

Rapidly dressing and taking a cup of tea with him, Sejong threw his papers onto the back seat while his chauffeur put the car in gear and raced to police head-quarters in Pyongyang. After a few unsuccessful at-tempts to call the *Justice*, Sejong's phone rang, and to his astonishment, the admiral was on the line asking if he had heard of their hair-raising experience in Cuba.

"Admiral Shumi-un, it is so good to hear from you. Yes, we are very proud of you for the courage you dis-played. Our nation will rejoice when you return. How-ever, I have the following new orders. You are to proceed on a northerly passage up the East Coast of the United States two hundred miles due east of land, into international waters. Now, this is imperative—you are to remove the cargo as soon as possible from their con-tainer and throw them overboard into the sea. Do you understand me?" Sejong said quite explicitly.

"I am to proceed on a northerly course up the East Coast of the United States, maintaining a two-hundred-mile distance from the United States. I am to also throw the cargo overboard as soon as possible. Is that correct?" the admiral asked.

"Correct, and dispose of the cargo without being seen by anyone or anything."

"I have your orders and will comply," the admiral said.

"One more thing. I want you to check in with me every eight hours," Sejong said.

"I am to check in with you every eight hours," the admiral dutifully repeated.

"Thank you, Admiral Shumi-un," Sejong said, then broke the connection.

He immediately called Kylo with the good news that the missiles would be disposed of at sea. Relieved, Sejong told his chauffeur he didn't have to drive over 100 miles per hour and then sat back, finishing his cold cup of tea.

41

Officer Brenda's on fire.

With the fires of injustice burning in her soul, Officer Brenda set out to right a wrong. She knew a woman who once confessed to her that she had been raped by a prominent politician, a man who was held beyond reproach by his constituents in California, the honorable State Senator Rollins Levitt.

"Kitty, this is Brenda. Long time, no see," Officer Brenda said to her by phone to a confused acquaintance. "Remember, we met at the Bellagio in Vegas? I'm the cop."

"Yeah, you live in Nevada, right?" Kitty guessed.

"Right, that was quite a night," Officer Brenda reminded her.

"Like two kids out on the town," Kitty said, vaguely remembering.

"Kitty, I need a favor. A friend of mine is doing time in California for a crime he didn't commit, and you said that if I needed anything I should call you, remember?"

"Uh-huh… what do you need?" Kitty asked.

"You told me you knew someone in the California Senate, Rollins Levitt," Officer Brenda said.

"I used to work for him. He was a piece of work," Kitty said.

"I know, I know… but I need someone who's connected to help me get my friend a hearing, and I wouldn't ask if there was any other way. So, will you help me?" Officer Brenda pleaded.

"What can I do? It's been years since I worked for the bastard." Kitty said.

"I realize that, but in a way, that might help," Office Brenda said.

"How? I don't understand."

"He's probably forgotten about you and what he did, but deep down he probably regrets his actions," Officer Brenda said for effect.

"I doubt it, but what can I do for you?" Kitty asked, trying to end the conversation on a harmonious note.

"I need an introduction, that's all. Once I get in the door, I'll plead my case for my friend's hearing. You'll never have to see him. That's it."

"What do you want me to say to him?" Kitty asked.

"Got a pencil and paper. I'll tell you… and thanks,"

Officer Brenda said as she dictated a brief introduction for Kitty to make to Senator Levitt on her behalf.

Next on her agenda was getting the last surviving victim of the pickup truck driver who played chicken with oncoming motorists on video. This was a guy in an SUV, one Russell Phillips, who hit the truck head on and survived while the pickup driver with a death wish, Clyde Robertson, died on the scene. Brenda tracked Mr. Phillips down using the California Department of Motor Vehicles and found that he lived in Asbury. After she called and explained what she wanted, he agreed to see her, especially once he heard that an innocent man was in jail because of Robertson.

Asbury was a pleasant, middle-class suburb of Sacramento with a population of 9,500 and a median resident age of sixty-three. Most of the homes were single-family, two thousand square feet, with four bedrooms and two baths, on one-acre lots. Here and there were gas stations, supermarkets, used-car lots, medical offices, a large assisted living and nursing home. The town had an elementary, middle, and a new high school. The homes were well kept and the streets clear and lined with mature trees and manicured lawns.

Mr. Phillips's house was a white colonial with black shutters reminiscent of many stately homes in New England. Officer Brenda guessed Mr. Phillips was originally from there, and she found out that she was correct. Hingham, Massachusetts, his birthplace, was the spitting image of Asbury. Mr. Phillips was a man with a gentle smile and gray hair in his late sixties, who walked with a crooked cane fashioned from the branch of a maple tree.

"How are you, Brenda?" Mr. Phillips said, extending his good hand while balancing himself with his cane.

"Fine. It's a pleasure to meet you, Mr. Phillips," Officer Brenda said, gently shaking his hand.

"Come through," he said, leading the way to his living room.

"Did I note a familiar British colonialism in your choice of words?" Officer Brenda remarked.

"Very observant, but then again, that's the mark of a good detective, isn't it?" he said.

"Maybe I've seen too many British movies where 'come through' is used,"

Officer Brenda admitted.

"May I offer you a refreshment?" he asked.

"No, thank you, but as I mentioned during our phone conversation, I am here to record your retelling of your experience of the night on Route 17, when a pickup truck driven by a Mr. Robertson deliberately hit your SUV head-on while he was traveling in your lane."

"Correct. Where should I begin?" he asked.

"First, with your permission, let me set up my video camera. After that I'll ask you several questions for the record, OK?" After Mr. Phillips nodded, Officer Brenda went about setting her video camera on a tripod and loading a blank cassette into the camera.

"I'm ready," she stated with a smile.

"Am I OK sitting where I am?" Mr. Phillips said, closing the top button on his shirt.

"Yes, and you look like Sir Laurence Olivier," Officer Brenda said, which brought a smile to Mr. Phillips's face.

"I wish," he said.

"Then we'll begin," Officer Brenda said, pressing the record button.

She then put Mr. Phillips through a series of questions to establish, for the record, who he was, where he lived, and so on, until she asked him to go back to the night of his accident.

"At what time and in which direction were you driving on Route 17?" Officer Brenda asked.

"I was driving my SUV north at nine p.m.," he said.

"Describe Route 17, please."

"Route 17 is a two-lane road with vehicles travelling north and south."

"And what were the weather conditions that night?" Officer Brenda asked.

"It was dry and clear; the visibility was excellent," he said.

"Where there any passengers in your car?" Officer Brenda asked.

"No, I was alone."

"Now, take me back to that night, the night of the accident. In your own words, what happened?"

"Well, as I said, it was nine p.m. on a clear night when I saw a vehicle traveling south on Route 17, flashing his lights from high to low and then completely off. A few seconds later he started flashing his lights from high beam to low beam. He was about a quarter of a mile away when I realized that he was coming at me in my lane. Shocked, I thought of slowing down and moving onto the shoulder, but there were only a few feet of shoulder leading to a steep embankment into a treelined stretch, and before I knew it he was upon me, in my lane, and hit me head on. That was the last thing I remember. I understand that the fire department had to use the Jaws of Life to extract me from my SUV. I was hospitalized with broken ribs; my right leg was crushed, and my right arm was dislocated. But thankfully, I survived to tell my story, which I did in detail sometime later. I also remember one of the policemen said offhandedly that it was the third such accident he'd seen on Route 17. I think he referred to them as the 'guy who plays chicken on Route 17.'"

"And did you ever give testimony at the coroner's inquest or trial?" Officer Brenda asked.

"No. As far as I know, everything was brushed under the rug, so to speak."

"That's strange. When a traffic accident ends in the loss of life, an inquest is conducted," Officer Brenda said.

"No; nothing was done," he said.

"Is there anything you would like to add to your testimony?" Officer Brenda asked.

"Yes, there is. I understand that this happened to another driver on Route 17, and I want to make it clear that this Clyde Robertson had a death wish and desperately wanted to kill someone and himself using his pickup truck as a weapon. I further understand that this person was sentenced to ten years in prison, which is a travesty of justice, and I urge a re-examination of his case in light of my testimony, which is true to my Holy God."

"Thank you, Mr. Phillips. I also pray that with your testimony, Brad Navarro will be pardoned."

42

Elizabeth is officially dead,
long live Grace Hayworth.

"OK, let's continue, and this time without the theatrics. Where's your brother?" Juan asked the sobbing boy, Mrs. Romano's son.

"He's at his girlfriend's place," Joseph said truthfully.

"Where's that?"

"Number 42 Viale San Gabriel."

"Tell him to get a taxi and come home immediately," Juan instructed.

Some forty minutes later a contrite Michael arrived at the villa with his tail tucked between his legs.

"Why couldn't you just ask me to help you?" Mrs. Romano asked, hugging her other son.

"We were afraid to," he said.

"Why? Have I ever denied you anything?" she cried.

Her boys were silent.

"You're both home, you're both safe, and you needlessly worried your mother over debts. Some gambling debts, is that right?" Juan asked.

"Yes," Michael confessed.

"How much do you owe them?" Juan asked.

"They say fifty thousand euros, and that's a lie," Joseph said.

"You gambled how much? Fifty thousand euros?" Mrs. Romano exclaimed.

"Tell me, did you sign any markers?" Juan asked.

"What's that?" Michael asked, confused.

"No? Then how did you get your chips?" Juan asked, realizing that the boys were merely amateurs in over their heads.

"They gave us chips to play roulette," Michael said as if in his world what you asked for, you got.

"Really? They just gave you chips without your signing anything?" Juan was pretty certain that lying was second nature to these spoiled brats. "All right, then what did they say? Give me their exact words when they demanded the money. Did they threaten your lives?" He knew there were different types of threats, and you didn't want to confuse an implied threat with a real threat because a real threat could get you killed.

"I don't know," Joseph said.

"Then remember," Juan demanded.

"The guy said, 'We want our fuckin' money, or else.' That's what he said; those were his exact words," Joseph said.

Michael agreed with a nod.

Juan wasn't sure how to take the threat or if the boys were in real danger, but to be on the safe side, he knew that putting an end to the situation was beyond his paygrade. So, he dismissed the boys and had a heart-to-heart talk with Mrs. Romano.

"My dear, thankfully the boys are temporarily safe. I'm not sure if the threat is real or imaginary, but in any case, we must proceed as if it's real. In that case I need your help."

"What can I do?" Mrs. Romano asked, holding Juan's hand.

"I need to employ your friend," Juan said.

"You need Tony?" she said, shocked.

"We want to end it amicably. Get the markers, pay off the debt, and warn them never to threaten a Romano again, capisce?"

"You're right. I'll attend to cleaning up the rest," she said.

"I wish I could do more, but..." Juan began to say, but Mrs. Romano embraced him with tears in her eyes and he knew it was time to go.

· · ·

The trip home was tiring. There were taxis, long lines through immigration and customs, then flight delays in Italy, so that he almost missed a connecting flight to Morocco, and to top it all off, a baby on his flight was crying at the top of her lungs; the Maria Callas of first-class was seated directly behind him. The best part of the trip was seeing their chauffeur Mohammad waiting to collect him at the airport.

"A successful trip, I pray," Elizabeth said back at the villa, embracing Juan as he took off his sport jacket.

"All's well that ends well," Juan said, taking off his shoes.

"What would you like to drink?" Elizabeth asked.

"Nothing now. I'm going to shower and take a nap," he said, slowly making his way to their bedroom.

Two hours later, Juan was a new man and begged for that drink.

"My darling, I'd love a spritzer, a nice, sweet sangria with soda on the rocks."

"Your wish is my command," she said with a silly bow on her way to the living room bar to fetch her master's libation.

"And get one for yourself," he called out.

Returning with a pitcher of sangria, a bottle of club soda, and two frosted tumblers, she placed the tray on a cocktail table by his chair and begged for the details of his trip. Mixing a drink for himself and Elizabeth, Juan sat back, took a sip and shared what can happen if you are an Italian mother who dotes over two spoiled brats.

"They're called *mammoni*, boys who live with their mothers way beyond their adolescence—into their twenties and thirties in some cases," he said, taking another sip for fortitude.

"What was her place like?" Elizabeth inquired.

"A typical Italian villa with a moat around it and a stone wall fifteen feet high surrounded by hundreds of acres of freshly cut lawn," he said, embellishing the description of Mrs. Romano's home.

"No, really?"

"Well, maybe the moat was dry, but anyway, she *is* called the Countess of Milan," he jested.

"What did the mammoni do that she had to summon you to her villa, pronto?"

"Nothing serious. They were kidnapped by some gamblers and held captive until they paid back their debts."

"How much did they owe?" she asked.

"The gamblers wanted fifty thousand euros, or, according to the mammoni, they'd kill them."

"So, what did you do?"

"I let the gamblers kill them... to teach them a lesson," he said with a grin.

"You're so bad. I bet you did," she said, smiling at his joke.

"No. After five minutes one of them confessed that it was all a ruse; there was no kidnapping. They just wanted to squeeze some money from their mother to pay off their gambling debts," he said.

"So, she paid off the gamblers, and all is well in Milan," Elizabeth said, tying it all up in a bow.

"Exactly," he said, omitting Mrs. Romano's need to have one of her deceased husband's soldiers carry out the payoff and advise the gamblers what happened to those who crossed the Countess of Milan.

"Are you ready for some good news?" she asked.

"I'm all ears, my love."

"I found the perfect villa for us, one that won't draw too much attention. It's overlooking the Mediterranean on a cliff; you must see it. This is its listing," she said, opening her laptop to show him.

"Oh, my dear, it looks just beautiful, and it's a fraction of what you paid for our current villa. Bravo, my love; you're a keeper," he said.

"Now do you want to hear the best news yet?" She hesitated for effect before saying, "Elizabeth Kleinshure is officially dead."

"What do you mean?" he asked, confused.

"A coroner's inquest in Virginia ruled yesterday that Elizabeth Kleinshure of Virginia Beach died by suicide," she said.

"You mean the running and hiding is over?" he said happily.

"Yep, we can go almost anywhere, my love," she said, falling into his lap and kissing him. "But for now, I beg you to make mad, passionate love to Grace Hayworth." She took his hand and led him to their boudoir.

43

Advisory Council
People's Assembly

At an emergency meeting of the Advisory Council, Chairman Pak Thae-bok was ready for a votc on the major changes to the North Korean constitution. The council members had debated the new rules, and now was the time to memorialize them.

Stepping up to the podium, the chairman began by summarizing the new articles and then putting them to a vote:

"Article One: The Kim Dynasty as we know it is at an end. From here on Kim Jong-un will be known as a symbolic figurehead and not an autocratic leader, a sovereign without a crown. I now ask for your vote. Those in favor, please raise your hand."

The article passed: twenty-six ayes, with two abstentions.

"Article Two: The People's Assembly will now be known as the Democratic Socialist State Assembly. Those in favor please raise your hand."

The article passed: twenty-four ayes, four nays.

"Article Three: The Democratic Socialist State Assembly is now the sole governing body in North Korea. Members of the State Assembly will henceforth be chosen by a council of elders similar to the one which ruled our land peacefully for over two thousand years. Those in favor please raise your hand."

The article passed: twenty ayes, eight nays.

"Article Four: It is hereby resolved that our nation should comply with the United Nations Resolution 220C, calling for the denuclearization of the Korean Peninsula. Those in favor raise your hands."

The article passed: twenty-four ayes with four abstentions.

"Article Five: It is hereby resolved that in compliance with the United Nations Resolution 220C, North Korea will transfer all its nuclear weapons to the nation of China. Those in favor raise your hands."

The article passed: twenty-four ayes, two nays, and two abstentions.

"Article Six: It is hereby resolved that North Korea shall seek a mutual defense treaty with the nation of China. Those in favor raise your hands."

The article passed unanimously with twenty-eight yes votes.

The chairman gaveled the meeting to an end, and the assembly members rose from their seats to applaud the first constitutional meeting of a new North Korea. As Chairman Pak Thae-bok made his way through the assembly, he was embraced by cheering members who were thankful for his courage and guidance in bringing a form of democracy to their nation.

With that done, there was no rest for the chairman. He now needed to plead his case to the nation of China for a mutual defense treaty as approved in Article Six. For this the chairman assembled a cross-section of delegates to accompany him to Beijing. In total forty-three men and women boarded a sleek, five-star Hainan Boeing 737 to Beijing Capital International Airport. Of the forty-three men and women, eight were translators, three reporters, two security, and ten aides of one form or another.

In the back of Pak's mind was how Article Six, a mutual defense treaty with China, would play with the top brass in the North Korean military. Was it an affront to their responsibilities as the protectors of the nation from foreign and domestic threats? Would there be pushback to their new roles in light of the defunding of their military budgets? What about the thousands of soldiers who would need to find new jobs in society? 'Democracy comes with challenges,' he thought, but for the glow of a new beginning, he decided it was worth it.

. . .

Meanwhile, Kylo and Sejong were planning their trip to see President Doris Kearns Goodman in Washington, DC, to discuss the end of hostilities between North Korea and the United States of America. Sejong suggested that if and when a formal declaration was signed by both nations, the sinking of the *Justice*, an American Victory ship, in American waters could symbolize the end of the war between the parties. In essence, the proud ship had fought its last battle and would now rest where it belonged, in home waters.

They also had to assemble a delegation of dignitaries to represent the newly endorsed constitution, men and women from many different fields, all the major sciences, technology, education, the military, and experts in Korean history, a history rich in the philosophy of Sejong the Great, who reinforced Confucian policies, created the Korean alphabet, encouraged scientific technology, and brought prosperity to Korea. Sejong planned to bring an ancient brass statue of his namesake as a gift to President Goodman.

Naturally, everything they were planning was contingent on the meeting being held in Beijing between the delegation led by Chairman Pak Thae-bok and President Xi Jinping of China. But the denuclearization of North Korea had always been on President Xi Jinping's mind—the last thing he wanted was a nuclear conflagration between North Korea and the United States—and here, the mutual defense treaty, plus the withdrawal of all nuclear weapons from North Korea, was a golden opportunity to bring peace to the region with the stroke of a pen. Both Sejong and Kylo were confident that they would soon be joined by Chairman Pak Thae-bok's delegation in Washington, DC, with their delegation for peace talks and the end to the Korean War, and several days later Kylo received a call from Chairman Pak that at nine o'clock that night, with all the world watching, the Nation of North Korea and the People's Republic of China would sign a historic agreement, a mutual defense treaty.

Elated by the news Kylo and Sejong began assembling their delegation for the trip to DC. Meanwhile, North Korean advance men in the United States were busy preparing visas for the hundred or so men and women who would participate in the meetings. They, with their American counterparts, organized the agendas, accommodations, dinners, and, most important, the news releases for the media.

Then, as television stations all around the world interrupted their programs for breaking news, an announcer addressed the world from Beijing, stating that "peace is at hand." Seated at a large table at the presidential mansion in Beijing was Chairman Pak Thae-bok of North Korea, and beside him was President Xi Jinping of The People's Republic of China. Smiling for the cameras, they signed the mutual defense treaty and rose to embrace each other to the cheers and applause of the witnesses of the historical event. Breaking away from the festivities in Beijing, news anchors read releases describing the treaty for their audiences.

"Are you as happy as I am?" Kylo asked Sejong over the phone.

"I never dreamed that we'd ever get here. What did the announcer say in Beijing? That 'peace was at hand'? What a wonderful thought... to live in peace,"

Sejong said.

"My boy, this is just the beginning. Now we have an opportunity to build a nation based on justice, harmony, equality, and human rights," Kylo said.

"Are you sure it's not a dream?" Sejong asked.

"If it is, I don't want to ever wake up," Kylo said.

44

Officer Brenda in action

Officer Brenda waited twenty-five minutes in Senator Rollins Levitt's reception room at the California statehouse in Sacramento. She figured that he kept his visitors waiting to impress upon them how busy and important he was when actually he was only cutting his nails.

"You can go in now," a perky young thing said.

When Brenda entered Levitt's small, dark office, she noticed a bookcase filled with the obligatory, leather-bound books attorneys display to show off their scholarship of the law, when in essence these books never left the shelf. Hiding behind piles of manila folders was Senator Levitt, a skinny, unshaven, crooked-toothed character out of a silent movie… the ones who collect the rent from poor women in distress. He was perfect for the role.

'...and this was the guy who raped Kitty?' Brenda thought.

"What do you want?" Levitt asked, avoiding the customary greeting of "Hello, good morning, please have a seat." He was a real charmer.

"I'm here this morning"—'after cooling my heels for twenty-five minutes in your waiting room,' she should have said—"to right a wrong."

"What?" he asked incredulously.

"Yes. A young man is now in prison after serving nine years because he had shit for a lawyer," she said.

"I think, young lady, you're in the wrong place. You gotta—"

But Officer Brenda walked in front of his desk, slid some files onto to the floor, and placed her laptop on his desk. Flabbergasted, the old geezer popped out of his chair and, reaching across his desk, tried to slap Officer Brenda, who grabbed his hand and twisted it. She got hold of his index finger and bent it back in a very painful manner.

"Sit down, you piece of shit. This is how we'll play it from now on. I've got two depositions on my laptop; one is from a victim who survived a crash on Route 17, and the other is from my friend Kitty. You know her; she used to work for you. That's the one you raped in Vegas. Which do you want to see first?" she asked, twisting his finger.

Near tears and afraid of what this woman might do,

Levitt sat. Officer Brenda played the tape of her interview with the SUV survivor, Russell Phillips, then told Levitt what she wanted him to do. If he didn't, she would upload her other recording, the interview with Kitty that described the rape, to YouTube for thousands, maybe millions, of viewers to witness the crime the senator had the depravity to foist upon a young mother of three who once worked for him in the California State Senate.

"I'd say you'd get fifteen, maybe twenty years at a federal pen," she said, letting go of his hand.

"I think you broke my finger," he said, looking at it.

"I'll give you twenty-four hours to contact the governor and plead my case for a pardon. I'm leaving with you this thumb drive with Russell Phillips's deposition and a file on the case highlighting how the police, attorneys, and courts railroaded a young boy into jail. It's a fuckin' slam dunk. Do it and I'll deep-six Kitty's tape."

On the ride home, Officer Brenda called Judy to brief her on her meeting with Senator Levitt. Judy told her that, if she hurried, Brenda could witness her attacking ship mockups in the desert with an F-15 fighter equipped with four AGM-158C laser-guided missiles.

"I want to see that," Officer Brenda, said pressing on the gas pedal.

"But tell me what he said for God's sake," Judy asked.

"Oh, he was a real gentleman, and will speak to the

governor to have them reopen the case based on my interview with the SUV crash survivor and all the supporting documents," Officer Brenda said to reassure
Judy.

"Oh, I was so worried! Brenda, I can't tell you how
relieved I am," Judy said.

"No problem. So, are you sure I can witness this
bombing run in your trailer? I don't want you to get in
trouble," Officer Brenda asked.

"Wear your uniform. They'll think you're my police
protection."

"Who's 'they'?" Officer Brenda asked.

"I don't know. They told me to wear my dress uniform for photos," Judy said.

"In that case, I'll wear my police uniform and my big
six-shooter," Officer Brenda said for effect.

"Atta girl! But seriously, I hope I don't fuck up in
front of the brass," Judy said hesitantly.

"What are you afraid of? You're a pro. You're their
ace in the hole."

"But this is the first time I'll be filmed by a chase
plane," Judy said.

"Really? Why?"

"They said they're sending a F-22 Raptor to film the
attack."

"What's that?"

"It's a supersonic fighter that can run rings around a
F-15, that's what."

"Just remember you're a lean, mean killing machine.

If he gives you any trouble, shoot him down!" Officer Brenda said, pounding on her steering wheel.

"Brenda, I'm not so lean anymore," Judy said.

"That's what happens when you get a lotta of love in... a good appetite."

On the way to the base, Officer Brenda called Rose to join her at Judy's trailer to witness the upcoming apocalyptic event in the desert, but Rose had a high-level meeting at the base to discuss a band of feral cats living in or around the dumpsters. She said that she was torn between her loyalty to the base and to her friend Captain Judy Sluzac, but had to take a pass on the forthcoming historic event.

Dressed in her recently cleaned uniform, Officer Brenda arrived at Judy's trailer to find several black government SUVs parked around it.

'Hmmm, must be something important going on inside that trailer,' Officer Brenda thought. 'I shall investigate.'

She mounted the steps and entered the trailer to the surprise of the colonels and generals who were there to witness Judy's attack on a variety of plywood ships in the desert. Officer Brenda smiled at the brass and removed her hat, and no one dared to inquire why the local constabulary was there. They assumed there was a good reason and paid no attention to her presence. Off to one side of the narrow trailer stood the base's information officer in front of a hastily installed sixty-five-inch high-def monitor. Glancing to her right, Brenda saw that at the end of the trailer Judy sat in her pilot's console surrounded by a maze of monitors, gauges, controls, buttons, levers, handles, and switches. To many, Judy's command console looked like a scene out of a Star Wars movie, and Judy was Captain Solo.

"Gentlemen, I call your attention to our monitor, using a video feed on the runway," the information officer said. "The plane on the right is one of our autonomous F-15 fighters under the command of Captain Judy Sluzac, here, and the other plane is an F-22 Raptor with Commander Paul Steele in the cockpit.

"Captain Sluzac is a veteran drone pilot, who served with distinction in Afghanistan, taking part in 'strike and destroy' missions against the Taliban. Here at Creech Air Force Base, Captain Sluzac is part of the Third Army Airforce, piloting autonomous F-15 fighters in defense of our nation's capital.

"Commander Steele is a thirty-year naval pilot who has flown missions in Iraq, Afghanistan, and Syria. He is currently director of the pilot training center at the Piedmont naval base. The F-15 fighter will be the delivery platform for the advanced AGM-158C long-range anti-ship missile. This missile was built by Lockheed Martin and carries a thousand-pound warhead. The unit cost of the warhead is 3.96 million dollars. The F-22 fighter will tape the operation and send links simultaneously to us, the Pentagon, and to Lockheed Martin. Before I begin the operation, are there any questions?"

That being done, he radioed the planes to begin the demonstration.

The F-15 under the command of Captain Sluzac smoothly advanced down the runway, gaining speed until it reached 275 miles per hour. Judy pulled her stick back, sending the fully laden fighter into a clear, blue sky. Upon reaching five thousand feet she gracefully banked to the west to conduct a wide circle of the base.

Commander Steele in his F-22 Raptor began his takeoff down the runway until he, too, reached 275 miles per hour and also pulled back on his stick to bank west. He began his role as a chase plane recording the operation. Once he was alongside, Judy radioed Commander Steele that she would lead him to the targets.

"Roger, I'll follow you to the targets one mile to your starboard and one half mile to your stern," the commander said.

"Roger," Judy said, increasing her speed to 450 miles per hour.

The plan was for them to do a flyby to inspect the targets in the agreed-upon formation, then return to a point five miles from the target to attack and record the operation.

When they approached the four plywood targets spaced three hundred feet apart, Judy advised the commander that she'd attack from left to right at five hundred miles per hour at an altitude of one thousand feet, the navy's standard attack mode over water to avoid a ship's anti-aircraft guns. Both planes increased their speeds to five hundred miles per hour, and Judy dropped to one thousand feet while the commander recorded the attack from twenty-five hundred feet. Judy activated her number one AGM-158C missile and, using her laser guidance system, painted the target on her extreme left. One mile from the target, she hit the red button with her palm, sending the missile on its way.

"Missile away," she radioed for all to hear, and she banked to port to avoid any fragments from the blast. There were some she almost flew into, so she asked for permission to fire her remaining missiles from one and a half miles from the target...and was given an OK from the Pentagon, who were impressed by the power of the AGN-158C missile.

The remaining test firings went extremely well, and all who witnessed them were impressed by the professionalism of the pilots both in the cockpit and on the ground. Judy, sweating in her bulky uniform, was praised by one and all to her delight. She'd made it, and the result was on tape for all to see. Taking her leave, Judy grabbed Officer Brenda, and they raced across the field to thank Commander Steele, who was getting out of his flight suit.

"Can I give you a big hug, commander?" Judy asked.

"Of course you can, Captain Sluzac," he said, picking her up and hugging her to his chest.

"You know, the last time a soldier hugged me like that was in the Helmand Province in Afghanistan," Judy said.

"Why don't you ladies tell me about it over a beer?" the commander offered.

"It's OK if it's on us," Officer Brenda blurted out to Judy's surprise.

The three of them went to an on-base watering hole to let off steam and trade war stories.

45

Bringing the Military on Board

With their ducks in a row, the problem of a military pushback loomed ever stronger in Kylo, Sejong, and the chairman's minds.

"What can we give them to join us in a democratic form of government?" Kylo asked.

"A role in the government?" Sejong replied.

"Isn't that superfluous?" Kylo asked.

"How?"

"With a mutual defense treaty with China, why do we need an army, navy, or air force?"

"To develop and sell their expertise to other nations; the military services will supply the manpower," Sejong suggested.

"You're right, we can become a supplier, not a consumer, of weapons,"

Kylo said.

"We should take military men as delegates who can pitch a sort of subcontractor role for our military. That's how Japan industrialized after World War II; it gave them an entry into new markets," Sejong said.

"It might work. If anything it will show we've been thinking about them, and that's part of the solution. Let's set up a meeting," Kylo said.

Later that night, as Sejong and his lovely partner, Amor, relaxed after a dinner of bibimbap, Sejong broached the subject of his upcoming meeting with representatives of the armed services to sell them on the idea of taking an active role in the new government and switching their emphasis from defending the nation to one of producing products and services that would give their men and women good-paying jobs.

"What would they produce?" Amor asked, preparing a water pipe with cannabis.

"The same weapons they use today: missiles, large and small arms, rocket launchers, things like that," Sejong said as he lit the water pipe and took a long drag.

"Hmm, but I thought you came in peace," Amor said with a seductive smile.

"That's what they know; that's what they're familiar with," Sejong said, passing her the pipe.

"But as you say, you go in peace yet continue to build weapons that kill. Isn't that what they call hypocrisy?" Amor suggested.

"True, my love, but as they also say, you can't teach a dog new tricks."

"But you must also think of how the west, the American president, will take the idea of producing weapons that kill people," Amor said, putting her long, lovely legs on Sejong's lap.

"But I have to find jobs, good-paying jobs, for thousands of soldiers under the treaty," Sejong said as he stroked Amor's legs.

"But they don't have to be weapons; they can be products of peace. The navy can build pleasure boats; the army can produce camping equipment, tents, recreational equipment, and bikes; and the air force can build fleets of uber-commuter aircraft for rural towns opening up a world to people living in remote villages. Our nation will use its power for peaceful ends." She smiled, opening Sejong's robe and wrapping her legs around him.

Needless to say, the colonels and generals who attended the meeting the next day were impressed both by Amor's presentation and her shapely figure.

"You were marvelous," Sejong said as they drove away from the army base.

"We were marvelous, my dear," Amor replied.

"I knew that after hearing you discuss their options, how they had to project peace into the world, that only you had the ability to sway them. And boy, were they swayed." Sejong shook his head, thinking about how incredibly lucky he was to share a life with such an intelligent and beautiful woman.

Later that afternoon, at their home, Amor's father was expected to join them for lunch. He had just returned from a business trip to Hong Kong and was eager to congratulate them on the news that North Korea had both signed a mutual defense treaty and would be meeting with the American president to discuss the official end to the Korean War.

"Congratulations, my dear children, on your wonderful achievements for our nation and for the world in the cause of democracy," Thi-sen said, bowing to Sejong and Amor.

"The honor is ours, my beloved father, for it has been your teachings that sent us on the path to enlightenment," Amor respectfully said.

"Before we partake in the bounty Amor has prepared for our reunion, let me tell you how she cast a spell on our military leaders this morning," Sejong said. "With the impeding reduction in military personnel due to the treaty, Amor presented an alternative. The military will now produce products and services for the world based on their technical skills, but the products and services must meet the needs of society in a peaceful manner."

He turned to Thi-sen. "Tell us: What's the news abroad of our new experiment in democracy?"

"To be honest, a mixed bag. The tyrants who rule

most of the world abhor the idea of self-rule and democracy, but the other leaders are ecstatic as to your brave moves toward peace," Thi-sen said.

"Did I tell you that we're leaving to meet Chairman Pak Thae-bok in Washington, DC, with our delegation? We will present a united front to sue for an end to the Korean War," Amor said.

"No! But that's something to toast," Thi-sen said, raising his glass.

After a dessert of fruit, cheese, and cookies, Thi-sen had some advice for Sejong and Amor. Sitting back in his recliner, he said, "You were raised to appreciate the teachings of Confucius. He did not seek to be considered a god. First and foremost, he was a teacher. His teachings were based on the importance of kindness, harmony, and order. This concept, or better yet, philosophy, is not shared in America where religion is a form of mental slavery: people are told what to do or they will be punished by an imaginary god who watches every move they make and every thought they have. Using this imaginary god, American society is rife with charlatans who fleece their flock from their money and resources with one aim, the perpetuation of their own power. Care must be taken; it is imperative to never mock their gods. The other taboo is to never engage an American in any political discourse; like religion, assume they have been brainwashed and are incapable of any reasonable thinking. Finally, when in doubt, smile and nod. Americans desperately seek approval."

"Thank you for your wisdom, Father, but what about President Goodman?" Amor asked.

"She is an exception to the rule. She was chosen to balance their party's ticket as a woman, a scholar, a presidential historian, a liberal progressive in a country with massive financial inequality and tribal fighting across racial lines.

It's been widely published that six Americans have more personal wealth than half the country; that's more wealth than one hundred fifty million American men and women. And, as one of the richest counties in the world, they have no national health insurance like us and forty million Americans live in poverty."

"A point well taken, Father, but we have been ruled by a succession of godlike dictators during the Kim Dynasty," Amor reminded him.

"True, my wise and beautiful daughter, and with that in mind, we must endeavor to seize this historic moment and make our new republic, in which the power is in the hands of the people and not a deity, a reality."

46

The Bonnie & Clyde
Concierge Consultancy

When Juan told Elizabeth that he had to see a new client on business, she told him she had a great idea: she'd come too.

"But it's business. No hanky-panky," he said.

"I know, but I've been thinking that I'd like to be part of your concierge consultancy. I can be your sidekick. I even thought of a company name: The B&C Concierge Consultancy."

"What do the B and C stand for?" he asked.

"Well, letters in a company name are always very official, dignified. You know what I mean, don't you?" she said, winging it.

"No. What do they stand for?" he said with a smile.

"Picture this: we at B&C mix business and pleasure

in pursuit of helping damsels in distress. There's an air of mystery, intrigue, and danger."

"I see you're being evasive for some reason," he said, "but if I agree to bring you on board you'll tell me?"

"You'll be the first to know. So, where're we going boss?" she asked, diving right into her new role.

"Our new client is a referral. She is being sponsored by a former client, Lady Ramsford in Sussex, England. She said she's bringing her into the fold on how the consultancy works."

"Are most of your clients referrals?" Elizabeth asked.

"Yes, I guess the old guard is now passing me on to more fertile pastures," he said, thinking he should have used a different example.

"Who is the new client?"

"It's a Ms. Gayle Santos, who lives and works in London," he said, referring to his crib notes.

"What does she do?"

"She's a hedge fund manager at Piedmont Sachs."

"Are they a part of Goldman Sachs?"

"I don't know. Maybe."

"Then when do we leave?" she eagerly asked.

"As soon as I make an appointment with her, then we'll make our trip reservations. Say, didn't you run the CIA's travel office?" he asked.

The call to Ms. Santos was short and sweet.

"I'll expect you on Tuesday the twenty-second at seven p.m. My address in Mayfair is 222 Bootle Row NE," she said rapidly and hung up.

'Well,' Juan thought, 'she doesn't waste time with formalities.'

Now that Elizabeth had a date and time for them to be at Ms. Santos's residence in London, she was in a quandary as to which passport—or better yet, passports —to use from one locale to the next.

'Should I use my Grace Hayworth, which I use in Morocco, or the Sara Murphy that I used getting to the Canary Islands? Definitely not the Allison Bryant; she's the one who left the US,' she thought.

"What do you think our assignment will be?" she asked Juan to procrastinate making her decision.

"I dare not speculate because I'm usually off the mark. Sometimes you can get a sense from speaking with the client, but this gal probably communicates via text or email exclusively," he said.

"You might be right. That's the 'in thing' in business, you know. It's called leaving a paper trail, especially if you're covering your ass," she said from experience.

Elizabeth opted to depart Morocco using her Grace Hayworth passport since there weren't any record of her under that name and Moroccan security wasn't as sophisticated as the immigration authorities in Europe. From then on, she decided to use her Sara Murphy passport. In any event, both were diplomatic passports, which were usually waved through. However, to avoid the prolific use of CCTV surveillance and its facial recognition software in England, she and Juan opted to take the Eurostar train to London. Arriving an hour early in Mayfair, they decided to grab a bite at a bistro near the subject's townhouse.

"Not so glamorous, the life of a concierge?" he said after ordering a pint.

"It is when I'm with you. That's all that matters." She stroked his arm. "I wonder: Why did you accept the case if you didn't know the assignment?"

"I usually don't, but her sponsor, Lady Ramsford, was extremely generous back when I was prospecting for clients." He also ordered a baguette and a wedge of Stilton to share with Elizabeth.

"Where are we staying tonight?" she asked.

"A place near the Marble Arch. I've stayed there before, and they serve an excellent traditional English breakfast, which is the only food edible in England. The rest is ghastly."

Waking over to Ms. Santos's townhouse, they passed a long row of similar buildings that were probably built postwar, circa 1946, since this area of London was destroyed during the Blitz. When they got to 222 Bootle Row, Elizabeth went up the three steps to the front door and rang the buzzer. This was followed by a voice asking who was there and waited for a response.

"This is the B&C Concierge Consultancy, Ms. Santos," Elizabeth said to the brass box on the door and then smiled at the video camera above the door.

"Please enter," the voice said as the door locks disengaged from the frame.

As they entered the vestibule, a tall, wiry woman in her fifties with a mop of yellow hair and a toothy smile rushed toward them with her hand extended. At first, Elizabeth thought that Ms. Santos was greeting them with an obligatory handshake, but no, no... she was stopping them from entering her living room with their shoes on.

"Leave your shoes where you stand," she ordered.

Obliging her demand, Elizabeth and Juan removed their shoes and followed Ms. Santos into a large, white living room. Everything was white—the leather furniture, wall coverings, lamps, tables, artwork, and, of course, a magnificent, white, wall-to-wall Berber carpet. Dressed in a gaudy, pink jumpsuit and Nike sneakers, Ms. Santos plopped her skinny ass on a white, egg-shaped, fiberglass designer chair and lit up a cigarette while holding in the palm of her hand a small, white ashtray. Without any preliminary chitchat, she began her tale of woe.

"I gave him everything... money, clothes, jewelry, and one day, after a long, busy, stressful day, he was gone. He left me a note. I'd show it to you, but I shredded it into a billion pieces," she said, nervously fumbling with her cigarette.

"Ms. Santos, do you know who we are and what we do?" Juan asked.

"Of course, I do. You're detectives," she snapped.

"No, we're not. My associate and I provide a unique service outside of typical law enforcement. In that way, our clients remain anonymous and the services we provide are private. Do you understand?" Juan said.

"Are you going to help me get Marco back? Yes or no?" She crushed her cigarette into the ashtray on her lap.

"We will endeavor to bring Marco back on the following conditions. First, we accepted you as a client based on Lady Ramsford's sponsorship. She, in essence, guarantees that our fees and expenses will be paid by you. If, for whatever reason, you do not fulfill your financial part of our agreement, she will pay us. Do you understand?" Juan said patiently.

"What's the bottom line?" she asked coldly.

"I was prepared to go over our terms and conditions on the phone, but you abruptly hung up on me. Based on that, I believed that we should discuss business face to face," he said.

"Can you get Marco back?" she asked in a more civilized manner.

"Naturally, we'll need more information, but the way we work, we guarantee success or you're not obligated to pay our fee. That being said, you must pay our expenses either way, whether we succeed or fail. Is that understood?"

"Lady Ramsford said you have a flat fee of one hundred thousand pounds sterling, is that correct?" Ms. Santos asked soberly.

"That is correct and memorialized in our contract, which requires your signature of acceptance."

He walked over and handed her the contract, which she briefly scanned and then dropped on the carpet by her feet.

After returning to his seat, Juan took out a leather-bound pad and Montblanc fountain pen. From there on, Ms. Santos was more civil and receptive to their help. She told them that she took in this waif, this vagabond, out of the goodness of her heart, and he ran off one day. She wanted him back at all costs. She admitted that she might have had him on a short leash, but it was for his own good. He took pills and did cocaine. She also admitted he stole cash from her purse.

"Where is he now?" Elizabeth asked, taking out her own pad and pen.

"He's in Amsterdam... where he can get all the drugs he wants."

"How did you find him?" Juan asked.

"Money. He needed money, so he called me. That's how."

"How did you sent it? The money, I mean?" Elisabeth asked.

"FedEx," she said dryly.

"Do you have the receipt?" Juan asked.

"Get it," Elizabeth quickly demanded. She was quickly running out of patience for this eccentric, melodramatic client.

Slowly, Ms. Santos went into her office. After she rummaged through some papers, she returned with the FedEx receipt. Not sure at first who to give it to, she handed it Elizabeth.

"And this, to the best of your knowledge, is his current address?" Elizabeth asked.

"I tracked the envelope every inch of its way and received a notification at the exact time it was handed to him," she said.

"And this phone number on the receipt, it's his cell phone?" Elizabeth asked.

"Yes. That's his mobile number," Ms. Santos answered.

"If you called him now, would he answer?" Juan asked.

"No. I've tried. He won't talk to me or anyone who calls his mobile," she said sadly.

At that point, Elizabeth used her cell phone to call Marco. She let it ring a dozen times to no avail.

"There's no voicemail capability?" Juan asked.

"It must be disabled," Ms. Santos guessed.

"Is he technically proficient to disable the messaging function?" Juan asked.

"No, he's as dumb as a nail. Someone must have done it for him... one of his druggie mates," she speculated.

"How long has he lived here with you?" Elizabeth asked.

"Approximately eighteen months," she said.

"And has he run away before?" Juan asked.

"Once, in the beginning, and that was because he was high and forgot where I lived."

"Do you, as a couple, socialize with friends?" Elizabeth asked.

"God, no. They'd never understand… We rarely go out together anyway."

"Then how do you spend your time together?" Juan asked.

"We fuck. All the time… day and night… that's what we do," she said bluntly and unabashedly.

"OK, I think we get the picture. If you would be kind enough to sign the contract, we'll be on our way," Juan said, approaching Ms. Santos, pen in hand.

With the formalities out of the way, they departed 222 Bootle Row and flagged a taxi to Claridge's Hotel. After checking in they ordered a traditional English breakfast delivered to their room, followed by showers, lovemaking, and naps.

47

Peace at hand

The Air China flight from Beijing landed at Washington Dulles International Airport at seven a.m., carrying forty-three members of the North Korean delegation. It was a long trip for them since they had never flown farther than Hong Kong, a mere three hours from Pyongyang. However, it was an experience that they would tell their friends and family about for ages—how they flew over the top of the earth, the great, arctic ice sheet, to the capital of the United States, a twenty-two-hour journey. Once on the ground and escorted through immigration and customs by a contingent of military guards, they found that a bus was waiting to take them to the Sheraton Hotel, where an entire floor was reserved for them. So far, the arrangements made by the American and Korean advance men were seamless.

"They've landed," Kylo said to Sejong and Amor, who were waiting to board their flight to Washington, DC.

"It's one small step for man, one giant leap for mankind," Sejong said.

"Well said, my Commander Armstrong," Kylo replied with a smile, though he understood the gravity of their mission.

"I think they are ready to board," Amor said excitedly, looking at the giant American Airlines plane parked at their gate. Adding to her excitement, Sejong had told her their charted flight to the United States was the first nonstop flight of its kind from Pyongyang to America. Heretofore, the only way to fly to the United States from North Korea was to fly to Hong Kong and then take another plane that had the range to fly to America.

"How many are in our party?" Amor asked, rolling her suitcase to the boarding ramp.

"Including our translators, security personnel, and experts in education, the military, health care, transportation, trade, tourism, the economy, banking, human rights, farming, and global warming... eighty-nine men and women," Sejong rattled off from memory.

.   .   .

Meanwhile, on the other side of the world, the first group of delegates from North Korea was lining up in a private dining room at the Sheraton for their buffet breakfast, American style—scrambled eggs, home fries, bacon, sausage, orange juice, oatmeal, cold cereals, muffins, fruits, pancakes with maple syrup, and either tea or coffee. To some, this was more food than they'd ever seen in one place, and to top it off, they could eat as much of it as they wanted.

After the meal, Chairman Pak Thae-bok gave an impromptu address to the delegates.

"Fellow delegates, I trust you've enjoyed the bountiful breakfast our hosts have prepared as a welcome to America. Speaking for myself, I can see why America is the greatest country in the world... they certainly feed their guest until they burst." This brought laughter and applause from the delegates.

He then reviewed the first day's agenda.

"I advise that you return to your rooms and enjoy a restful nap because you'll break out to attend your meetings with your American counterparts beginning at one. We've prepared this sheet, which will tell you where and when your meeting is. In addition, as we previously advised, business attire is required of all delegates. I assume you've chosen an interpreter for your group? Excellent, it is now your job to explain how we've turned our country from a dynastic country to a republic. That henceforth, North Korea is a country in which the power is held by the people, not a monarch. That North Korea has denuclearized in concert with the

United Nations Resolution 222. That we have sent all of our nuclear weapons to the People's Republic of China, and in doing so, we have entered into a mutual defense treaty with China. And most importantly, we come in peace. We are now a transparent country; we seek the end of hostilities between North Korea and The United States; we want to bring an end, for once and for all, to the Korean War."

Also having breakfast just a little way down the street, at the White House, President Doris Kearns Goodman was dunking her toasted bagel in her soft-boiled eggs. It was reminiscent of her mornings growing up in Brooklyn. On Sundays she was the chosen one to run down to Wasserman's Bakery on Church Avenue and get three bagels, two bialys, a quarter pound of Philadelphia cream cheese, and a third of a pound of belly lox for her family. They'd be literally waiting for her to arrive with the bags of goodies, sitting around a small Formica table in the kitchen. Then, it was chaos over who could cut, toast, layer cream cheese, and add lox first without cutting themselves or burning their hands in the toaster. The memory of those days was indelibly pressed into her being. She always thought that she was a better person for having grown up as a poor girl in Brooklyn. Actually, they weren't poor; they just didn't have any money.

"If I'm remembered for anything as president, ending that cursed Korean War is what I want," President Goodman was saying to her Secretary of State, Michael Bloomberg, who had joined her for a breakfast meeting in the State Dining Room.

"Good things come to those who wait, and they've waited seventy years for this day," Secretary Bloomberg said, then took a bite of his blueberry muffin.

"I understand that a man named Sejong is attending the talks," President Goodman said. She sipped her herbal tea.

"Is he a delegate?" Secretary Bloomberg asked.

"All I know is that he's Kim Jong-un's brother," President Goodman said. She patted her lips with her napkin, then threw it on the fine china before pushing back from the table.

"Interesting. The CIA has said that Kim is being retired from running the country."

"Yes, this new man—I forgot his name, but he's the chairman of their assembly—is now running the show. But Michael, do you know who 'Sejong the Great' was?" President Goodman asked.

"No, I'm not up on my Korean history," Secretary Bloomberg said, pouring himself a to-go cup of coffee.

"Well, I brushed up on him last night, and he was undoubtedly one of greatest thinkers since Confucius. He lived in the fifteenth century and turned Korea from a backwater state to one of enlightenment by creating a language that could be written and spoken by the people, rich or poor. He believed in the teachings of Confucius that people were basically good and that, by helping others, society would reap the rewards of peace with its neighbors. He was revered by the people, and I think this new Sejong may have the same destiny," President Goodman said.

"Wouldn't that be a twist! A leader of the people and not a despot. Quite a change from its former leader, his brother," Secretary Bloomberg said.

"When are we hosting the delegates?" President Goodman asked.

"I don't have that info at this time. I was advised that it depended on the peace talks, and they haven't started."

"Well, let me know. I have to write a speech worthy of the occasion," President Goodman said, then returned to the Oval Office.

48

Free at Last…Free at Last

The call came at 4:06 p.m. from the Susanville Correctional Center in California.

"Will you accept a collect call from a Mister Brad Navarro?" the operator asked.

Stunned, Derek accepted the call to hear his brother say, "I'm coming home. Can you pick me up?"

Gasping for air, Derek sank to his knees and began to sob.

"Yes! Yes… when?" he asked.

"After noon tomorrow," Brad said.

"I'll be there at noon," Derek said. "Wait. Do you need anything?" He could not believe that his kid brother was coming home.

"Nope. See you," Brad said.

"I love you, kid." Derek hung up, overcome with joy.

There he sat, thinking of what he wanted to tell Brad when he saw him. But first, he had to tell the family... his dad, Pamela, Judy, Joey, Rose, and especially Officer Brenda, who made it all possible. There were just a few people who meant the world to him, and after rehearsing what he'd tell them, he called them one at a time to tell them the good news.

Derek was there, at the Susanville Correctional Center, at eleven thirty, where he sat in the visitors' parking lot staring at the front door for Brad to appear. At 12:07 p.m., the door opened and Brad appeared, carrying a green plastic bag filled with his meager belongings. Derek braced himself against his truck; his legs buckled as his brother approached. When Brad was a few feet away, Derek threw his arms around his kid brother and, after taking a deep breath, began to sob on his shoulder in happiness.

On the ride home Derek tried to tell Brad how sorry he was about not coming to his aid, but Brad shook it off, saying he understood and that it was his fault. But the one thing on Derek's mind was how he could make it up to his brother. Even after they arrived home and Brad's father came out to greet his son, Brad bushed him off, saying that he deserved what he got and that everyone should forget it and move on with their lives.

However, when Derek met with the three amigos

the following week to thank them for all they'd done to get Brad out of prison, Officer Brenda had a different spin to the story. She had found additional information regarding the case to support an accusation of wrongful imprisonment on the part of the police and prosecutors who knew about the truck driver who played chicken with motorists on Route 17. They withheld this information from the defense, knowing that an innocent man was pleading guilty to, as he was told, get a lesser sentence.

In addition, the toxicology report had found traces of an amphetamine in a sample of Brad's blood. It seemed the sample from the police was tampered with before it reached the lab. The report from the technician who conducted the test noted on her report that the seal on the evidence bag was broken and resealed, making the test invalid. This, too, was not submitted to the defense as required. The police had used White-Out on the technician's comment, then submitted a photocopy of the lab report without the comment and put that one in the file, ignorant that the lab kept a copy of the original report. That was not only illegal; it was a felony punishable with serious jail time. Based on this new evidence, Officer Brenda urged Brad to consult an attorney; she happened to know one in California who would take it on a contingency basis.

"You've got nothing to lose," Officer Brenda insisted.

"But I've had enough of the legal system," Brad said.

"Look, they've taken nine years out of your life. It's time for payback,"

Judy insisted.

"You know, they've probably done this before. Break open the bag and sprinkle some fairy dust inside," Rose added.

"I'll take you," Judy said without even knowing where the lawyer was located.

"He's in Vegas but can practice in California," Officer Brenda added.

Reluctantly, Brad agreed to the meeting, and he and Judy took off a few days later with the file on the accident and the new evidence in hand to meet Attorney Josh Davis. Davis's office was in a large shopping center, surrounded by upscale clothing stores, restaurants, a ten-screen movie theater, and a Whole Foods Market.

Davis was a man in his sixties, impeccably dressed in a Harris Tweed sport jacket, gray wool pants, and a powder-blue shirt opened at the neck. He wore a gold Omega wristwatch and solid gold cufflinks.

"Can I offer you something to drink?" he asked as he shook their hands. "You must be the fighter pilot Brenda spoke about."

"Yes," Judy said, smiling and shaking her head.

"Brenda told me a little about your case," Davis said, turning to Brad, "but I'd like to hear it from you... if that's all right?" He led them to a cluster of chairs before sitting back in one with a notepad on his lap.

Brad straightened himself in his chair and began his story from the very beginning—what he was doing work-wise in California, his drug use, his dropping out of community college, his girlfriends, and how he was trying make a life for himself that his family would be proud of, especially his father and his brother, Derek.

He then went through what happened the night of the accident, the young girl hitchhiking home, the pickup truck driving into his lane with his high beams on. He shared that there was no shoulder to turn onto, how he had crashed into the trees, the ambulance, the police, the two days of nonstop interrogations and the plea deal… and the nine years behind bars.

"Do you have the materials with you, the ones Brenda spoke about? What about that copy of the original toxicology report before it was doctored?" Davis asked.

Brad passed a manila envelope to the attorney, who carefully placed the contents on his desk and inspected each piece of paper, making notes on his legal pad. After Brad and Judy had squirmed in their seats for almost twenty minutes, Davis pushed back from his desk and, folding his hands, presented what he thought of Brad's case.

"It is my opinion that a severe miscarriage of justice has taken place," Attorney Davis said. "I'd be happy to redress the wrongs inflicted in Brad's case."

"On a contingency basis?" Judy asked.

"Yes, and I'll explain what this entails. First, you pay me nothing to represent you in this matter. I take a percentage of whatever you receive in damages. In this case I will take thirty percent."

"How much will you sue for?" Judy asked.

"I'd rather not say yet because I have to speak to several people before we agree on who and what we deserve from each party, and from what I've seen, there are several parties to this case. In any case, you'll be part of the process and make the final decision. Agreed?" He then prepared a contract for Brad to sign and told them he'd be in touch when he decided on the best course of action.

Elated, Judy called Officer Brenda with the good news, and Brad thanked her for helping him. Brad demurred from calling his brother, wanting to tell him in his own words in private. However, when Judy asked Officer Brenda to convey the good news to Rose, Officer Brenda invoked the rarely used emergency meeting clause mandating a face-to-face meeting of the three amigos... pronto. So, the very next day, the three amigos met at rear of the high school baseball field to discuss important business. On the agenda was:

1. Tell us about Brad's lawyer.
2. What's going on among Brad, Derek, and their father?
3. What was it like to perform in front of the brass?
4. I'm in a panic; I don't know what to wear to the wedding.

Piling into Rose's car with coffee from the McDonald's drive-thru, the ladies were eager to share what they knew about anything and everything.

"So, first things first, Judy, you took Brad to see the lawyer. What was he like?" Rose asked.

"I can sum it up in one word: very professional," Judy said, burning her mouth on her coffee.

"That's two words. He's taking it on contingency, right?" Rose asked.

"Why do they make it so fuckin' hot… and yes, he'll take it on a contingency basis." Judy put her coffee in the cup holder and crossed her arms.

"What's his cut?" Rose asked.

"If he wins, he gets thirty percent of whatever the court decides."

"What're his chances?" Rose asked quickly.

"Look, I got the impression that it wasn't his first rodeo and he wouldn't waste his time if he didn't think there was a pot of gold on the other side of the rainbow, right?" Judy said, bringing item number one to a close.

"How's it going between the father, son, and Brad?" Officer Brenda asked.

"Like walking on eggshells. Brad's keeping to himself, and Derek is antsy about speaking to him about… anything." Judy tried to sip her coffee, but it still was too hot.

"But is Brad looking for work?" Rose asked.

"Don't you think it's a little early to start looking

for work? He just got out of prison," Judy said in Brad's defense.

"Easy, our little fighter pilot. Sitting around the house and watching television isn't the best idea. He's got to be thinking ahead soon," Officer Brenda said.

"Moving along, what is it... number three?" Rose asked.

Judy dove right in. "It was terrifying. I was sitting there surrounded by generals, colonels, and Officer Brenda, sweating my ass off. The F-15 was carrying four thousand-pound missiles with enough explosive power to destroy a battleship. To make matters worse, everything I did, every move I made, was being recorded by a chase plane and broadcast to our trailer, the Pentagon, and Lockheed Martin."

"But it was a success, right?" Rose said.

"Sort of. There was something I didn't tell them," Judy said in confidence.

"What? I was there, and your attack was flawless. They were ecstatic with your performance," Officer Brenda said.

"Maybe, but I could feel that something was amiss controlling my F-15 with all that ordinance. When I fired my first missile, I could feel—or better, I could sense—the wing bending under the stress," Judy said with a shudder.

"What do you mean, bending under the stress?" Officer Brenda asked, now concerned.

"Look, I was travelling four hundred, five hundred miles per hour, and I suddenly launched, fired a thousand-pound missile from under my wing. I sensed the wing bending when I banked to avoid the impact of the blast. Like I could hear it in my mind's eye. My F-15 was telling me, 'Easy, baby, or you'll lose it.'"

"Lose what?" Rose asked.

"The fuckin' wing, that's what."

"Do you think you should tell them?"

"Tell 'em what? That I had a premonition of losing my wing? They'd put me in a straitjacket," Judy said, eager to change the subject.

"OK, we can revisit the matter later. Now to the last but not least important subject on our agenda… the wedding of Princess Judy," Rose said to the cheers of the three amigos.

"Did you pick out a dress?" Officer Brenda asked.

"When have I had enough time to do it?" Judy replied,

"Well, make time," Rose demanded.

"I'm going to check out some of the shops in Vegas on the internet tonight.

I'll let you know if I like one," Judy said, though she had the lingering feeling that Rose was right. She had to tell someone about her premonition.

With that the meeting was adjourned, and the three amigos pealed out of Rose's car for a celebratory high-five and hug.

49

Marco... Polo
Amsterdam, The Netherlands

Bright-eyed and bushy-tailed, B&C Concierge Consultancy headed for the Eurostar to Amsterdam to convince Ms. Santos's boy toy to return with them to London. They had a recent photo of him, his last known address, and a cell phone he didn't receive calls on.

Arriving in Amsterdam they booked a room at a hotel just a few blocks from the target's address and decided that there was no better time than the present to smash and grab him, so they strolled over to his address and knocked on the front door. There was no any answer.

"Maybe they're doing 'you know what,'" Elizabeth said.

"Doing what comes naturally for our Marco Polo," Juan agreed.

"It's probably too early for him. Let's find a restaurant along the canal and hit him at ten-ish," Elizabeth suggested.

Stopping at a seafood restaurant with outdoor seating, they relaxed and ordered a bottle of white wine and an appetizer of mussels in garlic served with a crusty loaf of fresh-baked bread. Sitting back, sipping their wine, they watched the people pass hand in hand.

"It should always be like this," Elizabeth murmured, playing footsie under the table.

"After this case we're stopping in Barcelona before returning to Tangier," Juan said.

"Do we have another case?" Elizabeth asked.

"No, it's personal. You're going to meet my daughter, Maria." Juan said, topping off their wine glasses.

"How old is she?" Elizabeth asked.

"Let's see, she's now... twenty-two or twenty-three." He was embarrassed that he couldn't remember her age.

"Does she live with her mother?" Elizabeth asked, venturing into what might be a delicate matter.

"No, her parents are dead," Juan said sadly, though to Elizabeth's confusion.

"Maria is my adopted daughter," he explained. "When my sister Isabela and her husband, José, were killed travelling in Peru, I adopted her." Juan remembered going to Peru to claim their bodies and the girl who would become his new daughter.

"Oh, Juan. I'm so sorry for bringing up such sad memories." She placed her hand on top of his.

"Life is full of sad memories." He stroked her hand. "Shall we try our Marco Polo?"

"No, not tonight, my darling. They're probably clubbing and won't be home.

Tomorrow is another day. Let's get back to the hotel. I want to hold you and love you," she said before paying the bill.

The next morning was fresh and clear with temperatures in the seventies. It was just one of those mornings you felt like being outside. If anything, Amsterdam was a bright, vibrant city with happy people who rode bicycles and grew flowers and enjoyed life to the fullest. People said good morning and tipped their hats to each other, and the kids played music and danced in the streets.

This time, when Juan and Elizabeth pounded on the door, a sleepy-eyed Marco answered wearing a woman's bathrobe.

"Marco, this is your lucky day," they said, pushing past him and entering his three-room apartment.

"Who are you?" He sniffled.

"I'm Juan, and this is my partner, Grace. We represent your friend Gayle Santos who loves you and needs you back with her."

"No, no, I don't want to see her. She's bad news," Marco said, looking for something to drink.

"Sit down, Marco," Elizabeth demanded.

'Huh. He's obedient too,' she thought as Marco flopped on his couch.

"Let me tell you a story, Marco," she began. "There are two Marcos here. There's the Marco who will never have enough money to make it through the day, who will end up on the street panhandling and die unwanted and unloved, and there's the other Marco, who is loved and needed and well taken care of. This Marco can be you if you play yours cards right. Which one are you, the boy who ends up dead in the street or the other one, the smart Marco, living the life of a prince, with a home and the love of a woman who will be with him through thick and thin?" Elizabeth said, intentionally shaking him up before he could have a drink to calm his nerves.

"I need a drink. Do you want to get a drink?" Marco begged.

"Maybe later. First let's see what it takes for you to come back with us to London."

"You don't know her. She's a witch. She's bossy... and cheap."

"Atta boy, Marco, let it all out. You'll feel better," Juan said, taking the baton from Elizabeth.

"You know what she did? She wouldn't let me buy things I needed. Do you call that love?" Marco asked.

"From now on you'll get one thousand pounds sterling a week to buy anything you want. How's that sound?" Juan asked.

"Really? Anything?" Marco asked, feeling he may be ready to try love again.

"Yes, Marco. The world is your oyster. You can bathe in money... you can finally enjoy life," Elizabeth said.

"Are you ready to grab the good life?" Juan asked, holding out his hand. "Take my hand, and we'll be on our way to the good life. A happy life... a long life... Grab my hand."

He did, and Juan lifted Marco from the couch, guiding him to his bedroom to pack his clothes.

When Marco arrived at Ms. Santos's townhouse, the first thing she did was slap him in the face, grab him by the hair, and drag him into the bedroom.

"She let him in with his shoes on," Elizabeth said, closing the front door and joining Juan in the back seat of their taxi.

"All's well that ends well," he said as their taxi sped off from 222 Bootle Row to their next appointment in Barcelona with Juan's daughter, Maria.

Later that day, on their flight to Barcelona, Elizabeth was interested in getting more background information on Maria without appearing to be prying into areas that were painful to Juan. But, since Juan was now a part of her life, the more she knew, the better she could help him. Her idea was to embrace Maria into their life so that there wouldn't be any jealousy between them for Juan's attention and love.

"I'd like to get to know Maria better. She's twenty-two; is she still in school?" Elizabeth asked.

"Yes, she attends a university in Barcelona. It's a postgraduate school in music," he said.

"Oh, she's a music student. Does she play an instrument?" Elizabeth asked.

"She studied piano and now plays the guitar," Juan said.

"What does she plan to do after she finishes her studies?" Elizabeth asked.

"I don't think she knows what she wants to do after university," Juan confessed.

"If I'm touching on matters you'd care not to discuss…"

Juan interrupted to say, "No, no, you have a right to know this part of my life since you are now a part of it too."

"I love you with all my heart and soul," she said, kissing the palm of his hand.

"Now, what do you want to know?" he asked with a smile.

"Do you provide support for her studies?"

"Yes, I've established a trust fund to pay for her university and all the necessary costs to live in Barcelona for the rest of her life," he said proudly.

"You mean she's a bona fide trust fund baby?" Elizabeth said.

"If that's what it's called, yes."

"Have you gone to any of her recitals?"

"Not as many as I'd liked. I've been busy making money to support my lavish lifestyle as well as my trust fund baby," he joked.

"No, but really, when was the last time you heard her play?" she asked.

"Now, let me think... about four months ago she and her group of musicians and dancers held a recital at the villa of Countess Borgenessa," he said.

"What kind of music did they play?"

"To begin with, the villa was a marvelous venue for the event. It was the perfect setting for the flamenco experience rooted in the Andalusian culture. You've undoubtedly seen pictures of flamenco dancers, yes? The women in long dresses clapping, swirling, and stomping while the men wear tight-fitting suits similar to those of a matador. It's exciting; it's what Spain is all about... passion. The passion, it's what our great artists portrayed in their work. Look carefully at an El Greco or a Velazquez, or better, at a Goya, and be taken in under their spell. These men were the alchemists of the mind," he said proudly as a son of Spain.

"Flamenco. Then she must have played the guitar?" she said.

"*Exactamente*... and she played like our most famous flamenco artist, the legendary Andrés Segovia."

"Bravo, my lord," she said, kissing him. "What time are we meeting her?"

"You're aware that in Spain we eat dinner later than other people do. So, I told Maria to meet us at The

Winter Garden Restaurant in our hotel, El Palace, at seven tonight." He checked his watch to see if there was a time difference between London and Barcelona; there was none.

"Has she been there before?"

"Yes, I think so. Anyway she'll be delivered by taxi."

"What's this Palace Hotel like?" Elizabeth asked, wishing she could use her computer to check out the hotel and, more importantly, the nearby shops.

"Oh, I think you'll like it. It's quite elegant and it's in the shopping center of the city," he said to Elizabeth's delight.

At precisely seven o'clock a well-dressed young lady entered The Winter Garden Restaurant with her head held high, as she had learned at a Swiss finishing school, and gracefully strolled, as she had learned taking ballet lessons in France, to Elizabeth and Juan's table overlooking the city.

Elizabeth said to herself, "She's like a dream walking," and held back tears. Elizabeth rose from her seat and immediately embraced the young dream girl before any formalities and introductions could be made. This was followed by a heartfelt moment in her father's arms.

"Well, now that we know each other, this, my darling daughter, and this is my life partner, Grace Hayworth," Juan said, looking approvingly at his young princess.

"It's nice to meet you, Ms. Hayworth," the princess said.

"Maria, please call me Grace," Elizabeth said, following Juan's lead.

"What would you like to drink?" he asked Maria.

"A Chardonnay, please," Maria replied.

"And I must compliment your command of English. Where did you learn to speak so well?" Elizabeth asked.

"That's funny—I studied English in Switzerland," the princess said with a bright, white smile. "And my father said you've joined his company, the concierge consultancy."

"Yes, I'm honored to be a part, albeit a small part, of your dad's consultancy," Elizabeth said looking at Juan.

The rest of the conversation centered on Maria's plans for the future: What were her dreams? What did she want to do? Where did she want to go? What did she want to see, learn, touch, smell, read, and love? Elizabeth found that asking after a boyfriend was a little too personal on such short notice, but Maria, like her adoring father, decided to plan holidays where they could enjoy being with each other as a family, something she had missed growing up.

Leaving was heart-wrenching for father and daughter, but they promised to be together soon. For the time being, their mission was to make it a reality.

50

Judy's intuition

"Commander Steele, this Captain Judy Sluzac at the Creech Air Force Base.

You, ah, chased me on a bombing run," Judy said, grappling for words.

"Yes, of course. How are you?" the commander asked.

"I've got to ask your something about the mission. Is this a good time?"

"Yeah, what's wrong?"

"Look, this might sound crazy, but I felt something happen to my F-15 when I fired one of the missiles," she blurted out.

"Like what?" he asked.

"Now, I'm not in the cockpit like you, but as I fired a

missile at one of the targets, there was, like, a hiccup as I banked away from the blast."

"Maybe it was caused by a concussion wave," he said.

"No, it was more like… the wing bent or twisted."

"Oh, I've never heard of that… and you saw it or felt it?" he asked.

"Yep. Did you see anything funny when I fired the missile?"

"All the missiles or one of them?" he asked to narrow it down.

"The first one."

"And you banked to port, right?" he said, getting a picture in his mind of what he saw or didn't see.

"Right."

"No, I don't remember seeing anything out of the ordinary."

"Well, what can I do?" Judy asked.

"You can submit an incident report to the base commander, but, you know, what can you tell him? You had a hunch?" he said.

"Can you review the tape and see if anything unusual happened when I fired the first missile?" she asked.

"That's the port-side outer missile?"

"Roger."

"OK, I'll review the tape and see if there was any anomaly and get back to you."

"Thank you, Commander Steele," she said, thinking the call was over.

"You know there is one thing you can do," he added. "Get ten twenty-five-pound bags of sand from Home Depot and an infrared flashlight from Amazon. Then have one of the mechanics place the bags on the end of the port wing, the very end of the wing. Then shut the lights off and have him walk the wing using the flashlight to look for cracks. Now, this is important, have him do the same thing under the wing. If you don't see any cracks on the port wing, conduct the same inspection of the starboard wing and call me," he said, then asked her for her cell phone number.

Judy thanked the commander for indulging what must have sounded as a bizarre request. She respected the manner in which he approached the problem and his suggestion of how to follow up on the matter.

Meanwhile, as the North Korean delegates and their American counterparts scurried from one meeting to another, a feeling of camaraderie was ever so slowly building. The two sides were not enemies; they were doing their best to find common ground with one aim in mind: that the treaty would establish the ground rules they could use to go forward on an equal footing.

At the end of the day, in a joint meeting of Chairman Pak Thae-bok and Sejong and Kylo's delegates, the results of their meetings were shared. In a freewheeling give-and-take, several suggestions from the American military were enthusiastically accepted by the North Korean military delegates. They called for shared design and manufacturing in North Korea, in essence putting tens of thousands of soldiers to work on peaceful products, thanks in part to the speech Amor gave to the military delegates. The icing on the cake was the draft of an agreement that would bring the Korean War to an end.

It was leaked by an anonymous source that Sejong and Amor were invited to the White House to meet with President Doris Kearns Goodman. The very next day, a black SUV brought them to the White House.

"Good morning," President Goodman said as Sejong and Amor entered the Oval Office.

"This is Sye-li; she'll be acting as our interpreter, OK?" President Goodman paused, allowing Sye-li to translate what she had said to Sejong and Amor. When she had finished, the president asked, "Are you enjoying your stay in our nation's capital?"

"Yes, and we plan to visit many of your famous sites after our meetings," Sejong said.

"I understand that great progress has been made so far," President Goodman said.

"Yes, at a meeting last night, the consensus was that a draft of an agreement was ready for signatures, ending, once and for, all the Korean War," Sejong said with a tired smile.

"It's been a long time and it's been sorely needed," President Goodman said. "As a teacher and a presidential historian, I studied the root causes of the war and

President Truman's conduct at that time, and I must confess that our commander, General Douglas MacArthur, waged a brutal campaign of carpet-bombing the Korean people. It was unconscionable, the loss of life suffered by North Korea."

"Yes, it's true, and it colored both sides' actions for seventy years," Amor said.

"So, tell me. Are you the first to carry the name of the illustrious Sejong the Great?" President Goodman asked with an inquisitive smile.

"I was given the name Sejong when my father Kim Jong-il adopted me, and as far as I know, I am the only one who has had the honor to be named Sejong," he said, holding his head proudly.

"And a great honor to carry forth the legacy of a great man, a man who led his people by the teachings of Confucius, whose philosophy shaped half of the world," President Goodman said respectfully.

"I'm honored to be thought of as a successor of Sejong The Great, but in no way do I deserve it," Sejong said.

"Who knows what fate lies ahead?" President Goodman said.

From there on, the conversation was one of getting to know one another. The president asked what life was like in North Korea and the thoughts and dreams of the new republic.

Amor said that she looked forward to meeting people from other nations and travelling to Europe again, something she hadn't done since boarding school. She hated that North Korea was called the 'Hermit Kingdom' because of the rich history they had once enjoyed.

But although the conversation flowed and they shared a desire to put yesterday behind them and focus on tomorrow, Sejong needed to find a way to extricate himself from his horrendous plan to annihilate a nation of innocent civilians in the name of revenge. He proposed an outlandish plan to park the Victory ship at the Norfolk Naval Base in Virginia, coincidentally the largest naval base in the world, and offload the officers and crew and bus them the three hours to their hotel. Then they would drain the fuel tanks and tow the ship six miles out to sea and sink her. Sejong had read that their Victory ship was christened in 1945 as the *Saint Augustine* after the oldest town in America and that of all the 531 Victory ships built only one was sunk by German U-boats. The other Victory ship, the *Jacksonville*, *Saint Augustine*'s sister ship, was sunk six miles from the Norfolk Naval Base on its way to Murmansk, loaded with supplies for the Russian army.

Here was a way to memorialize the role these great cargo ships played during World War II, and by sinking her where the *Jacksonville* met her demise, now and forever, the *Saint Augustine* and her sister would be together. This almost brought tears to President Goodman's eyes, and though it was outlandish, she agreed to Sejong's plan and called the Secretary of the Navy personally to carry out her presidential orders.

51

Three amigos
Baseball field Top down
Sunshine and Whoppers

"Where is she?" Rose asked Officer Brenda as she unwrapped her Whopper and took a bite.

"She'll be here," Officer Brenda said, looking around.

"Well, I'm eating. My burger's getting cold," Rose said, fishing in her bag for the ketchup.

"Here she comes," Officer Brenda said as she saw Judy's car whipping around the batter's cage and heading for right field.

Pulling up beside Rose's car, Judy popped out, bag in hand, and got into the back seat of Rose's convertible.

"Oh, how I love it when we can get together on a sunny day and have the top down," she said, "getting all those yummy rays."

"Why are you so happy?" Rose asked.

"Didn't I tell you? She's in love." Officer Brenda stretched out and put her boots on the dashboard.

"If you're going to put your feet on the dashboard, kindly take your fuckin' boots off," Rose complained.

"Ladies, please! I've got good news," Judy said, unwrapping her chicken nuggets.

"Pray tell us, our little fighter pilot," Rose said.

"Well, you remember I told you about the issue with the wingy thing," Judy said.

"Your premonition of disaster thingy?" Officer Brenda said, pulling her boots off the dashboard before Rose could hit her on the head.

"Well, I spoke to Commander Steele, and—"

"Did you tell him he can put his boots under my bed whenever he wants?" Officer Brenda said.

"Please, do you want to know what he said?" Judy asked tersely.

"Not really, but tell us anyway," Rose said, taking a bite of her cold burger.

"Well, he told me to buy packages of sand and put 'em on the end of my wings and in the dark, inspect the wings with an infrared light," Judy began.

"He told you to do what? Is this a three-part series? 'Cause I've got to pee," Rose said.

"Hold it in, partner. She'll eventually spill it out," Officer Brenda remarked with a laugh.

"Do you know who I am?" Judy said, pretending to hit Rose in the head with her bag of chicken nuggets.

"Oh, forgive us, Captain America. Please continue. We'll be good." Officer .

"Just for that, I'm not going to tell you." Judy crossed her arms over her chest in defiance.

"Oh, for God's sake! Just tell it," Rose said.

"OK, fine. So, I did what he suggested and inspected the wings for cracks on top and bottom, and guess what?" Judy asked.

"What?" Rose asked, frustrated.

"There were no cracks," Judy said triumphantly.

"That's it? That's what you wanted to tell us? That it was just a bad dream?" Officer Brenda said.

"No, no, no! In doing that, we found out what really happened that day," Judy said.

"God bless you, Judy, can you get to the fuckin' point?" Rose pleaded, staring lustily at the Porta Potty across the field.

"When we looked under the wing, we found that part of the brace that holds the missile in position was torn off."

"So?" Rose said.

"So, it must have jammed. What the brace is supposed to do is release the missile from the wing. It just drops it, then the missile's rocket kicks in and propels the missile to its target. What must have happened is that one of the braces, the rear one, partially opened; the missile's rocket broke off the brace; and the missile flew as if nothing happened. These missiles have a mind of their own and find their targets regardless of where they're pointed," Judy said to the amazement of her colleagues.

"And you found it?" Officer Brenda asked.

"Not exactly. A couple of members of the ground crew helped me and found, to their surprise, what remained of the brace under the wing. They said that if a pilot was in the cockpit, he could have been killed." Judy nodded seriously in response to Rose's low whistle.

"So, what did you do about it?" Officer Brenda asked.

"Each one of us, me and the two ground-crew techs, wrote up incident reports and submitted them to the base commander."

"What did he say?" Rose asked.

"He was pissed. Said he's going to call Lockheed 'cause they supply the braces for their missiles and that he'll run it up the chain of command."

"Good work. You may have changed the course of history. Maybe you'll even get a medal," Officer Brenda said.

"Oh, one more thing. I called Commander Steele with our findings, and he said he's coming back to our base to bang the shit out of you, Brenda."

"Dream on, Officer Brenda," Rose said, slapping her friend's leg good-naturedly.

"Oh, if you speak to him again, tell him I just got a king-size, adjustable, vibrating bed," Officer Brenda snapped back with a leer.

"Changing the subject," Judy said, giving Brenda a reproving look, "Brad's lawyer asked us to return for a meeting. I think he probably has some numbers to go over with Brad."

"Let us know," Rose said, ushering the girls out of her car and heading, hell-bent, for the Porta Potty.

"Judy, get in my car. Let's talk about Brad's case," Officer Brenda said, opening her passenger door. "So, what time are you leaving?" She looked at her watch.

"Derek and Brad are picking me up at two at my trailer."

"What did Josh say? What were his exact words?" Officer Brenda asked, sounding very much like the law enforcement official she was.

"Do I need a lawyer?" Judy asked, pretending to look for Officer Brenda's handcuffs.

"No, really. It's important. And my handcuffs are in the glove compartment."

"He said he's had an offer and he wants to bounce it off Brad," Judy said.

"FYI, whenever a lawyer gets an offer, good or bad, they must bring it to their client's attention. That being said, I want to caution you not about the offer but about what Brad will do with the money."

"Well, in that case, how much money are we talking about?" Judy asked.

"Let's see—and this is purely hypothetical—there's the police for roughly five million. Then there's Brad bogus defense lawyer for roughly five million. I'd say ten million less attorney fees and taxes."

"Really?" Judy said, sitting back in her seat.

"Look, I told you I don't think Josh would have taken the case unless there was a big payday," Officer Brenda said.

"Then what have we to fear?" Judy asked.

"Whenever there's a sudden windfall, people come out of the woodwork to get a piece of the action. So-called family you haven't met and friends you've never known. They'll come at you from all sides with stories of how they loved you and want to help you. Yeah," she snorted, "help you spend your money. Then there's the investment advisers with every scam in the world—tax shelters, insider stock offers, technical money market funds guaranteeing unbelievable returns. If there's a scam, there's a broker willing to sell it to you... for the long run, until they drain your account dry in fees. But probably Brad's greatest threat is in his pants.

"There is a breed of leaches out there to suck the money out of a boy like Brad," she explained. "They spread their legs in hopes of bearing a child from the Brads of the world, as they've done many times before with other men, for the child support or alimony or cash settlements... I can go on and on. It's a business; I call them 'childbearing capitalists.' I've also heard stories about men and women who've inherited vast sums of money who were broke in six months. I don't know what to tell you, but he'll need guidance in how to spend his money so that it lasts long enough to make a new life without worrying about money ever again."

. . .

With that in mind, Derek, Brad, and Judy ventured forth to Josh Davis's office to hear who had offered what to settle their pending lawsuits. And just as Brenda predicted, the police offered $3,700,000. After a brief discussion, they refused the offer. They knew they could get more.

52

Sejong/Kylo/Chairman

S itting up in bed, Sejong watched his lovely partner, Amor, moving gracefully from bath to bedroom, laying out her wardrobe for the day. She was an eyeful, he thought, and he could not get enough of her both physically and mentally. She was his life and he welcomed every day they could spend together, but this morning she was meeting their military delegates to finalize a news release announcing a joint agreement with Boeing to set up manufacturing in North Korea of components for lightweight training planes. Granted, it was a small and limited contract, but it did open the door to future business down the road. Like many of Boeing's subcontractors, North Korea had to prove itself worthy of their business.

"Can you meet me for lunch?" Amor asked as she applied her makeup.

"I'm meeting the officers and crew of the Victory ship here for lunch," Sejong said, slipping into his robe.

"Oh, when will they be arriving?" She turned to look at Sejong with a smile.

"The Victory pulled into the Norfolk Naval Base last night, and their bus is collecting them sometime this morning."

"You said that the journey from the base to our hotel is about three hours… then yes, they should be here for lunch," Amor said, slipping into a tight, red silk dress.

"My love, you look spectacular in that outfit. Are you sure the men will pay any attention to what you say?" Sejong said with a lover's smile.

"Have you heard any of the details regarding the disposition of the Victory?"

Amor asked, ignoring his flirtatious remark.

"The way we've left it, the naval base will prepare the ship to be sunk in a dramatic fashion befitting an American warship. The fuel tanks will be drained, the compartments sealed, and it will be towed out to join her sister ship at the bottom of the sea."

"That's wonderful how it will honor their memories," Amor said.

"Yes, well said. In addition, the base has painted the ship's original name on both sides of the bow, *Saint Augustine*, so that her sister the *Jacksonville* will recognize her," Sejong said, giving his love a long hug.

• • •

Sejong paced the lobby of the Sheraton, waiting for the bus carrying the offices and crew from the Victory ship to arrive. When it finally pulled up to the entrance, the sailors, dressed in sparkling, new, green-and-white uniforms, exited the bus followed by the officers, the captain, and lastly, as tradition called for the last one to leave, Admiral Shumi-un. Greeted by Sejong with a bow they shook hands in front of the entrance, to the flashes of press cameras and the questions of reporters, who were advised that there would be a press briefing later that day.

Once the formalities were attended to, the crew was escorted to the floor reserved for the North Korean delegation. The sailors doubled up in rooms with two beds, the officers and captain received private rooms, and the admiral was given a spacious, three-room suite.

After the crew had freshened up, they all marched down a flight of stairs to the dining room, which was filled with delegates eagerly anticipating their arrival for lunch. When the doors opened, leading the officers and the crew of the Victory ship was Admiral Shumi-un in his parade dress uniform. Upon seeing their comrades, the delegates sprang to their feet to applaud and cheer their successful journey.

Finally coaxing the delegates to their seats, Sejong addressed the Victory's officers and crew on how proud their nation was of their bravery under dangerous conditions to bring their ship home to the United States, where it would be memorialized as the first step toward peace between the United States and The Republic of North Korea, which was the first time in history that anyone had referred to North Korea as a "republic."

After his remarks, Sejong took his seat to the right of Admiral Shumi-un and, smiling, whispered how proud he was of him. The admiral patted Sejong's hand and nodded in understanding.

Following the festive luncheon, Sejong was contacted by a liaison officer of the US Air Force that plans had been made to tow the *Saint Augustine* to the spot where the *Jacksonville* rested, and that an autonomous F-15 fighter plane would send it to the bottom of the ocean using guided missiles. He explained that this anonymity was because an American pilot could not carry out a mission against an American warship. He also told Sejong that a chase plane would record the mission and broadcast it to the world as President Doris Kearns Goodman and Chairman Pak Thae-bok signed the treaty ending the Korean War.

At the same time, Captain Judy Sluzac was ordered to the base commander's office. Caught off guard by the order, Judy scurried about, looking for fresh clothes to wear, and after showering and deodorizing every part of her body, she struggled to fit into her ever-shrinking uniform. She knew that she would have to have the waist taken out a couple of inches but kept putting it off. Feeling that what you see is what you get, she ran over to the base commander's office. When she arrived, she knew something was up because his secretary quickly got up and knocked on the commander's door announcing that Captain Sluzac was here. Thinking that she'd been called on the carpet for some infraction, she wondered if this meeting was a prelude to a firing squad. When she entered the commander's office, she was surprised to find he rose to his feet and saluted her. She returned his salute and was told to take a seat.

'Oh shit,' she thought nervously. 'They're drumming me out of the service. It must have because of the incident report. They're right; one should let sleeping dogs lie.'

"Captain Sluzac," the commander began, "you have been chosen by the United States Navy to sink the *Saint Augustine*, a United States Victory ship, off the coast of Virginia. In addition, you are confined to base for the next forty-eight hours. Further instructions will follow."

"What?" she exclaimed, not believing what she heard.

"That's what it says." He waved the paper sharing commands from the highest ranks of the navy in disbelief.

"When?" she asked.

"Doesn't say when, but it does say you'll receive further instructions," he said, re-reading the last line of the message.

He then got to his feet and handed her the paper with her orders. As the two faced each other, they saluted each other, and Judy, remembering how to properly turn around, exited his office holding her breath, thinking to herself, 'Wait till I tell my amigos.'

Later that day, Kylo requested a meeting with Sejong and Chairman Pak Thae-bok in his suite to discuss unfinished business. After helping themselves to drinks and plates full of hors d'oeuvres, the men got down to business.

"Thank you for your presence here tonight," Kylo said. "I know this has been a long day, but if I might say, a very productive one. We have successful brought our sailors back into the fold without any loss of life. In fact, from what I've read in the press, they conducted themselves with honor while in Cuba, a friend and valuable trading partner.

"I want to bring you up to date on some recent developments in the attempted assassination of Kim Jong-un. Two of the CIA agents responsible for the attack were returned by South Korea to the United States, which has promised to investigate and punish anyone involved in the plot. They further have identified the CIA ringleader who is reported to have committed suicide.

"In the case of *The Republic of North Korea v. General Zoko*, the state has taken into consideration the general's years of service, his age, and possible dementia, and granted him leniency in sentencing. He will serve seven years in prison. Regarding the deposition of his co-conspirators, we are still litigating their cases, and it will be several weeks until the court decides.

"Finally," he said, "I can now confirm that our nuclear weapons have been successful transported and received by the People's Republic of China in accordance with United Nations Resolution 222.

"I am happy to report that Kim Jong-un has been installed as the national symbol of the Kim Dynasty that once ruled our nation. Now that we are a republic the power has been transferred to the people and their elected representatives."

"How is my brother doing?" Sejong asked.

"I can report that Kim is happy being a husband and father to his wife and children and is often seen with his family at public events," Kylo said.

"Thank you for sharing the good news with us," Sejong said.

"Oh! Last but not least, plans are set for the signing of the peace treaty, which will formally bring an end to the Korean War two days from today. The signing will be held in the chambers of the United States Senate. Representing the United States will be President Doris Kearns Goodman and representing the Republic of North Korea will be Chairman Pak Thae-bok of the People's Assembly." He paused to nod at his guest. "At the conclusion of the signing an American autonomous F-15 fighter plane will sink the Victory ship we returned to the US naval base in Norfolk, Virginia. This symbolic act is in accordance with Americans' desire to reunite two sister ships. Both will now rest together in the waters off Virginia."

53

Elizabeth and Juan
Move to Barcelona.

Elizabeth felt that Juan had been acting strange since returning to their villa in Tangier. It wasn't anything he did or said; it was his mood. He seemed pensive and withdrawn, not his usual carefree self with his untroubled swagger. He was hesitant and reflective, often sitting alone on the veranda, writing. When she asked him if she could get him something, he pretended not to hear her or waved her away, seemingly deep in thought. After a few days of seeing him like that and torn as to whether he needed help, she begged him to tell her what she could do.

Putting down his pad and pen he sat back in his chair and, looking out at the sea, he sighed.

Something was wrong, very wrong, she knew.

"Juan, what have you been writing? Is it something you can share?" she asked.

"I don't belong here," he said.

"Yes, you do. What's troubling you, my dear?" she asked, holding back tears.

"This life we've chosen... we're like nomads, pitching our tent here and there and constantly moving on. We have no family or friends, no sense of a community of like minds. Strangers, that's what we are... strangers." He shook his head.

Speechless, Elizabeth could only nod because, deep down, she knew he was right. Here were two people, one on the run from her past and the other a vagabond bouncing off one damsel in distress to another.

"Is this life normal, or is there such a thing as a normal life?" he asked, as if he could read her mind.

"My love, the greatest minds have asked those questions, and they've come away without any answers. I guess what we do is try to survive as long as we can and not think about why."

"But can we in good conscience separate ourselves from those we love, just walk away?" he said sorrowfully.

It was at that moment that Elizabeth understood the struggle Juan was having. He was torn. She should have seen it coming when they said their goodbyes to Maria. The look in his eyes and in his daughter's eyes said it all. Once again, he was pushing her aside for another woman, another stranger. The poor girl's life was filled with women clinging to her father and at the same time pushing her away.

"Yes, my love, our life is filled with madness and the only resolution is to circle our wagons." She looked at him, and like a miracle, they shared an unusual epiphany. They knew exactly what they had to do.

First, they asked their agent in Marrakesh to sell their villa and return the Mercedes to the leasing company. In addition, they requested his assistance in placing their servants in another home with compensation until they could find gainful employment. They then made reservations at a hotel near Maria, booked one-way flights to Barcelona, packed their bags, and had Mohammad drive them to the airport. They were moving to Barcelona... for good.

They landed in Spain with lists of what they could and would do to simplify their future life together and, finally, to embrace that little girl hiding inside of Maria. So as not to frighten Maria with the onslaught of change, they decided to make her part of the process. She would help them choose their new abode, tell them in what part of the metropolis they should live, and help them decorate it. They were circling their wagons, and Maria was safely inside where she belonged.

But Juan being Juan couldn't control himself with joy. He was being a father in the only way he knew: with a passion for life, as a Spaniard. It was in his DNA; it was what made the Spanish man, a man—love, the unbridled love of family and life. It was walking the crowded streets at night, hand in hand. It was smiling at strangers; it was harmless flirtation; it was tipping one's hat in respect for elders; it was the pride in being Spanish. And in some indescribable way, Juan was now more of a man in Elizabeth's eyes. He had found peace at last; he didn't need to prove himself with one-night stands with wealthy strangers. He was finally home where he belonged, in the place of his birth with the people he loved.

54

Judy calls emergency
Three-Amigos powwow
at her trailer on Base.

Both Rose and Officer Brenda arrived at Judy's trailer at the same time, carrying cups of coffee and a bag of donuts.

"Hello, Captain Sluzac," Rose said, entering the dark confines of Judy's trailer.

"Man, does it smell in here," Officer Brenda remarked upon entering Judy's inner sanctum.

"Did you bring a coffee for me?" Judy asked, squinting from the glare of sunlight pouring through the open door.

"No, do you want to share mine?" Officer Brenda offered.

"Does it have sugar?" Judy asked.

"Yep, two spoonful's," Officer Brenda replied.

"Never mind. I'm on a diet." Judy sighed.

"Since when?" Rose asked.

"Since I can't fit into my uniform, that's when," Judy said, biting the diet bullet.

"How often do you wear your uniform anyway?" Officer Brenda asked, despite the fact that she was dressed in her own bright blue uniform.

"Now, I go to bed wearing it," Judy said sarcastically.

"Ladies, amigos, why do we meet today?" Rose asked, getting the meeting back on track.

"Well, something's up and I had to share it with you. That's why I called this emergency meeting," Captain Judy Sluzac stated, loud and clear.

"Pray tell, oh wise one," Officer Brenda said.

"Well, the other day the base commander requested the pleasure of my company to discuss a matter of national security. During this meeting he showed me a document from on high commanding me to remain on base for the next forty-eight hours until further notice. The document said that I had been chosen by the naval department to sink the *Saint Augustine* Victory ship off the coast of Virginia. Now here's the kicker; I later got a call from you know who," Judy said, making them guess.

"Who? Who called you?" Rose implored her to just get to the point.

"None other than Brenda's heartthrob, Commander Steele," she said, teasing the police officer.

"What did he want?" Officer Brenda demanded, not amused.

"My body, of course," Judy said winding her up.

"Come on, you know she longs for the commander. What did he say?" Rose begged before Officer Brenda could withdraw her six-shooter.

"He said that he received similar orders from the navy, just that in his case, they ordered him to immediately fly his F-22 Raptor with its video equipment to the Norfolk Naval Base in Virginia. He said based on the long-range capability of the Raptor he'd only need to refill just once, halfway at the Higgs Air Force Base in Oklahoma. And here's the best part, they cleared him to fly coast to coast at sixty-thousand feet, way above commercial aircraft."

"So, it sounds like you're reenacting what you did in the desert... just this time you're sinking a Victory ship," Rose said.

"What's a Victory ship?" Officer Brenda asked.

"I Googled it, and it was a World War II–era cargo ship," Judy said.

"Doesn't sound like much. Why are they sinking it?" Rose asked.

"Commander Steele thinks it has to do with the peace talks being held in Washington between us and the North Koreans."

"I did see something on CNN about it... they're going to sign a peace treaty ending the Korean War, right?" Officer Brenda said.

"But why all this shit about sinking an old cargo ship?" Rose asked, not seeing any connection.

"Steele didn't know, but orders are orders," Judy said.

"So, you're confined to the base?" Officer Brenda asked.

"Yep, for at least the next forty-eight hours," Judy said.

"Well, that's OK unless it interferes with the wedding. In that case we're calling it off," Rose said.

"What, the wedding?" Judy said incredulously.

"No, not the wedding… sinking that old tub in Virginia," Rose clarified.

"Now, when are you going to clean up this place?" Officer Brenda asked, holding her nose.

"If I speak to Commander Steele, is there anything you'd like me to tell him?" Judy asked, teasing Brenda and ignoring her question.

"Yes, invite him to your wedding."

55

The Big Event Is
Here…Peace at Last.

Sejong and Amor were relaxing after enjoying a sumptuous breakfast in their room.

"The coffee is very good here," Amor remarked, refilling her cup.

"Yes, I think it has a hint of hickory?" Sejong said.

"Do you think we can buy some before we leave?" Amor asked.

"Of course, my love. I'll ask the concierge."

"Tell me, what will you wear to the signing?" Amor asked.

"I thought the blue suit you picked out for me," Sejong said, taking a sip of his coffee.

"Yes, you look very handsome in it. Very dignified too." She contemplated what she'd wear to accompany him. She'd love to wear her red silk dress, but after Se-jong's comments about how sexy it was, she thought black was more appropriate.

"What time is the bus planning to pick us up to take us to the ceremony?" she asked, holding up two dresses for her consideration. Not pleased with how they looked, she was tempted to reconsider the red dress. She remembered watching the Oscars ceremony on the television and the fuss the actresses made of showing off their frocks on the red carpet. Maybe, in front of the whole world, a lady from the Hermit Kingdom could strut her wears for all to see? Still, she thought it inappropriate and tried on the black dress.

"Did you get a program?" she asked.

"No, they'll most likely have them at the ceremony," Sejong said.

"What did Kylo say about the seating?" she asked, frowning and taking off the black dress.

"He said we'll be sitting next to him in the balcony with our delegation," he said, looking for his cufflinks.

"It seems that everything in America is fodder for the TVs," she mused, looking at the coverage of their upcoming signing ceremony. "Look, Sejong, that's your Victory ship." She pointed to the widescreen television on the wall.

"Yes. If they only knew what the ship's purpose once was, there wouldn't be a peace ceremony today," he said.

"That's for us to know, my dear, and sending it to the bottom of the sea was just genius. I don't know what you said to President Goodman to convince her to memorialize a rusted, old cargo ship and, to top it off, to have it destroyed by one of their Top Guns for everyone to see. It takes my breath away," she said, holding up the red dress again for reconsideration.

"My dear, everything is America is for show. Life in America is one sound bite after another. The art of capitalism is a product of Madison Avenue, and they pull all the strings by which the country dances." Then he said yes, throwing caution to the wind and giving her his approval that she should wear the red dress.

Meanwhile, in a different time zone, Judy was trying to set up her console with the script for the upcoming circus in the sky. She walked over and around the cables the cameramen were running to feed audio and video to a hungry television audience estimated to be in the millions.

"Captain, this won't be in the way, will it?" the cameraman asked, lining up one of the two cameras in her trailer.

"Yeah, yeah, that's OK, but you can't use a spotlight behind me like that one." She pointed to a Klieg light mounted on a tripod.

"I'll put a filter on it," he said, rummaging in his case. "How's that?"

"No, it still causes a glare on my monitor," she said, punching in some preprogrammed commands to her weapons computer.

"I'll fix it," he said reassuringly, which he did to her satisfaction with a darker filter.

"Guys, I've got to talk to the pilot in my chase plane. No recordings, OK?" Then she turned to her microphone. "Captain Sluzac here... do you read me?"

"Roger, Captain Sluzac, and how are you this morning?" Commander Steele asked as his image appeared on her screen.

"Oh, don't you look handsome in your jumpsuit?" she said, smiling into the camera trained on her.

"What's that behind you? Is that the crew of the *Star Ship Enterprise?*" he joked.

"No, just the usual paparazzi that follow me around." She adjusted her seat.

"Don't joke. It may be an omen of what's to come," he said seriously.

"Well, get used to it because today we live in Camelot, my dear Lancelot, and you've got to chase my chariot all over the sky," she said with a phony British accent.

"Roger, my Guinevere," he said, going over his pre-flight checklist. "Do you have your script in front of you?"

"Roger," she replied.

They then went over their route from the Norfolk Naval Base to a figure eight over the Pentagon, then a figure eight over the US Capitol, before heading for the *Saint Augustine* Victory ship parked six miles offshore. They'd scope out the ship before commencing the attack that would send it to the bottom of the sea.

"Pretty cut and dry," Judy remarked.

"Roger," he said, adjusting his straps.

"By the way, are you coming to my wedding?"

"Wouldn't miss it for the world," he said, smiling at her.

"Oh, wonderful!"

"Did I tell you the guys from Lockheed Martin replaced the braces on the missiles?" he asked.

"No, but I feel reassured that they did. Wouldn't go over well on prime time," Judy joked.

"Also, I see you've increased the distance from one mile to two miles from the target to avoid flying through shrapnel," he said.

"They thought it was a good idea too. Why scratch up my pretty, forty-million-dollar fighter plane?"

"Any questions before we get started, Captain Sluzac?" he asked, saluting her.

"None, Commander Steele," she said, returning his salute.

Outside Judy's trailer, camera three had a live update from a local staff reporter with the Vegas News Service.

"Good morning, America, this is Scott Walker of the Vegas News Service, broadcasting from the Creech Air Force Base in Indian Springs, Nevada. It's a bright and sunny day here, and in a little while, inside this nondescript trailer, Captain Judy Sluzac will fly an autonomous F-15 fighter jet around Washington, DC, with two thousand-pound, laser-guided missiles. Again, yes, this is all from her flight control station in this trailer. Amazing what technology it took to create a marvel like this, sitting here and flying a plane over a thousand miles away. What will they think of next?" He smiled at the camera.

On the steps of the United States Capitol, another reporter with tonier General American Diction and a national-news haircut looked into his camera.

"Good morning, America, this is Roger Dumont speaking to you from the steps of the United States Capitol. In a little while, the president of the United States, Doris Kearns Goodman, and the chairman of the newly formed Republic of North Korea, Pak Thae-bok, will sign a historic treaty that will after seventy years end the Korean War.

"As you can see, there are thousands of people here to celebrate the signing of this historic document. Look over there"—he instructed his cameraman to aim his camera into a crowd—"onlookers are carrying signs saying, 'Peace At Last.' They're waiting for word that the treaty has been signed and for the peace-at-last flyover, where a F-15 fighter plane will make a figure eight over the US Capitol, symbolizing what many believe was man's first peace sign."

Inside the hallowed confines of the United States Senate, North Korean Chairman Pak Thae-bok was finishing his speech celebrating the meaning of a republic to the North Koreans.

This was followed by an impassioned address by the brilliant spokeswoman for the American people, President Doris Kearns Goodman.

"It has been a long and rocky road for the people of North Korea, a people rich in the brilliance of leaders like Sejong the Great who, over five hundred years ago, brought enlightenment and peace to his country when all about sought war and conquest.

"So, to reaffirm our commitment to the world of nations, we, the United States of America, will go anywhere, help anyone, in the name of peace. As it's written in the Book of Isaiah, 'Many people shall come and say, "Come, let us go up to the mountain of the Lord, to the house of the God of Jacob; that he may teach us his ways and that we may walk in his paths." For out of Zion shall go forth instruction, and the word of the Lord from Jerusalem. He shall judge between the nations, and shall arbitrate for many people; they shall beat their swords into plowshares, and their spears into pruning hooks; nation shall not lift up sword against nation, neither shall they learn war any more—'"

As the sound of a F-15 fighter plane laden with advanced air-to-ground, laser-guided missiles circled above the building.

After making figure eights over the Pentagon and the US Capitol Building, Captain Judy Sluzac, in her F-15 fighter, chased by Commander Steele in his F-22 Raptor, headed out to sea to find her next prey, a Victory ship named the *Saint Augustine*.

"F-15 to chase," Captain Sluzac barked into her radio.

"F-22 to F-15," Commander Steele replied.

"Heading 152 degrees southeast, altitude five thousand feet," Sluzac advised.

"Roger, F-15, 152 degrees southeast, altitude five thousand feet," Commander Steele confirmed.

At a speed of 350 miles per hour it was only a few minutes until they came upon the *Saint Augustine*. Judy noticed that the ship's orientation for attack to strike at midship required her approach to be from the southwest, specifically 243 degrees southwest, which she so advised her chase plane.

"F-15 to chase," Captain Sluzac barked.

"F-22 to F-15," Commander Steele replied.

"Attacking from 243 degrees southwest. Do a doe z doe till I'm in position."

"Roger, F-15," Commander Steele confirmed.

With her instructions broadcast to everyone listening, Judy banked and made a wide circle around the *Saint Augustine*, lowering her altitude from five thousand to two thousand feet. Leveling off, she came to 234 degrees as she painted the target at midship with her laser, armed her port and stern missiles, increased her speed to 450 miles per hour, and, with her finger on the firing pin, launched both missiles simultaneously two miles from the target.

"Bombs away, running true!" she screamed as she

immediately banked to port to avoid the concussion blast as the two thousand-pound bombs, flying side by side, raced ten feet above the waterline to the center of the *Saint Augustine*.

Judy said later in an interview that although she was fifteen hundred miles away, she felt the fuckin' blast, which was recorded by Commander Steele in his F-22 Raptor chase plane, as an enormous fireball consumed the ship and sent her mercifully to the bottom of the sea.

EPILOGUE

Four weddings and a Funeral

W ell, I guess it's time to bring closure to our tale and tell you what happened after all the festivities. Our protagonist, our pugnacious little fighter pilot, Judy Sluzac finally made it to the altar and married her Prince Charming, Derek Navarro, in one of the largest and wildest weddings ever held on the Vegas strip. Thousands of people crowded the sidewalks dressed in vintage military uniforms and flight jackets, topped off with steampunk aviation helmets and goggles. Pickup trucks roamed the street with loudspeakers playing Purcell's Trumpet Voluntary as Captain Judy Sluzac walked down the aisle to the cheers of onlookers who were lucky enough to squeeze into the tiny Candlelight Chapel. This was followed by an all-nighter on the rooftop Sky Liner

Lounge in the Elegante Hotel and Casino. The groom's best man was his brother, Brad, who recently settled several lawsuits in California for damages estimated to be in the tens of millions of dollars. Judy and Dereck now reside in North Las Vegas where Judy is a spokesperson for the National Veterans Assistance Program. Judy's brother Joey and Derek's daughter Pamala, moved into a newly acquired 200 acre ranch near Las Vegas with Brad Navarro an his father.

One of Judy's bridesmaids was Officer Brenda Carson of Indian Springs, who was escorted by Commander Paul Steele of Pasadena, California. Officer Brenda Carson and Commander Steele were later married at the United States Air Force Academy in Colorado Springs, where the commander graduated summa cum laude.

Elizabeth Kleinshure (alias Grace Hayworth) married Juan Carlos of Barcelona in a traditional Spanish wedding in El Convent de Blanes in Calella, Spain. In attendance was Juan's daughter, Maria, a music student at a university in Barcelona. Elizabeth and Juan are directors of the international B&C Concierge Consultancy de Espana, Ltd. Their consultancy caters to an international clientele who enjoy their personal touch securing yacht charters, event planning, and real estate and property sales and rentals in the French Riviera.

• • •

The fourth wedding took place in the city of Pyongyang, North Korea, joining Amor-Ra, daughter of Thi-sen, and Sejong, son of the late Supreme Leader of North Korea, Kim Jong-il and brother of Kim Jong-un. Amor and Sejong are the directors of NK Development, Ltd., which designs and builds hotels, shopping centers, and restaurants throughout the Republic of North Korea.

Finally, I must inform the reader that the funeral speaks to the death of the impractical and unrealistic plans to make North Korea into an industrial state that could compete on the international stage in manufacturing goods and products for sale on world markets. After an initial investment, American investors saw how futile the venture was and quickly backed out. But Amor and Sejong realized that a capitalist society with all its flaws was the only way to bring North Korea the funds and investments that would create good jobs and a vibrant economy. That being said, it also required a sea change in the current North Korean laws and culture. To begin with, Amor had to convince the People's Assembly that legalizing the sale and use of cannabis would bring tourism by rich millennials throughout the area, China in particular, to their country in droves. In addition, Sejong promoted new banking laws to the People's Assembly to open their banks to western money investments as done in most of the world. This in turn would allow investors opportunities to shelter their investments in projects like hotels, shopping centers, and restaurants, also a common practice throughout the world. Soon, others jumped on the bandwagon, adding sporting events like soccer to the offerings by building stadiums to accommodate the hundreds of thousands of fans who would come to their nation. With these new laws, it didn't take long until the country was building new homes for the workforce needed to staff and run these projects. By and by, the Hermit Kingdom became a player on the world stage, and they never looked back again.

THE KOREAN WAR

Near the end of the Second World War, two American colonels, Charles Bonesteel and Dean Rusk, tore a page out of a world atlas of the Korean peninsula and arbitrarily drew a line across the 38th Parallel, giving the land north of the parallel to the USSR and the land south of it to the USA without any regard for the inhabitants, thus setting the stage for future conflicts. Contrary to American propaganda, Syngman Rhee, the president hand-picked to rule South Korea, invaded North Korea for the sole purpose of unifying the north and south under his tyrannical regime.

REVENGE

General Douglas MacArthur was widely considered a coward for his role during World War II, especially for his conduct in Bataan and Corregidor when he ran to Australia while his men suffered and died. It was the largest capitulation in American history. When Mac-Arthur was given the chance to burnish his reputation by commanding the American forces in Korea, he massacred millions of men, women, and children by first carpet-bombing everything standing, then burning the survivors to death with firebombs (now called napalm). His end came when he refused to heed the advice of his intelligence officers and sent his men into the Chosin Reservoir where they were trapped and massacred. Desperately needing to divert attention from another military disaster, he came up with a plan to end the war by dropping thirty to fifty tactical atomic bombs on the border of North Korea and China; however before he could get his hands on the nuclear bombs, President Truman fired him for being "a dumb son of a bitch."

ALSO BY PHIL SILLS

Ghosts of Sackett Lake

The Hunt for Madoff's Treasure

www.ingramcontent.com/pod-product-compliance
Lightning Source LLC
Chambersburg PA
CBHW020238200626
46816CB00001BA/29